THE
MERCHANT
and the
ROGUE

OTHER PROPER ROMANCES
BY SARAH M. EDEN

Ashes on the Moor

Hope Springs
Longing for Home
Longing for Home, vol. 2: Hope Springs

Savage Wells
The Sheriffs of Savage Wells
Healing Hearts

The Dread Penny Society
The Lady and the Highwayman
The Gentleman and the Thief

THE MERCHANT and the ROGUE

SARAH M. EDEN

SHADOW
MOUNTAIN

All rights reserved. No part of this book may be reproduced in any form or by any means without permission in writing from the publisher, Shadow Mountain®, at permissions@shadowmountain.com. The views expressed herein are the responsibility of the author and do not necessarily represent the position of Shadow Mountain.

This is a work of fiction. Characters and events in this book are products of the author's imagination or are represented fictitiously.

PROPER ROMANCE is a registered trademark.

Visit us at ShadowMountain.com

Library of Congress Cataloging-in-Publication Data
Names: Eden, Sarah M., author.
Title: The merchant and the rogue / Sarah M. Eden.
Other titles: Proper romance.
Description: [Salt Lake City] : Shadow Mountain, [2021] | Series: Proper romance | Summary: "Russian-born shopkeeper Vera Sorokina and Irish-born penny dreadful author Brogan Donelly join forces to take down a criminal enterprise that is threatening shopkeepers in South London in 1865. Along the way, the two find love and romance as they fight for a chance for their own 'happily ever after.'"—Provided by publisher.
Identifiers: LCCN 2020056724 | ISBN 9781629728513 (trade paperback)
Subjects: LCSH: Russians—England—Fiction. | Authors, Irish—England—Fiction. | Nineteenth century, setting. | London (England), setting. | LCGFT: Romance fiction. | Historical fiction.
Classification: LCC PS3605.D45365 M47 2021 | DDC 813/.6.—dc23
LC record available at https://lccn.loc.gov/2020056724

Printed in the United States of America
Lake Book Manufacturing, Inc., Melrose Park, IL

10   9   8   7   6   5   4   3   2   1

To Jolene,
who convinced me not to give up on this book,
then stepped up and helped me
make it a story I could love

CHAPTER 1

London, 1865

If laughter truly were the best medicine, Brogan Donnelly would have been the healthiest Irishman in all of England. Jests came as easy to him as breathing, and that was more-or-less all anyone knew of him. He preferred it that way.

On one particularly dreary early-winter afternoon, he jaunted with his usual air of revelry down the streets of London, headed for his home-away-from-home-away-from-home. Dublin would've been his first choice, but if he had to be in London, he much preferred enduring Town in his favorite corner of it.

Brogan walked the pavement near Covent Garden, spinning his pocket watch on its leather strap, whistling "Whiskey in the Jar," and pretending he had no determined destination. He'd been summoned by a fellow member of the Dread Penny Society, a group of vigilante do-gooding authors most of London had heard whispers of but no one outside their ranks could actually identify. He was known in this area—a man with hair the color of burning embers could hardly go unnoticed—but he'd made such a point of appearing devil-may-care that few wondered what he was about, and fewer still cared enough to sort the mystery.

As he approached King Street, he tucked his watch in his fob pocket. He slipped up to the blue door. It was a destination no one was meant to take note of. Secrecy required he not draw attention to it, and he was blasted good at secrecy.

Brogan slipped inside. He set an engraved penny on a nearby table. The coins were tokens that granted members entrance to their society's headquarters. There were no other pennies present, meaning Brogan had arrived first for his meeting.

"Much obliged, Nolan," he said to the sleeping butler, slouched in a chair by the door.

The butler, eyes still closed, head hung low in a posture of sleeping, lifted his hand just enough to wave in acknowledgment. He didn't say a word. He very seldom did.

As there was no formal meeting of the entire membership called that day, Brogan continued onward, past the usual meeting room and to the front staircase.

The unassuming town house boasted a great many odd rooms: a small-scale House of Commons, a boxing saloon, a room filled with wardrobes containing a variety of disguises. Many gentlemen's clubs contained coffee rooms or dining rooms, and most afforded members the opportunity to purchase and be served spirits, but as far as Brogan knew, only the Dread Penny Society, in all its secretive oddity, had built for itself an actual pub.

It was small—only three tables and the bar with its bottles and barrels—and 'twas of the serve-yourself variety, but every consideration had been given to making the room cozy and comfortable. The dark wood paneling put one in mind of a centuries-old neighborhood watering hole. A fireplace adorned one wall. Curtained windows filled another. They'd even hung a shingle declaring it "The Quill and Ink."

Brogan lit a fire, poured himself a glass of Guinness, and sat at a table to wait. His summons had come from none other than Fletcher Walker, a legend on the streets of London and the acting head of the Dread Penny Society. He'd never before asked Brogan to meet with him personally and alone. Truth be told, Brogan was more than a touch nervous.

Mere moments later, Fletcher slipped inside. "Brogan," he greeted as he made his way to the tap.

"Can't tell you how pleased I am to have converted you to the superiority of Guinness," he said, noting what Fletcher had chosen to pour himself.

Fletcher sat in a chair at the round table Brogan had chosen. "What's the scandal broth, mate?"

Brogan spun his glass slowly, almost mindlessly. "*You* summoned *me*. Best be asking your own self what's what."

"Fair enough." Fletcher took a quick pull from his glass. "Last meeting we had, you made quite a speech about the sister organization you've been puffing up to us."

"I did, yeah." Too many of the Dreadfuls had families, and growing ones at that, and keeping their work a secret from the very people who shared their lives was proving harder and harder.

"And you still think it a plumb idea?"

Brogan nodded. "The ice is thin enough already. It'll take no more than the tiniest crack to crumble the entire thing.

Without a means of giving our loved ones an explanation that ain't an entire fabrication, that crack'll come sooner than later."

"Supposing, once we get a gathering of the membership large enough to vote on the matter, it don't carry?" Fletcher's gaze turned more pointed, more studying. "What'll you do?"

What would he do? He'd avoided requiring an answer of himself. He was too torn, truth be told. His membership in the DPS had given him a purpose in London, a sense of belonging, his only real friends in the entire city—the entire country, really. But it took a toll. It risked his connection to the only family he had left. If he lost that, he didn't know how he'd recover.

He rubbed at the back of his neck, tense and worried, but trying to tuck that away as usual. "I can't keep lying to m'sister."

A grin tugged at Fletcher's mouth. "Afraid of her, are you?"

"Anyone with sense is afraid of Móirín." Brogan was only half kidding. "But that's not m'reason for needing to add some honesty to this charade. Móirín's no simpleton. She's likely already suspicious about what I get up to with you lot. She'll sort this eventually. Secrecy keeps the Dread Penny Society safe and able to do our work. If I can't keep this a secret, and if I can't do it without spinning an unending tale . . ." He swallowed back the rest of the sentence. He'd feared for some time that, without the ability to tell Móirín something real and honest, he'd have to give up the only connection he had besides her.

"Would you leave the DPS?" Fletcher pressed.

Brogan rose and paced away. He knew the truthful answer, but saying it out loud felt too final, too severing. "I'd hope it wouldn't come to that, but . . . I'm not sure what else I could do."

"That's what I'd hoped you'd say."

He turned back to look at Fletcher. "You'd *hoped* to be rid of me?"

"Hardly." Fletcher pulled a folded and sealed letter from the inside pocket of his jacket. "If leaving was your answer, I was told to give you this." He held the missive out to Brogan. "From the Dread Master."

Brogan's mouth dropped open. After a bit of sputtering, he managed to mutter, "The Dread Master?"

Fletcher was the *acting* head of the DPS. The Dread Master was the one running it all. No one other than Fletcher had any idea who he was, though theories ran rampant. Some believed he was one of the members, posing as no one terribly important. Some insisted it was Fletcher himself. Some theorized the Dread Master was someone none of them knew or had met. No matter the man's identity, his authority could not be questioned, neither could his judgment.

Brogan lowered himself back into his chair. The Dread Master had sent him a note? *Him?* Brogan was good in a pinch; he'd give himself credit for that. And he made a good team member during missions. But nothing about him would've warranted the direct notice of someone as important and secretive and authoritative as the Dread Master.

He took the letter but didn't open it immediately. "Do you know what this is about?"

Fletcher took a swallow of amber liquid. "I've an inkling."

"Is he tossing me out?" Brogan had rather expected that from almost the moment he'd joined up. "I know I'm not the asset you are. Or Stone or Hollis or Doc. Dominique. Kumar. Martin."

Fletcher shook his head in amused annoyance. "Just open the note and read it before you end up listing the entire membership."

He could have. Brogan worked hard on behalf of the society and their mission, but he wasn't the leader any of the others were.

No use putting off the inevitable.

Brogan broke the seal and unfolded the stiff parchment.

Donnelly,

Whispers are coming from the Russian embassy that Ambassador von Brunnow has been asking for additional security and protective measures. My source there does not know why.

What did this have to do with him? He looked to Fletcher, but the man was making quite a show of paying him not the least attention.

The ambassador has taken to watching the street and pacing about, anxious and restless. He was visited recently by someone whose business proved upsetting, though the identity of this visitor is not known.

This would be no concern of ours except the ambassador has been overheard muttering about a man with four fingers.

"Four-Finger Mike," Brogan whispered. The Dread Penny Society had had a string of run-ins with that gutter dweller and the notorious criminal he worked for known as "The Mastiff," but the slippery snake always managed to wriggle away. It seemed he was slithering after more exalted prey now.

We have failed to stop Four-Finger Mike and the Mastiff. If the ambassador is being targeted by them now, we need to know. But a mission involving someone of his standing is too great a risk. Should our efforts be discovered, it would destroy the DPS and endanger everyone connected to us.

"Why is he telling *me* all this?" Brogan looked to Fletcher, completely flummoxed.

"Dread Master don't tell me everything, mate."

We need information, and you are our best hope of managing it.

"Me? Is he mad?"

Fletcher wiped a drop of Guinness from the corner of his mouth. "I'm not actually reading the letter with you, Brog, I'm not certain which part has you so twisted up."

My proposal to you is this: resign your member-ship from the Dread Penny Society under the pretense of being unwilling to continue the ruse for the sake of your sister.

Brogan looked at Fletcher. "He's asking me to quit being a Dreadful."

"Said he might," Fletcher muttered.

Being distanced from the Dreadfuls will protect them. As I said, we need information, but you'll have to work alone to get it.

Alone. *Great jumpin' toads.* He'd never taken on a mission alone before. None of the Dreadfuls had, really. And he was the last one among them who ought to be given an assignment like that. Give him a task that'd help someone else's efforts, and he was bang up. But some people were leaders and some people were . . . him.

The Sorokin Print Shop in Soho is run by a Russian immigrant who has been seen in the area of the ambassador's home. Discover, without tipping your hand, if he was the one who called on von Brunnow. And learn whatever you can about the situation with the ambassador without giving away your aim.

Fletcher and I alone will know of your activities. Report to him only as absolutely necessary. Your secrecy in this matter is crucial.

Give your answer to this proposed assignment to him then destroy this letter.

DM

Brogan sat a moment, stunned, confused. Why would the

Dread Master ask *him* to do this? Any of the others would've done a better job.

"What's it to be?" Fletcher asked.

"Failure, probably."

Fletcher did not look the least swayed. "You're our best option, and if the ambassador is in danger on account of someone we've failed to bring in time and again, we can't simply ignore it."

"I'm the worst choice to send out on m'own—the rogue elephant, as it were, operating outside the herd."

"Completely outside the herd?" Fletcher set his empty glass on the table.

"Unable to call on the Dreadfuls if I get myself in a fix."

Fletcher shook his head slowly. "Likely not."

Brogan pushed out a tense breath as he began tearing up the note. "You'd be a better choice for something like this. Or Stone. Or Hollis."

"Don't go listing the membership again," Fletcher said. "The Dread Master picked you, on purpose."

"Because I have an easy excuse to leave the group," Brogan said.

"I'm certain that ain't the only reason."

Brogan wished he felt that confident.

"The lad's dependable," his first employer had said when Brogan was still very young. "Give him instructions, and he'll see them through. Leave him to sort his own instructions . . ." The man had shrugged and laughed a little. "'Tisn't a thing wrong with being a foot soldier."

A foot soldier. That's what he'd always been. But the

Dread Master was asking him to be a general in this high-stakes battle.

"What happens if Four-Finger Mike really is causing trouble with the ambassador and we don't stop him?" Brogan asked.

"Four-Finger Mike works for the Mastiff. If *that* brute gets hold of any part of the government, then all the good we've done for the poor and unfortunate these past years won't matter a lick."

"But no pressure on my shoulders, yeah?" A threat that big couldn't be ignored, but neither could he help thinking the Dread Master had chosen the wrong person. "'Tis a high ask, Fletch."

His tone as dry as a field in drought, Fletcher said, "So, don't bungle it."

Brogan pushed out a smile. Lightness, even if forced, helped cover a great deal of uncertainty. He only wished he could laugh this off entirely. "You're assuming I'm going to accept the task."

"Am I wrong?"

The Dread Master's letter was now in minuscule fragments, but that didn't change the reality of what had been in it.

"People will be hurt if Four-Finger Mike and the Mastiff *are* involved with the ambassador and aren't stopped?" Brogan pressed.

"More than 'hurt,'" Fletcher said.

What choice was there, then? Brogan didn't abandon people in need, neither did he wait for them to be hurt before stepping in. But undertaking this alone . . . that was out of character, and, he feared, outside his ability. "The rogue elephant it is, then."

"The rogue Dreadful, more like." Fletcher held out a hand to him. "Here's hoping you'll not be on your own for long."

Brogan shook it. "Here's hoping a whole lot o' things."

CHAPTER 2

Vera Sorokina stood in a corner of her family's print shop, out of sight of the back room. Her father was back there, and he'd be spitting mad if he caught her reading. She'd spent the morning unpacking the newest crate of penny dreadfuls—stories sold in installments, a week or more apart, for a penny a piece—and she had carefully arranged them so the customers would be all the more tempted to buy one. She'd made the mistake of opening one, the first installment in a new series by an Irish author, and had been so immediately engrossed that she was completely distracted from her work.

That happened more often than it ought. Had the stories been less exciting, she might have been able to resist. But adventure, mystery, romance, monsters, crime—the penny dreadfuls were as varied as they were irresistible.

She jumped at the sudden sound of the bell chiming over the shop door. She fumbled a bit but managed to quickly slip the tale out of sight.

The newly arrived customer was George, who worked as a clerk for a bookkeeper nearby.

"Mr. Harris is wanting his usual supplies," the clerk said. "He's in a rare taking today, so I'll not have time to chat."

Though Vera had never met George's employer, she was certain George's days working for the man were an unending misery.

"Mr. Harris would yell at a dog then kick the beast for good measure."

George nodded his agreement. "Trouble bein', I'm the dog at the moment."

"We'd best wag a tail, then, mate," Vera said.

"You'll have my unending gratitude."

She opened the drawer holding the lightweight parchment the bookkeeper always asked for and pulled out the amount he'd be wanting.

George turned toward the door to the back room but didn't walk closer to it. "Halloo, Mr. Sorokin."

"George," Papa acknowledged. He preferred to stay in the back room on days when a new set of penny serials were on display, but he did talk to the customers when they gabbed at him. "Is Mr. Harris still causing you grief?"

Papa hadn't lived in Russia for sixteen years, but the sound of his home rested heavily in his voice. Vera, on the other hand, hadn't retained even a hint of the land of her birth, a land she'd left when only five years old. Anyone listening would mark her as a South Londoner and never guess she'd been born in St. Petersburg. Sometimes she forgot herself.

"He's always kicking off over something or other," George said. "Today it's ink."

Vera pulled open the cupboard holding ink bottles. Mr. Harris demanded a very specific shade of black and would tear George to bits if the poor clerk returned with the wrong bottle. Vera checked the label four times, just to be certain.

"I see you still have your sign out saying you're hiring on," George said. "Have you had any inquiries?"

"A couple," Vera said, "but one applied while roaring drunk, which didn't bode well. Another said he'd be willing to stock shelves but drew the line at making deliveries, as he didn't care to exert himself overly much. I told him we didn't care to pay people to be lazy."

She set several sheets of blotting paper beside the other items. She knew this purchase well enough to fill it by memory. She quoted George a price a ha'penny below what was normal between them.

He raised an eyebrow in hesitation.

"I happen to know Mr. Harris fancies a bargain," Vera said. "You saving him a bit of coin will leave him pleased as a pig in the mud."

He breathed a sigh of relief. "Thank you, Miss Vera." He turned toward the backroom door. "And my thanks to you, Mr. Sorokin."

"Nye za schto," Papa returned.

George looked to Vera with an expression of confusion and expectation.

"Papa said, more or less, 'you're welcome.'"

Their transaction was quickly completed, and George slipped out.

Papa's occasional lapse into Russian had bothered their customers and neighboring shop owners when they'd first opened their doors six months earlier. But most had seemed to shrug it off in the end. Soho was filled with people from all over. Papa didn't cause anyone any grief, so the locals decided not to be bothered by him.

With George sorted and on his way, Vera, after one quick check that she wasn't visible to her father, took up the penny story she'd been reading. Papa objected to having the tales and stories in the shop, but Vera knew every author and which stories belonged to which, and the order of every installment. She eagerly devoured every one that arrived, waiting with empty lungs for each shipment. Papa didn't have to know that.

The shop would be full to bursting tonight as the working men and boys dropped in to grab copies of their favorites on their way home. It was the part of her job she liked best. Selling them had been her idea, and she was proud to say that that decision had pulled their the shop out of the suds.

After an hour or so, the first wave of readers arrived, eager for a copy of the popular tales and the chance to lark about in made-up worlds, far from the heavy lives they lived. Men, boys, women, girls, all clamored around the penny serials. If the shop was bigger, it likely would've seemed less successful. As it was, looking like they had a crowd was good for business.

"Miss Vera?" Olly called her over. He was eight years old, always a bit filthy, and as keen as mustard to be part of anything and everything. He was always knocking about the shop when new tales arrived, though he seldom had money to spend. "This one's new, i'n't it?" He held up a copy of Brogan Donnelly's latest.

"It is, yeah." She crossed over to him. "Have you read this author before?"

"I ain't, no."

Vera had suspected as much. She addressed the gathered boys as a whole. "His stories ain't about children like Fletcher Walker's or Lafayette Jones's. Might be you'll not like 'em as well."

"We ain't weak as water," Burnt Ricky objected.

"And we ain't babies," added Bob's Your Knuckle.

The street children often had odd names.

"You're a regular pride of lions, I don't doubt," Vera said. "And you might well like it, but it's different from what you usually pick. I only want to make certain you know that."

"Is it gruesome?" Olly asked, a bit of doubt tugging at his soot-smudged brow.

"Not yet."

"Have you read it?" None of the boys posed that question, but rather a man standing nearby who sounded as though he hailed from Ireland.

She turned to look at him. He wasn't dressed fine and fancy, but neither did he look like he was a breath away from poverty. His hair was a startling shade of red. He watched her expectantly.

"I have. And I am eager for the next installment. Of his, and Mr. King's, and Fletcher Walker's, and Lafayette Jones's."

"'Twould seem you've read a great many of the penny dreadfuls." A grin blossomed on the man's face, and blimey if it didn't fully upend her. Ginger men were often dismissed as less handsome, less striking, but bless him if he didn't prove that utterly and entirely false with a simple upward tip of his mouth.

"I read them all if I get the chance. Pays to know the inventory, don't it?"

"I imagine." He eyed Brogan Donnelly's latest, the one they'd been talking of mere moments earlier. "Are you enjoying the tale?" He motioned to it.

She nodded. "Donnelly's quality at weaving a surprising story. And this one's set in Ireland, which I'd wager will appeal to you."

"Sorted that about me, did you?"

She tugged her ear. "These ain't just for holding up spectacles."

He gave her a sweeping glance. "You don't wear spectacles."

"All the more reason to put my ears to other uses."

"Put your ear to listening to my question, Miss Vera," Olly said, uncharacteristically impatient.

She motioned to Olly with her head and, to the ginger stranger, she said, "Right nutty little fella, this one."

"Miss Vera." Olly whined out her name.

She took pity on him. "What's your burning question?"

"Would *we* like 'The Dead Zoo'?" He flicked his thumb toward himself and his urchin chums.

She gave the boys her full attention once more. They were being patient, bless 'em. "Mr. Donnelly's other stories usually have dying and sometimes murder."

"Fletcher Walker writes that too, Miss Vera," Burnt Ricky tossed back.

"And *everyone's* dead in Lafayette Jones's tales," Olly said.

Vera lowered her voice to a dramatic whisper. "Not everyone."

Grins appeared on all the children's faces.

"Gab amongst yourselves. Let me know what you decide."

The children put their heads together, yammering low and eager. She adored the little ones who came into her shop. Too many hadn't families to look after them. She didn't fancy herself a replacement for their missing mothers, but she hoped she gave them some feeling of the safety of home.

The ginger-haired man crossed her path again as she saw to her other customers. "Are you meaning to refuse to sell Donnelly's latest to the lads?"

"Not if they fancy it." She straightened a stack of Mr. King's latest offering; the green cover was quite striking. "Once they've made their pick, I let 'em crack on with it."

"Then why go to such lengths warning them?"

An easy enough question. "It's tough times. Their pennies are hard-earned. If they mean to spend their coppers here, I fully mean to give them the best I can for their money."

She stepped behind the counter. The Irishman leaned a shoulder against the nearby wall, facing her. Studying her. She knew she was a bit tall for a woman, and that caught people's notice. Her features were often described as looking Russian, though those who told her as much couldn't ever say what specifically gave away her heritage. She knew so little of the country of her birth that she couldn't answer the mystery either.

"What brings you to the shop?" Vera asked the inquisitive new arrival.

"You've a sign in the window saying you're hiring on help."

Ah. She gave him a quick look over. He wasn't teetering like he'd tossed back a few too many at the local pub. Whether or not he was a lazy bones she couldn't yet say.

"We're looking to," she said. "There's a fair lot of hauling things about the shop and running deliveries out to customers."

"I was a delivery man when I lived in Dublin," he said. "Though I can't say as I've ever been hired on to haul things about a shop, I think I could manage it."

"Pay ain't luxurious, but it's fair."

He nodded, not seeming overly worried.

"And it wouldn't be all day every day," she further warned. "Two or three days a week at most."

"Fair enough." He popped his hands in his coat pocket and watched her. "Care to give me a try?"

"Come by day after tomorrow, and we'll see how the day goes."

"You have yourself a lugging-and-errand boy, Miss Sorokin."

"Sorokina," she corrected. Most people in England hadn't the first idea how Russian surnames worked.

"Sorokina." He dipped his head in acknowledgment.

"And what's your name?" she asked.

"Ganor O'Donnell." His lips tugged upward, sending her heart fluttering a touch.

Peter, who had a cart in the area and who regularly

dropped in to pick out a story, brought up a penny dreadful to the counter and paid her for it. He had it open even before reaching the door and was distracted enough by what he read to not manage more than a couple of steps outside.

"He bought that same one you warned the children might be a bit too frightening," Mr. O'Donnell said.

"It's a first installment in a new tale and selling well."

"Do you really think the wee urchins'd be upset by reading it?" he asked.

"Likely not." London's street children knew far too much of the world to be upset by tales of danger and dastardliness. "I simply want to make certain they never feel they've wasted their pennies."

Olly, Bob's Your Knuckle, and Burnt Ricky still stood at the display, apparently overwhelmed by their options.

Mr. O'Donnell pulled a penny from his pocket. Without a word he held it out to her.

"I don't understand," she said.

"For the little ones," he said. "They can try this new story without worrying over their precious pennies."

An act of kindness. That was a good sign, indeed.

"Thank you, Mr. O'Donnell."

"You can call me Ganor," he said. "I'll be working for you, after all." He moved to the doorway, pausing to tip his hat. "I'll be here day after tomorrow, Miss Vera."

Quick as that, she potentially had the help she needed in the shop, provided Papa didn't take a dislike to him and Ganor was willing and able to do the work. She ought to have been fully relieved. But something in it all gave her pause.

Perhaps she'd simply read too many penny dreadfuls, and their tales of intrigue and untrustworthy characters had her mind spinning far too easily toward conspiracies. Perhaps. But she'd keep her eyes open and her ears perked just the same.

THE DEAD ZOO

by Brogan Donnelly

Day One

In the heart of Dublin City, between the River Liffey and the Grand Canal, surrounded by Merrion Square, Trinity College, and St. Stephen's Green, sits the imposing and stately Leister House where meets the Royal Dublin Society. And housed in the newest wing of this residence-turned-Society premises is a museum of a most unusual nature. Its contents are not unknown elsewhere; its function is not strange for a museum. It is made unusual by the oddity of its name, a moniker both amusing and dark.

This place of learning and study and preservation is a museum of natural history, filled with the remains of animals large and small, bird and insect, mammal and fish. Skeletons sit alongside wax models that occupy displays alongside taxidermy of a most realistic nature. Whales and eagles, rodents and trout, a Tasmanian tiger and a polar bear. The species are too numerous to name here, but the museum is far from empty. And its contents have earned it, amongst the locals, the name "The Dead Zoo."

Early on a spring morning, Amos Cavey, a man who had earned in his thirty-five years a reputation for intelligence by virtue of having mentioned it so very often, stepped inside the zoo of no-longer-living creatures, having been sent for by William Sheenan, keeper of the exhibit of mammals.

William had asked this tower of intellect to call upon him at the zoo, not out of admiration but desperation. Amos never ceased to brag of his intellectual acumen, and William was in need of someone who could solve a very great and pressing mystery.

Amos walked with unflagging confidence up the Plymouth stone stairs to the first floor where the mammals were housed. He was not unfamiliar with the museum and its displays. Indeed, he had once proclaimed it "quite adequate, having potential to be impressive indeed." He had made this observation with a great deal of reluctance as it might very well be seen as a declaration of approval of the Royal Dublin Society, which he did not at all intend it to be.

Alighting on the first floor, he stepped into the grand hall where the preserved species were displayed, some on shelves, some behind glass, some posed on pedestals. The ornate ceiling rose three stories above the stone floor. Two upper stories of balconies overlooked the space beneath. Tall columns supported those surrounding galleries, giving the room a classical look, one designed to complement a place of learning.

He held back his inward expression of frustration at having to step over and around a mop employed by a janitor. The man offered no acknowledgment of their near collision, but simply continued his efforts, so intent on his work that one would assume he was expunging the worst of muck and grime rather than polishing the floor of a museum that was kept quite clean.

"Do not mind Jonty," William said as he approached. "He is so very dedicated to his work. We owe the beauty of this building to his unflagging efforts."

Jonty grunted but didn't speak, neither did he look up from his mopping. As William had declared, he was quite good at what he did, and no oddity of character would see him dismissed from his position. Do we not endure things in people when we value something else enough?

"Your note," said Amos with his usual air of superior intelligence, "indicated you are faced with some puzzle you find *unsolvable*." He spoke the last word with an unmistakable tone of doubt.

"Indeed, I am." William's tone held far too much worry for anyone to mistake his sincerity.

"I fancy a challenge," Amos said. "Tell me of your mystery, and I will find your answer."

The reader may find this declaration a touch too arrogant, but Amos did have a most impressive intellect. He was not wrong to rate his abilities so highly, though his tendency to regularly regale people with acclamations of his intelligence made him a difficult person with whom to spend any length of time. Were William not truly in need of Amos's particular assistance, the self-assured intellectual would not have been offered so sincere a welcome.

"How familiar are you with our collection?" the harried keeper asked as he motioned for Amos to walk with him amongst the displays.

"I have visited a couple of times." Amos looked over the nearest animals with an eye to evaluating them. "I found the musk ox mother and calf intriguing. The particularly large trout, however, I take leave to declare might actually be a salmon."

William let the criticism pass, not wishing to dwell on anything other than the matter at hand. They passed the dodo skeleton, a particular favorite of his, though why it was displayed amongst the mammals, he could not say.

"I am, however," Amos said, "quite intrigued by the polar bear."

As William was partial to the arctic predator, he found himself better pleased with his current company than he had been. "That bear was brought back by Captain Leopold McClintock after his arctic search for the lost Franklin expedition. The bear's fatal wound has been left in the fur, giving us a perfect picture of how the creature looked in its final moments."

They'd reached the taxidermied animal they were discussing. Amos eyed it with curiosity. Something about it was different from what he remembered. He prided himself on his eye for detail and would not be satisfied until he knew what had changed since he last saw the animal.

"We have recently added this Arctic ringed seal." William motioned to the large pinniped, displayed in all its taxidermied glory in a wood-framed glass box. "Our collection of ice-bound animals is growing."

Amos took pointed noticed of the seal before studying the bear once more. Two glances at each were all he needed to sort out the change in the massive polar bear. Its positioning had been changed from the last time he saw it. The museum had turned the bear's head to be looking not at the lions, as it had on Amos's previous visit, but at the seal.

Clever, he thought to himself, as the seal was a polar bear's natural prey. He hadn't realized the taxidermied animals could be repositioned.

The Dead Zoo possessed an unavoidable degree of eeriness, being so full of creatures that had met their demise. Row after row of skeletons, of long-dead and, at times, notlong-dead animals frozen in poses meant to mimic life but never fully capturing it. How chilling was the effect of a dangerous, deadly animal, focused unblinkingly on the very animal that constituted nearly the entirety of its diet, but both animals nothing more than skin and fur stretched over expertly formed frames.

The janitor trudged past, pulling his mop and bucket with him, grumbling something neither William nor Amos attempted to overhear. As soon as he was out of sight, William addressed the matter at hand.

"I've asked you here because pieces of our collection have gone missing. I dismissed the first few disappearances as items being misplaced or pulled off their shelves for repair or cleaning, but they have never returned."

"You wish me to solve for you a string of petty thefts?" No man in possession of as much pride in his cleverness as Amos could help but feel disappointed at the request.

"These are no ordinary thefts." William guided him past kangaroos, posed in mid-jump, and an armadillo preserved in full armor. All around were skeletons and glass-eyed forms. Tall displays cast odd shadows. Rows of displays broke up the large space into small, sometimes confining sections.

Amos glanced backward as they walked, fighting the oddest sensation that someone was there, watching or wishing for his attention. But he saw no one. Only row upon row of animals. Bears. Lions. A magpie.

From the long-ago years of his childhood came the familiar refrain of the well-known nursery rhyme about magpies.

One for sorrow.

Two for joy . . .

He'd long ago outgrown superstitions, but that lone bird sent a shiver over him, one he clamped down with effort.

The two men paused at a display of rodents, many of a variety unseen in Ireland. William indicated three separate empty places. "These are newly missing, but they were held in place by strong metal bands and thick bolts. Freeing them from their confines is not a simple task. These specimens couldn't simply be picked up and slipped in one's pocket. This required time and effort, yet we've seen nothing."

That bit of additional information did offer some degree of intrigue to the mystery.

"And what does the museum director have to say about these thefts?" Amos asked.

William glanced in the direction of the director's private office. "I would rather not tell Mr. Carte about this, not if we can discover the thief's identity and recover the stolen items."

While Mr. Alexander Carte was not a vindictive man, there was no doubt he would be none-too-happy to hear that the museum, whose collection was not yet what he wished it to be, was being diminished by thievery. The director's displeasure might very well cost William Sheenan his position.

"Are these the only specimens to have been stolen?"

"No," William said, "only the most recent. We have lost mammal skulls, taxidermied rodents, even a couple of small felines."

"And how long has this been happening?"

William's expression grew ever wearier. "For a week now. Something has disappeared every day. That is all I know for certain. The items disappear, though I know not when or how. I've seen nothing, can explain nothing. I am at a loss."

Amos took a slow look around the enormous display room. Row after row of specimens spread out over three floors, the ground-level floor not yet completed. The museum was quite popular, owing in no small degree to Carte's exhaustive efforts to raise funds, expand the collection, and build interest.

Discovering who amongst the many visitors could possibly be pilfering items would be a challenge, indeed. A challenge worthy of a finely honed mind.

Amos tugged at his right cuff, then his left. He smoothed the front of his sack coat, then straightened his neckcloth.

"I will return in the morning," he said, "when the museum is open once more to visitors. I will observe, study, sort, and, I have no doubt, solve these mysterious thefts."

William offered his gratitude along with expressions of confidence in Amos's ability to do just as he had promised. One would be quite justified in wondering if he offered the praise as a matter of sincerity or in the hope of convincing himself that the disaster awaiting him should his superior discover the thefts could yet be avoided.

"Until tomorrow." Amos dipped his head quite regally.

"Tomorrow," William repeated.

He watched as the would-be detective left, a spring in his step and an unmistakable confidence in his stride. He watched with heavy expression, tight pulled lips, and tension radiating from him. The situation was a dire one, more so than Amos Cavey yet realized.

CHAPTER 3

Brogan smoothed the front of his shirt, making full certain it was tucked in all around, and adjusted the fit of his rough-spun trousers. He'd assumed any number of false identities over the years. He'd done so when he and his sister had fled Dublin. He'd done so in his work for the Dread Penny Society. When he and Móirín made their regular journeys to the struggling corners of London, they did so in garb meant to blend in.

This persona felt different, though. It felt more uncomfortable, more uncertain. For the first time, he was undertaking a pursuit entirely alone.

Móirín came down the stairs with her usual air of mingled amusement and determination. "I see you're hoping to make an impression on your first day at the new job."

"'Tis physical labor I'll be doing. Wouldn't make sense to arrive dressed for a night at the opera."

She looked him over. "You opted for 'a night at the squalid pub' instead?"

"I ain't so scruff as that. I'd wager you have your usual boot accessory." He eyed her footwear.

"I've a knife on m' person even when I'm sleeping." She pulled on her plain, serviceable cloak.

"And where is it you keep your derringer when you're asleep? In your nightcap?"

"Of course not." She yanked on her bonnet. "The gun's under m' mattress."

Though Brogan laughed, he felt certain she wasn't jesting. "I suspect if I didn't love you, I'd be terrified of you."

She eyed him sidelong. "You ought to feel a wee bit of both."

"Likely." Brogan pulled on his wool jacket. "Shall we go for a merry jaunt?" He did his best impression of a proper London gentleman, the effort marred by the unshakable influence of Ireland in his voice.

She answered with a fairly well-executed version of a proper British accent. "A regular pleasure stroll it'll be."

They stepped out of their flat and onto the pavement.

"We need to make our way to Maida Hill by week's end," Móirín said as they walked on. "I've heard whispers of difficulty up that way."

"The usual sort?" Brogan asked.

Móirín gave a quick, single nod without slowing her step. "Poverty turning people desperate, tearing families apart, pulling people into crime."

London's underbelly was as putrid as a corpse on a hot day. Those who ran it and manipulated it were powerful and dangerous. Brogan and Móirín hadn't come from a particularly peaceful area of Dublin, so they knew all too well the poverty that kept people tied to places like Maida Hill and Somers Town.

They made regular jaunts to those seedier corners, bringing what they could afford to give to those in greater need than they. The poor of this city needed so much more than food and medicines and the meager bits of coin they managed to bring them.

"Think you'll have time with this new position of yours to keep helping with the deliveries?" Móirín asked.

Helping. He was far more comfortable *helping*. And, yet, here he was on his way to *doing*.

Móirín motioned to a street sweeper, leaning on his broom with a penny dreadful in his hand. "Mr. King's latest," she said. "That green cover can't be mistaken."

Brogan shook his head. "Wish I had the bloke's knack for writing a top seller. We'd be in fine fettle, Móirín. Fine fettle, indeed."

"Fine enough that you might not be taking on a second job." Móirín knew their situation as well as he did. They'd not had near enough since coming to London. They pooled what little they had, barely enough for sharing a flat. "You said you sold a good many copies of your latest tale just yesterday."

He nodded. "And got m'self a needed job at the same time."

Unmistakable mischief entered Móirín's eyes. "Hired on by a woman who has you thinking on her a full day later."

He knew that teasing tone. "Don't you go adding more meaning than's there."

"You've not mentioned any lass to me more than once in

years. Yet Miss Vera Sorokina's name has slipped from your lips more times than I can count in the last day alone. I'll be adding all the meaning to that I want, and just you try stopping me."

With his separation from the Dreadfuls, Brogan had no one else to talk with but Móirín. He couldn't tell her the real reason he'd visited the print shop nor his true motivation in jumping at the work offered there.

He'd spent more than a year telling the Dreadfuls how much he hated lying to his sister. He'd left the Society, more or less, and there he was, still lying. And lying to more than just Móirín.

"She was intriguing, I'll grant you. Seemed to enjoy her customers, yet she gives the impression of keeping something tucked away from them all. Haven't the first idea what that might be." He'd learn more the longer he worked there. That was his current plan. "Intriguing. That's all that needs saying on that matter."

"For now," Móirín said.

They turned a corner, drawing closer to their destination, when, from the shadows of a narrow alley, a man jumped out and grabbed the handle of Móirín's basket.

Quick as thought, she pulled a dagger from the basket with her free hand and pointed it at him without hesitation, without the slightest tremor. "Let go the basket or I'll cut you a third nostril."

"Best do as she says, lad," Brogan said. "She ain't foolin'."

The would-be thief hesitated.

"I'm in earnest," Brogan said. "She'll carve you like a block of wood and enjoy the doing of it."

He must've been convincing. The thief took flight, leaving them with both their baskets firmly in their possession.

"'She'll enjoy the doing of it'?" Móirín clicked her tongue. "You make me out to be a cold-blooded murderer."

"You're an Irishwoman with a temper. 'Tisn't a large gap between the two."

Móirín didn't always allow teasing about her potential for criminal behavior. She did this time, merely shaking her head and smiling at him. He loved his sister, of course. But he also deeply liked her. She was good and fierce and caring.

"Why is it you gave a false name at the Sorokin shop?" Móirín asked. "Seems an odd way to start a new position."

Heavens, that was a mass of muck he wasn't at liberty to explain to her. He offered, instead, a reason he could safely admit to. "They sell m'stories there. 'Twould be as uncomfortable as wearing sackcloth underclothes to be lugging and delivering as my own self in a place where I'm meant to have some small bit of prestige."

"A Donnelly having importance?" Móirín clicked her tongue. "Seems you've forgotten we were running from the law only five years ago on account of our being low-down, no-good sorts of people. Tucking ourselves in London didn't change what we are."

"Didn't change us because it ain't that simple," Brogan tossed back. "No matter what the Peelers think, you and I know who we are. Let the Dublin police sully our names all they want."

"And sully them from a distance," Móirín said with the tone of one offering both a prayer and a curse.

He tucked his hands in his coat pockets, gaze lowered. "I wish I could've done more to—"

"Stop it, now," she said. "You strike that exact posture—hands in the pockets and eyes on the ground—when you're fretting and feeling lower than the weeds. You've done so since we were tiny."

"You can read me like a book, can you?"

Her self-assured expression was not the least feigned.

They'd reached Great Windmill Street, where he needed to turn off and head toward Soho. Móirín's job took her farther on.

"Best of luck to you today, *Ganor*," Móirín said with a smirk. "I hope Miss Vera proves as intriguing on second acquaintance as she did on the first."

He needed all the luck he could get. Brogan readily acknowledged he made a fabulous second, but he'd never been one for filling the role of principle. Yet, he'd agreed to do just that. He very much worried the scheme would fall to bits sooner rather than later. Rogue elephants, after all, rarely survived long.

He knew why it had to be done the way it was, but he couldn't for the life of him sort out why the Dread Master had chosen him, the resident foot soldier, to undertake this assignment when any of the others would have been a better choice.

The print shop was quiet when he arrived. Miss Vera'd not given him a time when she'd wanted him to arrive. Perhaps he'd missed the mark and ought to have been there sooner.

She looked up from the green-covered penny dreadful in her hand when he stepped inside, the bell ringing overhead.

"Morning, Miss Vera." Brogan popped his hat off. "Hope you don't mind me calling you that. 'Twas what the customers called you when I was here last."

"I don't mind." She tucked the story on a shelf under the counter. "But when you meet my papa you'd best call me Miss Sorokina. Wouldn't do to set him against you straight off."

"Meet your papa?" He assumed an overblown look of horror. "I'd intended to apply for a job. Seems I overshot the mark."

She smiled at his jest, but in a way that told him quite clearly that she'd not intended to. "My papa owns the shop. Though you're working for *me*, you have to meet with *his* approval."

Ah. "'Tis why the shop's called 'Sorokin's' and not 'Sorokina's.'"

She nodded. "I'd wager most people will insist it's an error rather than admit there's things they don't know."

"They can't all be as well-versed as I am," he said.

"And what is it you know about Russian?" she asked, a twinkle of amusement deep in her eyes.

"I know that daughters and fathers aren't always going to have the same surname. Learned that a couple days ago, I did."

"At least I know you're a quick study," she said. "I'll mention that as a point in your favor if my papa decides he don't care for you."

"How likely is he to decide I'm a good-for-nothing?"

"Hard to say." She studied him, though, again, there was a teasing quality to it he wasn't certain she meant to let show. "How do you feel about writers?"

For a fraction of a second he couldn't sort out a response. She was striking far too close to the mark. "How am I meant to feel about them?"

She shook her head. "Ask my papa some time. He'll spill a whole heap of complaints in your ear."

"He's not overly fond of writers, then?"

"That's hitting *far* below the mark."

Oh, mercy. He was in a stickier spot than he'd realized. Fletcher or Stone would've known immediately how to navigate this. Brogan was going to have to do some fast thinking.

"Papa's downstairs working at the printing press," Vera said. "He'll need to give you a look over before you start." She motioned Brogan to follow her toward the back.

He needed to win the approval of a man who despised writers. Might as well attempt to restore hair to a bald man's head.

A small back room connected them to another door, beyond which were two narrow staircases, one leading up and one leading down. Brogan followed Vera to the basement. The space was not overly large, but was sufficient for the large printing press, the cupboard with equipment, the shelves of paper and ink bottles. It was organized and well-laid out.

At a tall table in the midst of it all, a man near about fifty years old sat bent over a row of metal letters. His sleeves were protected with coverings. He wore thick glasses perched at the end of his nose. His silver-streaked beard was long enough to nearly touch the table.

"Ganor O'Donnell's here, Papa. The bloke I told you was taking up the job we had on offer."

For not the first time, Brogan was glad he'd given a false name that he'd used before. He'd be less likely to forget 'twas his name in this shop.

Mr. Sorokin turned slightly on his stool and studied Brogan over the rim of his spectacles. He scratched at his beard. "You are not a very large man. This job requires a lot of physical labor."

While Vera sounded entirely London, her father spoke with the undeniable flavor of Russia.

"Most of m' countrymen aren't large people," Brogan said. "But we know how to work."

"Irish?" Mr. Sorokin's eyes narrowed.

Brogan nodded. "London's filled to bursting with people from other places."

"That it is." Mr. Sorokin returned his gaze to his table. "We'll give you the day to prove yourself. If you can and will do the work, and you aren't a drunkard, then you have a job, O'Donnell."

"A drunkard?" Brogan looked to Vera. "Is that a commentary on m' origins?" The Irish were often assumed to be in a constant state of inebriation.

Vera shook her head no. "One of the men who applied for the position arrived drunk as a wheelbarrow."

"Ah." 'Twas a far better reason for the comment than he'd feared. "I've been working since I was a tiny lad, and I've never once shown up tipsy as a two-legged cow."

"See that you keep that pattern, and this'll work out just fine."

Brogan followed her back out of the printing room and up the stairs.

"No drinking," he repeated, "and no writing."

"Not even *mentioning* writing or writers is likely a better approach."

"His disapproval is that looming?" That'd make his position at the print shop all the more precarious.

"He's miffed that I sell penny dreadfuls in the shop," she said. "He begrudges having to even step inside now that they're there."

"But he's not bothered by you reading them?" He'd been in this shop twice, and twice he'd come upon her reading one of the familiar pamphlet stories.

Vera didn't answer directly. Her guilty expression did it for her.

Blimey. Mr. Sorokin disapproved of penny dreadfuls in particular. What had the Dread Master tossed Brogan into?

"Why's he so set against stories and the folks that write them?"

"That ain't my history to tell," she answered. "But we have decades of reasons to keep our distance from the literary set."

We. Not *he.* "But you still read the stories."

A weariness settled over her. "I shouldn't. I feel guilty every time, but . . ."

She didn't seem to have any answers.

Heaven knew, he had plenty of questions.

THE MERCHANT
AND THE ROGUE

by Mr. King

Installment I
in which our lonely Heroine is forced to endure the
company of a Person with a most Roguish reputation!

In the village of Chippingwich was a confectionary shop where sweets of unparalleled deliciousness were sold by a woman who had not long been a resident. Tallulah O'Doyle's arrival in the picturesque hillside hamlet had gone mostly unnoticed until she opened her shop and became quite quickly a favorite of many villagers. She created and sold peppermints and taffies, anise candies and sweets with soft cream centers. She included cakes and biscuits in her offerings and showed herself quite adept at all that she made. Indeed, she had no equal in the matter of confectionary delights.

Alas, her life was not nearly so honeyed as the sweets she sold! Tallulah was quite alone in the world, without parents or siblings, without the dear friends she'd known when she was young, without the beloved granny who had raised her on tales of the Fae and warnings of creatures lurking somewhere between myth and reality. Tallulah now lived far from her childhood home in Ireland, far from the familiar paths and fields she'd daily traversed. To England she'd come to build a new life, and, for all her show of bravery and determination, she was lonely and terribly uncertain.

"Lemon drops, please, Miss Tallulah." Seven-year-old Belinda Morris clinked a ha'penny onto the shop counter, the top of her head barely visible.

"Not peppermints?" That was Belinda's usual choice of sweets.

"Marty likes lemon drops."

Tallulah leaned forward across the counter, the better to see the dear child. "And he has convinced you to try them?"

She shook her head. "He don't have a ha'penny. I'm sharin' with him." Her eyes darted toward the shop window.

Little Marty, near in age to Belinda, stood on the other side of the glass, watching with a look of earnest worry. She knew his family was not particularly flush; the sweets he purchased now and then came dear to him. That this girl, whose situation was not much better, would buy *his* favorite in order to brighten his day . . . Dear, kind Belinda!

"Perhaps I could give you three lemon drops and three small peppermint sweets," Tallulah said. "Then you would both have your favorite."

"How many candies is that?" Belinda asked.

"Count them on your fingers, dear."

Belinda did, her lips moving silently. "Six! But I usually only get four with a ha'penny."

Tallulah simply smiled. She pulled three of each candy from the glass display jars on the nearby shelf and wrapped them in a small bit of paper. "You are a good-hearted girl, Belinda," she said, handing the prized sweets over the counter. "And a very good friend, indeed."

"Oh, thank you, Miss Tallulah!" She skipped from the shop. Her exchange with Marty was visible through the windows, an innocent bit of kindness. A mere moment later, Marty rushed into the shop and behind the counter.

He threw his arms around Tallulah's waist. "Thank you, Miss Tallulah."

"Make certain you thank Belinda. 'Twas her ha'penny."

"I will, Miss Tallulah. I promise!"

He rushed out and rejoined his friend. Tallulah smiled at the sight and, after they'd slipped from view, at the memory. She'd once had dear friends like that as well. She was gaining acquaintances in Chippingwich, but she was often lonely. And far too often alone.

As she wiped down the counter, she allowed her thoughts to whirl in the winds of time, carrying her back to Ireland and the life she'd lived there. It had always been home to her. Could this tiny village feel that way? Could she find home again? How heavy was her heart with so difficult a question resting upon it!

The shop door opened once more, and the local squire stepped inside. Tallulah did not know him well. He spent far more time at the pub than the confectionary shop, a not unusual preference amongst the men of the village. Mr. Carman was a man of great influence and importance in the village.

Tallulah greeted him in a tone of deference. "Welcome, Mr. Carman. How may I help you?"

With a flick of his red cape, the squire placed himself at the counter but somehow seemed to fill the entirety of the shop. He wore a hat in the same shade of crimson. Tallulah had never seen him without either accessory. It made him quite easy to identify. As did the almost putrid smell of him. Tallulah struggled against the urge to hold her nose when he was nearby. Yet, no one else seemed the least bothered.

"I am hosting a fine family who are passing through the area, and I am in need of a very elegant cake."

"Of course." Tallulah jotted down his requirements for flavor, size, and style, and the time and date he would need it.

While they discussed the particulars, the door opened yet again. For a moment, she was entirely distracted from her purpose. The man who had just entered was known to her by reputation, and that reputation was not an entirely angelic one.

Royston Prescott was known for two things. First, he was the local haberdasher and quite good at what he did. Second, he had a reputation for being a rogue. Not a true scoundrel or someone a person ought to be afraid of. Rather, he was playful and mischievous. He made trouble, but in a way that people liked him all the more. Liked him, but perhaps did not entirely trust him. He was known to flirt with any and every female he came across. He was known to joke when he ought to have been serious, to take lightly those things which ought to be taken quite seriously.

Tallulah was not afraid of him. She doubted anyone truly was. But he was a rogue and a flirt. Men of that sort were best taken with an enormous grain of salt.

"I will be with you in a moment," she said.

He smiled a very personable smile and accepted his lot.

To the squire, she said, "Have you any other requirements for—"

A sound echoed off the walls—a gurgling noise that sent shivers down her spine.

Neither the squire nor Mr. Prescott seemed to have heard it. Odd.

She gathered her wits and tried once more. "Have you any other requirements for your cake?"

"Let me see your list, and I will make certain it is correct." He reached for the paper.

For just a moment, Tallulah thought she glimpsed, not a hand, but a claw. She looked again and saw nothing out of the ordinary. Her gaze shifted to his face, but the shadows of his hat hid most of it. An uncomfortable sensation tiptoed over her, but she dismissed it. Her mind, no doubt, was playing tricks on her.

"All is in order," the squire said. "How fortunate the village is to have you. Do you mean to make your home here permanently?"

"I do hope so," she said.

The squire, despite having posed the question, did not seem entirely pleased with the answer. Odd, that. He *had* said the village was fortunate to have her.

He stepped back from the counter and past Mr. Prescott. The two exchanged looks that were not easily discernible. Tallulah couldn't tell if the two men were on friendly terms or if 'twas animosity she sensed between them. The squire's crimson cape fluttered behind him as he left the shop.

Mr. Prescott stepped up to the counter. Even his swagger held a heavy hint of self-admiration.

Fortunately, Tallulah was rather immune to such things. She too could flirt and make lighthearted conversation. And she was known to toss about an expert bit of banter. But she was unlikely to fall under the spell of a scoundrel.

"You seem to have secured the patronage of our most significant local personage," Mr. Prescott said.

"And it appears I'm soon to have the patronage of our town's most *flirtatious* local personage."

He tipped her a crooked smile, one complete with a twinkle of the eye and a raise of an eyebrow. "My reputation precedes me."

"And what reputation might that be?"

The man chuckled lightly, far from offended. "You cannot deny that I have a reputation."

"I don't intend to deny any such thing. I simply wondered if *you* are aware of what is said of you."

He leaned an elbow against the counter, watching her with a gaze that was at once curious and assessing. "Let me see if I can sum it up. I am a man of exceptional taste. I run a successful business. I am quick with a word of praise, predisposed toward finding beauty in everything around me. I enjoy banter and flirting, but all the women in the village are warned not to take me too seriously."

It was, in all honesty, a good summary of what she'd heard.

"You've left something off," she said.

He tipped his head to one side, clearly attempting to sort out what he might have left out.

Tallulah went about her business, wiping the counters and removing finger smudges from the glass displays about the shop, not offering him the least clue.

"You have baffled me, Miss O'Doyle," he said. "What aspect of my rumored character have I omitted?"

"You neglected to mention the weakness you have for sweets, and"—she motioned to the colorful display on the wall behind her—"your intention to buy a great many confections while you're here."

That brought the smile to his face once more. Oh, he had an intriguing smile indeed! His reputation was widely spoken of, as was his ability to cut quite a fine dash. The fact that he was handsome and personable was mentioned at every opportunity. Yet, even with all of these warnings, Tallulah found herself ill-prepared for the impact of his roguish smile and knee-weakening good looks.

She would do well to be on her guard with this one.

CHAPTER 4

Vera's customers were quick to realize Ganor
O'Donnell knew everything about the penny
dreadfuls. He was in the shop on his second day
of working there, having spent the morning unpacking the
latest arrivals and helping get the displays in order. He'd even
taken up the job of arranging window displays, something
she'd not yet had the time to do that day. All respectable print
shops had eye-catching displays. Having that part of the business sorted would bring in more print jobs, and Ganor's easy
and personable discussions of the serials would bring in more
penny dreadful customers.

Hiring him had proven a stroke of genius. And yet she
couldn't shake a nagging sense of uncertainty. His knuckles
bore the heavy scarring of one who'd seen more than his share
of brawls. He was a fighter, though likely not a professional
pugilist. She was not unacquainted with men who swung fists
as a matter of course, but it still made her a touch nervous
having one working in the shop.

Ganor worked hard, but there was an air of distraction

about him. Sometimes his mind wandered enough that he didn't respond when she called out to him. His eyes would take on the strangest look when someone mentioned a penny dreadful author—didn't seem to matter which one. And he asked a lot of questions.

Still, having him there to lug and deliver things made everything run better. It also allowed her a few more un-guarded moments where she could read the penny dreadfuls she loved, despite her feelings of lingering guilt. The stories Papa resented having in the shop gave her a sense of friend-ship and adventure. She wasn't certain she could entirely give them up, even for him.

She was rereading the first installment in Mr. King's latest offering, searching for the clues that he always managed to sprinkle in his writing. Vera took pride in being able to sort out the mystery a little ahead of the story.

"Enjoying it?" Ganor plopped onto the chair beside hers, the both of them sitting at the table near the back of the shop where print orders were taken.

"I always like Mr. King's stories," she said. "The mystery and romanticalness." She stopped a minute. "I'm not certain that's a word."

He tossed back one of his heart-fluttering smiles. "Seems to me it ought to be."

"You have a nice way with the customers," she said. "Talking with 'em about the penny dreadfuls and helping 'em sort out which ones they'd like best."

"Are Mr. King's the ones *you* like best?" He motioned to the story she still held in her hands.

"I like most all of them."

"So do I." They were having a rare quiet moment in the shop, a lull between waves of customers. "Seems odd to me, though; you selling stories when your da is so opposed to 'em."

She glanced toward the back doorway, wanting to make certain her papa wasn't near enough to overhear. "The shop weren't doing well. We sell a good amount of parchment and pens and such things. But, without enough print orders coming in, we needed something else. I knew the penny dreadfuls were popular, and I'd read plenty enough of them to know how to go about selling them. He was spitting fire over it when I first brought 'em here. He still ain't happy about the whole thing. But it's kept us afloat."

Ganor leaned his arms on the table, appearing to settle in for a cozy chat. How long had it been since that had happened with anyone at all? Papa was sometimes talkative over their evening meals, but outside of him she didn't have a lot of gabs.

"Why is it your da, a man who despises books and tales and the written word, plies his trade as a printer? Seems a contradiction to me."

"He was a printer in Russia. It's the trade he knows and the skills he has." She shrugged, her hands held out to her side. "He never prints any books or stories or bits of fiction. He limits himself to documents and advertisements and pamphlets."

"Pamphlets are written by writers," Ganor pointed out.

"I know it's a contradiction, but I don't press him on it. If he limited his jobs even more, we'd be in the suds for sure and certain."

"Money remains tight, does it?"

"Always."

His ginger brow pulled as he focused more closely on her. "You're certain you've the funds for paying me? Don't misunderstand, it's grateful I am for the income as I'd not care to live with m'sister for the rest of m'life. But I don't want to be the reason your shop sinks beneath the waves."

"With how many penny dreadfuls you sold today alone, I'd wager you'll more than pay for yourself."

He grinned broadly. The man had a shockingly beautiful smile. "I've a fondness for the tales."

"I twigged that."

Still looking as amused as ever, he asked, "You 'twigged' it?"

"Sorted it out," she explained. "South London shows up in my words still."

He nodded. "Ireland wriggles its way into mine now and then."

She snorted. "'Now and then.'"

"What is it you're trying to say, lass?" he asked, eyes twinkling with laughter.

"That I'm not sure you know what the phrase 'now and then' means, that's what I'm saying." She couldn't remember the last time she'd smiled so much chatting with someone. "It'd be like me saying I crave hot roasted chestnuts 'now and then.'"

"Fond of roasted chestnuts, are you?"

"Desperately fond."

Papa's voice echoed from beyond the back door, raised

in a way that told her he was talking as he approached rather than being present already. "Have you read the paper, *kotik*?"

Vera lowered her voice and said to Ganor, "Another product of writers he's willing to endure."

Ganor nodded solemnly.

"I haven't, *papishka*," she called back just as Papa stepped through the doorway.

He didn't come all the way inside. She'd wager his distance was part of his ongoing protest over the presence of the penny serials. Vera rose from her seat and crossed to him. Ganor, thank the heavens, set himself to tasks on the other side of the shop. Papa had accepted his presence there, but he'd not seemed overly pleased at the need for hiring someone.

"It's about von Brunnow." Papa pointed to an article on the page he'd folded back.

"And what does the paper have to say about Russia's ambassador?"

"Rumors of a falling out with Lord Chelmsford." More curiosity sat in Papa's tone than alarm.

"Odd, that. They've something of a friendship between them." She took the paper from him.

Papa scratched at his beard. "I've heard whispers he's been acting strange."

"Which one? The baron or the ambassador?"

"The ambassador," Papa said as he pushed back his spectacles.

Vera scanned the article, looking for indications of oddity in Russia's representative. "Where've you heard these whispers? You haven't much contact with the Russian community here."

He stiffened. He always did when talk turned to his countrymen. She ought to have known better after so many years. But his bringing up the ambassador had lulled her into thinking the topic wasn't as forbidden as it usually was.

"I suppose von Brunnow will sort things with the baron soon enough," Vera said, hoping to end the discussion before Papa worked himself into a huff. "We've done a vast deal of business today. One of our most profitable."

"We'll have more print business soon enough, you'll see. Then you can get rid of all those—" He looked over at the display of penny dreadfuls. His nose scrunched as if he'd come across a putrid smell, sending his spectacles slipping once more.

"They're only stories, Papa. None of the people who write them are here, and they never will be. We're a small shop in Soho. We're too far below any of their notice."

But Papa was shaking his head in that mechanical way he did when dismissing an argument even as it was being made.

Little Olly hopped into the shop in the very next moment, offering a much needed distraction. "What've you got new today, Miss Vera?"

"Piles and piles, Olly." She stepped away from her papa, knowing he'd disappear downstairs. "You remember Mr. O'Donnell." She directed the boy's attention that way.

"You bought us a story last time." Olly popped Ganor one of his cheeky salutes.

"What'd you think of it, lad?" Ganor asked, leaning a

shoulder against the doorframe, his thick arms folded across his chest, light falling on the thick scars on his knuckles.

"It'll be frightening, I know it. All them dead animals."

Ganor nodded. "I suspect it will be."

Olly dropped his voice to a whisper. "Who do you think's taking the missing animals?"

Ganor matched the boy's volume. "If I knew, I'd not tell you, lad. 'Twould ruin the story."

That brought Olly's eyes to Vera. "Have *you* sorted it?"

She shook her head. "It's a mystery to me."

Raised voices echoed outside, pulling all their attention. Ganor stood nearest the door and was the first outside. Vera was there an instant later. A bit of commotion had broken out in front of the tobacconist's shop a few doors down.

Peter, the costermonger who worked on the street, stood in his usual spot just outside the print shop.

"Any notion what's happened?" Vera asked.

"I heard shouts of 'thief.' I'm guessing Mr. Bianchi's been robbed," Peter said.

"A common thing on this street?" Ganor asked.

She shook her head. "We've crime, sure enough. But thievery ain't much heard of." Vera hooked a thumb in the direction of her own shop. "Keep an eye on the place, will you? I mean to go learn what's happened."

"Surely will, Miss Vera," Ganor said.

No objection to being asked to remain behind while a woman investigated the danger. There weren't many men who'd accept that arrangement, especially those with a brawler's history.

Vera dipped her head to a few neighbors she passed, all

of whom were watching the proceedings outside the tobacco shop with worried curiosity. She reached the doorway in a matter of moments and eyed the scene.

The shop was a bit broken up. Mr. Bianchi sat atop an overturned crate with a wet rag pressed to one eye. Mr. Overton, the barber from across the way, stood beside him, a reassuring hand on his shoulder.

"What happened?" Vera asked.

"A couple of roughs demanded money of him, then tossed the place around."

"Because he wouldn't pay?"

Mr. Bianchi shook his head.

Mr. Overton answered. "He gave them what they demanded. They tore the place to bits anyway."

The damage didn't look irreparable, but it was a full mess. "I've extra hands at my shop today. I'd bet Ganor'd be willing to come help you set the place to rights."

"I'll not take away your employee," Mr. Bianchi said. "You'd be paying him and getting nothing for it."

"Not a bit of truth to that. Having your shop running as it ought and showing anyone wishing to follow these roughs' example that they'll not manage much are both well worth doing."

Whether Mr. Bianchi and Mr. Overton believed her, she couldn't say, but she kept her word. Ganor was more than willing to head to the tobacconist's and clean and sort things, though he too expressed concern about being paid *by* her for work he wasn't doing *for* her. While she was grateful so many people were concerned for her, she was a little frustrated that no one seemed to take her at her word.

She was still considered new in the area, and she was younger than a lot of the local merchants. Papa's gruff standoffishness likely didn't help. And, though she sounded London, she was told often enough that she looked Russian that she wondered if that might also be considered by some people a mark against her. There were plenty enough immigrants in this corner of London; it ought not to have been a point of trouble.

In time, she would find a way of forging connections here. She would make a home of this bit of Soho.

She would stop being so painfully alone.

CHAPTER 5

Brogan was stretched mighty thin. Between getting new installments to his publisher, the days he spent at the print shop, and his and Móirín's ongoing efforts in the poor areas of London, he had hardly a moment to breathe. It was likely a good thing he no longer met with the DPS. He'd have run out of time to sleep.

And yet, he missed being part of that society. He missed his friends there. He missed the connection. He longed for the assurance he had when undertaking missions *with* them instead of the unshakable doubt he felt being the rogue animal in the herd.

Móirín was working extra hours as well, apparently having taken quite seriously his explanation that he was earning additional money to allow them both the independence of setting up their own homes. So he didn't see her as often as he used to either.

As busy as he was, he was also horribly lonely. And exhausted. And far out of his depth.

He was making his way back home from Somers Town, a

56

particularly poor and all-too-often violent corner of London, having brought some needed goods to the struggling families there, when his path unexpectedly crossed with two of his old associates.

More than a fortnight had passed since he had left the Dread Penny Society. Two weeks in which he'd not seen a single one of his friends from that organization. Seeing them again was a salve he hadn't realized he needed. His heart lightened on the instant.

"Fancy seeing you in these parts," Fletcher said to Brogan. "Where you off to?"

"Returning from a trip to Somers Town."

Doc whistled low and long. "Struggling area, that," he said. "I hope you had Móirín with you."

Brogan shook his head.

"I don't know that I'd want to spend time there without her along for protection." Fletcher nudged Doc with his elbow, the two exchanging laughing glances. Even Brogan grinned.

Móirín's fierceness was well known among the Dreadfuls. Brogan was mostly known for being good for a laugh. Life's struggles had made her hard in many ways. He'd passed through many of the same things, but it hadn't changed him in the same way.

Perhaps that was part of the reason why the Dread Master had trusted him with this secret mission. No one, including his fellow Dread Penny members, would ever peg him as capable of undertaking a dangerous investigation alone.

"Martin says he's heard you're working in a shop now," Doc said.

Martin was another one of the Dreadfuls. The man was known for having eyes on near everything that happened around London. Brogan hadn't realized the man had sniffed out his arrangements. That could make things mighty difficult.

"We can't all have the sales Fletcher has." He adopted the conspiratorial tone he'd often used when bantering with his friends. "I'm needing a bit more coin in m'pocket."

"Is that why you actually left? You needed more time to take on more work?" Doc eyed him closely, with a look of suspicion Brogan wasn't accustomed to seeing on the faces of his one-time comrades. It cut him deeply.

Money trouble would've been an easy excuse for leaving the DPS. But Brogan hadn't realized at the time that the opportunity would present itself for a job at the very shop he was meant to be investigating. He'd seen the sign in the window and had jumped at the lucky turn.

He knew from years of investigating with the DPS that changing a story only made things more complicated. He'd have to stick to what they'd already been told. "I left for the reason I gave—couldn't keep lying to m' sister."

Doc didn't seem fully satisfied with that. Did the others feel the same way? Had Brogan managed to make a mull of even the simplest part of this assignment?

"With a bit more time, we might've managed to create that sister organization," Fletcher said.

Though Brogan understood Fletcher had to play along, it still hurt hearing him criticize the decision he knew Brogan had made at the behest of the Dread Master.

"I couldn't wait any longer," Brogan said.

"But you didn't give us any warning." Doc shook his head. "If we'd had the least idea you were so close to crying off, we'd have moved faster."

Mercy, this was getting complicated. "I couldn't keep it up. Too many lies. Too many false stories. Móirín was bound to see through it sooner rather than later. I couldn't keep risking accidentally spilling our secrets."

"We would have helped you if you'd trusted us." Doc turned and walked away, an angry clack from his bootheels. He was not a large man by any means, being of average height and very slender build. Yet, he had a presence that was commanding. His departure delivered a very clear message: Brogan's defection had driven a wedge.

He shoved his hands in his coat pockets, dropping his gaze to his shoes. He'd known this assignment would mean he'd no longer be a comrade-in-arms with the Dreadfuls. He'd not expected to lose their friendship altogether, though.

"Sorry about that," Fletcher said quietly.

"Is everyone that . . . disappointed in me?" Brogan asked.

"No one's terribly happy about it."

"Unhappy enough that they'll not even want to gab with me if we cross paths?" Saints, that'd be a lonely way to live his life.

"I can't say one way or the other. You're the first of us to ever desert the group." With Doc out of view and no one else hanging about, Fletcher pressed forward, speaking low and quick. "Please tell me it's at least proving somewhat fruitful."

Brogan made a minute gesture of uncertainty. "The job I have secured is at the shop I was told to look into, but I've not learned much yet. Mr. Sorokin apparently has very little interaction with his countrymen. There's a story behind that, I'm certain of it, but I don't know what it is yet. Even with that estrangement, he takes an interest in what's happening with the ambassador."

"Anything else?" Fletcher asked quickly and quietly.

"He hates writers."

Fletcher winced. "How'd you get around that?"

"I'm using a false name: Ganor O'Donnell."

Fletcher nodded in recognition. 'Twas a name Brogan had used before. "And you've not sorted too much about the Sorokin family yet, I'd wager."

"I haven't." Brogan wished he had more information to pass along.

"It's early days yet," Fletcher said. "Keep at it."

Brogan nodded.

Fletcher continued on his way, following Doc's path. Brogan watched them go, his heart dropping into his shoes. He'd thought a few times that it'd be nice to see his DPS friends again and gab for a spell. Watching them approach, he'd felt a ray of sunlight he'd been missing. But the chance encounter had, instead, cast a shadow.

There was a rift between him and the only friends he'd made since coming to London, the friends he thought of as brothers. Even when all this was over, assuming his activities could be revealed to them, would he ever be truly welcomed back? It pained him that he didn't know the answer.

THE DEAD ZOO

by Brogan Donnelly

Day Two

Amos did not begin his investigative efforts until the day after being asked. He'd told William Sheenan that would be the case but hadn't confessed that there was no reason for the delay. Truth be told, Amos simply wanted to seem quite in demand. A reputation was only as impactful as one made it, after all.

With an air of casual authority, he stepped into the expanse of the collection of death. From a scientific perspective, it was the very height of anthropologic intrigue. To one who possessed even a modicum of superstition, it was the very height of horror. Amos Cavey's logical mind was never permitted to have greater say than what he considered his inferior tendency toward anxiety.

The museum was not empty, but neither was it bustling yet. This was the perfect opportunity for gathering clues. Amos had armed himself with a small notebook and a lead pencil sharpened to perfection. With both firmly in hand, he began a slow, pointed circuit of the first floor where the mammals were displayed, along with a few oddities from other corners of the animal kingdom. He chose to overlook how utterly sloppy a bit of work that was. He had been asked to solve a series of thefts, not teach the keepers the proper classification of species.

All seemed well around the largest displays. Nothing appeared amiss with the rhinoceros or American bison. He walked slowly around the open-air display of a walrus. All was well. A bit of dust hung about the zebra.

The wooden frame of the glass case surrounding the seals was a bit beaten up. The museum really ought to place their older cases in lesser visited corners of the room, not on full display such as this.

Mr. Carte had gone to such lengths to build the reputation of the Dead Zoo. Carelessness would only undermine it. Then again, so would knowledge of the thefts Amos had agreed to try to solve. He ought not be surprised to find other flaws beneath the veneer.

His investigation took him up the stairs to the second-story balconies where the museum housed its display of birds and fish. Amos spotted a gap in the display of birds and made directly for it. Not seeing a placard indicating the specimen had been removed for repair or cleaning or such, he studied the spot more carefully.

As with the case that had once housed the now-missing rodents, this case containing the display of birds boasted a bit of injury, precisely what one would expect after someone had quickly and inexpertly used a tool of some sort to loosen the bindings. The scratches he saw were not scattered in every direction, as one would expect from the natural wear and tear of years of visitors, but concentrated, repetitive. Someone had removed this bird without the precision one would expect from the keepers of this odd zoo who valued their animal population.

A disconcertingly familiar sensation—that of being watched—tiptoed over him just as it had the day before. It set his neck hairs standing on end. He swallowed, but not without a little difficulty. There were far too many eyes in the museum, not all of them human, not all of them seeing, for some sensation of being observed not to be felt. He told himself it was merely a trick of the mind.

But his eyes fell upon a murder of magpies—made still by death—watching him. Seven. Seven magpies.

> *One for sorrow.*
> *Two for joy.*
> *Three for a girl.*
> *Four for a boy.*

He could not stop the rhyme from echoing in his thoughts.

> *Five for silver.*
> *Six for gold.*
> *Seven for a secret, never to be told.*
> *Seven for a secret.*

Amos pushed down the feeling of foreboding. He would not allow himself to be ridiculous.

William arrived at his side not a moment later, no doubt the real reason for Amos's premonition. He *had* been observed by the man who had asked him to be there. With his logical nature firmly in charge once more, Amos felt himself far more on solid ground.

"You should know that this bird has also been pilfered," Amos said. "The display shows the same subtle damage, the same pattern of gouging."

Though the keeper was, understandably, a bit embarrassed to not have realized the issue extended beyond the mammals exhibit, he did not grow offended. "I ought to have realized the thefts would not be limited to only my section of the zoo. Please tell me if you find any other specimens you believe we have lost to this unknown criminal."

"He will not be unknown for long," Amos said. "I can assure you of that."

William dipped his head. "There is a reason I asked for your participation in this."

It must be remembered that the Dead Zoo was run by none other than the Royal Dublin Society, the members of which were not precisely dunces. To not ask one of their membership to oversee a matter such as this was a good indication that either the mystery was indeed an exceptionally difficult one to solve or William Sheenan was particularly keen to keep the matter a secret. It is for the astute reader to ascertain which was, in fact, the case.

Amos continued his searching circuit of the museum, first on the second story, then making his way to the galleries on the third. He found in his perusal a number of missing items. Some showed not the least indication of having been tampered with. Others, however, were scarred with the same careless marks as the other hapless dead creatures. All totaled, he found eight specimens had been taken.

Seating himself upon an obliging bench at the far end of the mammal exhibit, Amos acquainted himself with all his notes, searching for the connection he knew he would find there. Visitors glided in and out, each awed by the displays and most filled with amazement at the collection. Few paid him the least heed. He did not mind.

Nine missing.

One feline.

Four rodents.

One fish.

Two birds.

One bicolored lobster.

All were small enough for an enterprising individual to tuck under a jacket or shawl. These thefts, he grew more and more certain, were not the work of a particularly gifted thief. Perhaps the items were taken by youths challenging one another to undertake what they saw as a lark. Perhaps it was a person with a propensity toward thievery for reasons even they could not explain; he had read that some people could not help the inclination. Perhaps someone wished to undermine the museum.

He rose from his place of pondering and meandered amongst the visitors, listening in with a degree of subtlety he felt quite proud of. None, he felt certain, would realize he was investigating them.

The mother and child peering at the whale skeleton were quickly eliminated. To undertake something like this in the presence of a child would be difficult indeed.

He hovered just beyond a group of young students from Rathmines as they spoke at length of how very bored they all were.

"We'd not be seen if we slipped off and moved a few things about," one lad said. "Could pose the animals for a rugby match or some lark like that."

His friend shook his head. "They're likely all bolted in. And the museum man said once the animals are put on display, they don't get moved about."

The boys, then, were certain the specimens couldn't be stolen or moved from their spots. They'd not think that if they were the ones making off with them.

Amos realized, of course, that the perpetrator might very well not be present that particular day and at that particular hour. But the museum was open only three days per week. For so much to have gone missing in so short a time, he reasoned, the person must have been coming in every open day to make off with something new.

On he wandered. As has been established already, he was not one to admit to any insufficiencies in his intelligence. And he certainly wasn't likely to admit defeat after a single morning.

His footsteps took him past the polar bear once more. It was really a magnificent animal. Something in its eyes was more realistic than the other creatures strewn about. The glassy expressions one saw in all directions made clear how very dead the Dead Zoo really was. But this bear somehow gave a person pause. Perhaps it was simply the decision to have him perpetually watching the animal that might once have been his dinner. Even the least scientifically inclined visitor could understand hunger at a glance.

Amos wandered on, listening in on every conversation. Back up the stairs. Past the fish. Back to the birds. He ignored as he went the eyes that were deceptively upon him. He knew better than to believe the trick this place played on the senses.

Two gentlemen stood near the ostrich skeleton, having a lively conversation. A quick assessment of their attire told Amos they were relatively well-to-do. Their manner of speaking confirmed that evaluation.

"A remarkable specimen," the taller of the two said to the other.

"Indeed," was the response. "And the mounted birds are quite exquisite, as well."

"Have you observed the penguins?" The taller gentleman indicated the birds in question by pointing at them with his cane. "I find myself quite envious. Something of that caliber ought to be in *my* collection."

"Indeed."

"There is, you understand, but one thing to be done." The man's mustache twitched. His silver brows arched haughtily.

"Indeed."

"I must have a penguin of my own. I will not rest until I do. I have certainly managed to add to my collection of late." The man's tone was both self-satisfied and suspicious. "It would be a small matter to do so again."

And with that, the miscreant sealed his fate.

"Sir, if you will be good enough to follow me." Amos assumed his most demanding, unwavering tone.

"I beg your pardon." The man eyed him disapprovingly.

"The keeper of the mammal exhibit requires a word with you."

"Does he?"

Amos motioned him toward the stairs, counting on the man's good manners to prevent a scene. He often depended upon people doing what he thought they ought. He was both cynical and trusting by nature, and he was not always a good judge of when to employ which. In this instance, he chose correctly.

William was easy to find. He seldom left his precious mammals, and there he was found.

"Mr. Sheenan, I have solved your mystery." Amos held himself in a proud and defiant posture. "Your collection is the envy of many, some to the point of abandoning their good breeding to obtain what you have that they wish to possess."

William looked from Amos to the tall gentleman and back once more. His confusion was lost on the self-assured detective, who was quite proud of having so easily solved a question that had baffled others. Had he paid greater attention, he would have noticed that William and the gentleman did not seem at all surprised to see one another. Neither had they asked for an introduction.

Confident in his conclusions, Amos pressed forward. "This man wishes for one of your penguins to be part of his collection. He spoke of it in quite strong terms, almost foregone terms. I contend that—"

"Pray pardon the interruption, Lord Baymount," William hastily said to the man at Amos's side. "I hope you will continue to peruse the collections here at your leisure."

"Lord or not," Amos resumed, undeterred. Oh, the follies one reaps when unwilling to give ear to others. "He spoke of his collection—"

"With pride, I hope," William quickly interrupted. He knew the path Amos meant to trod and intended to save him from it. "Do go look them over."

He breached protocol so much as to nudge his lordship away, desperate as he was to avoid the humiliation Amos had very nearly caused.

"You did not allow me to finish." The intellectual was all wounded dignity.

"And for that you are quite welcome." William pointed to the back of the retreating lord. "He has contributed a great many specimens to our museum. His 'collection' of items are on display *here*. That he saw the penguins and wished one were part of *his* collection was not a threat of thievery but a determination to add something of equal intrigue and significance to those items he has already donated."

Few times in his adult life had Amos experienced the odd sensation of being embarrassed. It was a feeling he had as much experience with as being wrong. That he'd experienced both at once would astonish anyone who knew him.

His pride whipped up a frenzy of determination. He refused to be defeated by so simple a task. And he further refused to be humiliated again. The mystery would be solved, and it would be solved by him. His worth would be proved to William Sheehan, to the haughty Lord Baymount, to himself.

And, if it were the last thing he did, he would find a way to shake the unnerving weight of an unseen gaze that followed him all around the Dead Zoo.

CHAPTER 6

A few days had passed since the robbery at Mr. Bianchi's shop. Every person who walked down the street was eyed closely, watched with suspicion. Anything of any value in the various shops had been tucked out of sight. They'd no good reason for the crime; Bianchi wasn't exactly wealthy. No one on this street was doing terribly well for themselves. Yet, it had happened, and everyone was worried.

Little Olly slipped inside the print shop, earlier in the day than usual. The enterprising urchin was a favorite of Vera's. He'd learned to read at a ragged school and devoured any story he could get his hands on. Unfortunately, he was also poorer than a church mouse.

"Hiya, Miss Vera." Olly snapped a salute, a common gesture for the boy.

"*Zdrastvui*, Olly."

He flashed her a mischievous, gap-toothed smile. "I like when you say the Russian words."

"Always knew you was dimber-damber, Olly." She ruffled his dusty hair.

Olly strutted a bit. "I *am* smart, at that."

"Smart as a fox."

"I read 'The Dead Zoo' again. Three times now." He made for the penny dreadful display but stopped at arm's length. The boy knew he couldn't touch them if his hands weren't clean.

Ganor spoke from his place updating the window display. "Do you like the story so far, lad?"

Olly's eyes pulled wide. "I want to know what happens next."

"The next installment came in today," Ganor said.

The boy's mouth pulled in an O. "I'd hoped it would."

"That first bit was fine feathers, weren't it?" Vera said

"It were." He stuffed his hands in the outer pockets of his jacket and bounced a little in place. "I ain't got any pennies. None I can spend, leastwise."

She wished she could give the poor children who came through her shop all the serials they wished for—the stories were good for their spirits—but she and Papa would land in the workhouse if she did. Many children had shown themselves too proud to accept charity, as it was.

"Have you some time to yourself just now?" she asked Olly. "There's work to do around here—enough to earn a penny."

He eyed her narrowly. "I could take on a spot of work."

"Dusting the display and the windowsills?" Vera suggested.

He nodded quickly. "I've done that before."

"And you've had to wash your hands before," she reminded him.

Olly eyed her with brow drawn and forehead creased. "Yous always after me to clean up. I cain't go about smelling like a blossom and looking clean as a toff. I'd get me nose broke."

"Your secret's safe with me," she said. "Get to it, then. No more knocking about."

Olly snapped one of his salutes and disappeared into the shop's back room, where they kept a washbasin and hand towel. He knew the setup well by now.

"Good of you to help the lad," Ganor said.

She knew how easily the street children's pride could be bruised. "He works hard for the coins," she said. "Fly me if we ain't getting the better end of the arrangement."

"What does Olly do when he's not dusting for you here?"

"A little of everything, from what I hear of him. He's like most urchins in London; he gets by on his wits."

Ganor stepped back from the window, apparently having finished his efforts there. "Dublin was like that, too. M'sister and I did what we could to get by. 'Twas sometimes a long while between pennies."

"Life don't hand out opportunities in equal measure," she said.

"Correcting that inequality is the work of a life well lived."

It wasn't a sentiment she'd have expected to hear from a man who bore the scars of a life violently lived. Not only was the idea gentle and compassionate, but the expressing of it was almost poetic. "You've a way with words."

"And I didn't even have to kiss the Blarney Stone." He grinned mischievously.

His brown eyes had a way of sparkling when he was jesting. That, combined with his breath-catching smile, was mesmerizing. Every time he tossed her that look, and it came often on account of his being fond of teasing, she wondered what it would take to keep the laughter from fading away.

"Do the Irish often kiss rocks?" She matched his tone of teasing.

One ginger brow quirked upward. "Oh, the Irish are brilliant kissers. Every last one of us."

Vera attempted to pull in a breath, but her suddenly pounding heart seemed determined to prevent it.

"And do you know what I've learned about Russian lasses?" His eyes danced about.

"What've you learned?" Her voice emerged a bit shaky.

"That you blush a very pretty shade of pink."

No one had ever flirted with her before, but she was certain that's what he was doing now. Bless her, she was enjoying it. Deeply enjoying it.

Olly emerged from the back room, holding up his newly washed hands. "Scrubbed raw, Miss Vera."

"You've piles of dust waiting to be wiped up." She waved the boy over. "Hop to it, *zaychik*."

Olly grinned, the gap in his front teeth making him all the more darling. The child was a delight, a right nutty little fella, and she adored him.

"What does *zaychik* mean?" Ganor asked, doing a fine job pronouncing the Russian word.

"'Little rabbit,'" Vera answered. "Can't say when I started calling him that."

"My da called me *sicín beag*, when I was wee thing."

"What's that mean?"

He straightened the display of pen nibs. "'Little Chicken.'"

Though Ganor wasn't a tall man, it was difficult to imagine him so small he'd be compared to a tiny chick. He had the hands of a fighter and the muscular build of one as well. She probably should have found his thick arms and broad shoulders intimidating instead of undeniably intriguing.

"Sicín beag." She tested out the feel of the Irish words, not having ever attempted anything in that tongue.

"Not terrible," Ganor said. "Likely better than my attempt at *zaychik*."

With a shrug of dismissal no one could possibly have mistaken for sincere, she said, "Not terrible."

He grinned at her teasing repetition of his exact evaluation.

Customers were wandering in, pulling them both back to work. They often had moments like that. Quick conversations scattered throughout the day. She'd worried at first about all the questions he asked, but she'd come to suspect he simply liked to gab. And, since they were nothing more than strangers when he'd begun working, questions were needed or they'd've had nothing to talk about. That would be a blasted shame.

"Oi, Miss Vera." Peter held up a copy of Mr. Donnelly's latest. "You've read the newest chapter, ya?"

"I have. A fine tale is unfolding, though Mr. Donnelly shows in it an odd interest in magpies."

"Magpies?" Peter whistled slow and low. "Bad omen, magpies. Depending."

"An English superstition," Vera acknowledged, having learned of it growing up in London. "But who's to say if it's an Irish one as well?"

"He'd know." Peter motioned with his head toward Ganor.

A good idea, that. And it'd give her a welcome excuse to chat with him again.

Peter reached into his coat pocket and pulled out two ha'pennies. "Thinkin' I'll pick this'n. I liked his last one."

She took up his coins. "Drop in and tell me how you like it."

"Will do, Miss Vera." He tipped his hat without taking it off. "Always fine seeing you. Offer your father my greetings."

"Will do, Peter."

Many of the other customers bid him a farewell.

"Have you read Mr. King's newest?" Clare asked. She lived somewhere nearby and tended to knock about the place, though she seldom had money to spend.

Vera suspected she was avoiding wherever she called home. This was Soho; Clare was hardly the only woman in the area wishing to avoid a bad situation. Vera would let her lark about all she wanted.

"I've read Mr. King's," Vera said. "There's the start of a bang-up tale in that one."

Clare nodded and returned to her perusal. A younger girl asked her a question. Two other customers talked in low but excited whispers about Mr. King's stories. Olly was wiping down the windowsills. All her customers seemed content.

She returned to the counter to put the ink bottles back in the nearby cupboard. A folded piece of paper sat atop the counter, with her name scrawled across the parchment.

Odd. It hadn't been there a moment earlier.

She caught Ganor's eye and held up the note, pointing to it. "From you?" she mouthed.

He shook his head. That was unexpectedly disappointing.

She slipped a finger under the top fold and pushed the paper open.

I have heard of the violence on this street. I'm able to safeguard your business. Only £1. If you're interested, someone'll come collect tomorrow.

It was signed "The Protector."

"Did you sort out what it was?" Ganor had approached while she was reading.

"The oddest note." She handed it over to him. "What do you make of it?"

His eyes scanned the paper. She watched him as he read. Ganor O'Donnell was a handsome man, and that was a little distracting.

"Someone's found a way to make a bit of money," he said.

She nodded. "Odd, though, that this bloke didn't sign his real name."

Ganor shrugged. "I've heard any number of odd names on the streets of London. Dublin too. 'Tisn't necessarily proof of poor character."

"It ain't exactly proof of good character either," she said.

"And strange that the offer was made in a note rather than simply asking you. You've been here all day." He flipped the paper over. "No marks. 'Twasn't sent through the penny post."

"Someone was here and delivered this note without saying a word." Criminy, she didn't like that. "And who's to say if I pay what's being asked that I'll get any protection at all? Could be the entire thing's nothing but a cheat."

"I wish I had answers for you." His usual teasing expression turned to sincere concern. "What do you mean to do?"

That he was confused by the note too didn't bode well. "We could use extra eyes and ears on the street. No matter that the chap went about it in a curious manner, if the offer is a true one, it'd be helpful."

"And if the offer isn't aboveboard?" He handed the note back to her.

She took it, but reluctantly. "Then not paying it might be a danger itself." Vera sighed, her body still tense. "The character of 'The Protector' ain't the only thing I have to worry over in this matter."

"What else, then?"

"What to tell my papa."

Ganor stepped away a moment to answer a question one of the customers posed to him, leaving Vera to ponder the one on her mind.

Papa struggled to trust people. He was gruff and off-putting at times. Life had taught him to be paranoid. What he'd told her of the struggles he'd passed through had given her many of those same inclinations toward distrust. She'd fought all her life to keep her faith in people intact.

Papa had spent the days since the robbery at the tobacco shop grumbling about crime and poor characters. He'd talked to some degree of adding extra precautions around the shop on the days when Ganor wasn't there. He'd even at one point mused that they'd have done better never to have left Southwark.

She didn't want to give up on this shop but feared Papa would if the matter of crime in this area was pressed too heavily. Someone finding it enough of a threat that they'd offer protection for a price would only add to that impression.

Ganor returned, eyeing her with curiosity.

"Nothing about this is truly threatening," she said, holding up the note. "Odd, yeah. But nothing to worry Papa over."

"Are you sure?" Ganor asked. "It might be he'd have some thoughts on the matter."

Vera very nearly snorted. "Oh, he would most definitely have thoughts."

He smiled. How was it she hadn't grown any more accustomed to that heart-melting smile of his after more than a week of working together? "Are you saying that you aren't interested in his thoughts? Or that you know what they would be and therefore don't need to hear them?"

"I know what they would be, and that would only make the situation worse."

He nodded. "And what is it you mean to do with the offer that was made?"

"I mean to accept. This 'Protector' is only asking a quid, and if that grants us a few extra eyes on the street, it wouldn't be a bad thing."

He nodded but didn't seem entirely convinced.

The customers pulled their attention in the next moment, and she hadn't a chance to ask him what his misgivings might be. In the end, she set aside a pound from the till and told herself all would be well.

They'd have some protection. The shop would be safer.

And Papa would be happier not knowing a thing about it.

CHAPTER 7

Brogan cut through Hyde Park after making a delivery for the print shop. 'Twas faster than going the long way 'round, besides being a fine opportunity for strolling along the Serpentine on an unusually mild winter day.

The fashionable hour hadn't arrived, but the park was far from empty. Half its inhabitants were dogs, truth be told. And a good number of those dogs were being followed by children known throughout London as "pure finders." They collected droppings that they then sold to tanners. The work was unpleasant and, at times, dangerous. But Brogan knew all too well that poor street children did what they could to survive.

Two very rough-looking men, their clothes stained and worn, their hair and beards unkempt, caught Brogan's notice as he went by. They eyed every person who passed, including him. 'Twasn't a rough area of Town; the two were entirely out of place.

Brogan stopped under an obliging tree and pulled a

penny dreadful—Mr. King's—from his coat pocket, pretending to read it. He watched the ruffians, paying particular attention to which of the park's occupants caught *their* attention.

One of them nudged the other with his elbow, then motioned toward a girl following the path of a large, thick-coated dog. She was likely about twelve or thirteen years old. Her hair was startlingly black and, in the spots where the sun hit it just right, the tiniest bit blue. She had a very striking look about her, and that was a very dangerous thing for young girls living on the merciless streets of London.

Bold rescues of children were Fletcher Walker's specialty, but Fletcher wasn't there just then. Brogan refused to leave the child in danger, no matter that he was ill-suited to the roll of knight on a white charger.

He pushed away from the tree and moved toward the girl, keeping one eye on the roughs and one eye on the girl, all while trying to formulate a means of helping the child without frightening her.

She spotted him as he approached and quickly slipped from the path and a bit out of reach.

"I'm not looking to do you any harm, lass," he said softly. "I only hoped to warn you."

"Something a body'd say to put me off the scent." The glance she tossed him was hard and untrusting. He didn't blame her.

"I'll not come any closer to you, and I'll keep m'hands where you can see them." He held them up for good measure, palms to her so his brawl-scarred knuckles didn't cause her alarm. He'd caught Vera staring at them more than once, and not as if she liked what she saw. "I truly wish only to warn you. There's two men back a pace who I'd peg as bullyboys, either seeking out their own enjoyment or working for a madame."

"Them rorty blokes back there?" She motioned to the two roughnecks.

Brogan nodded. "And I think you know why they're keeping so close an eye on you."

Without flinching she said simply, "I'm at the age when girls start disappearing. We all know what happens to them."

He hated how true that was. "You're not safe on the streets."

"I'm always on the streets," she said. "Urchins ain't got fine homes to run off to."

"I know it."

She eyed him up and down. "You're a bit big for an urchin."

He shrugged. "I grew out of it."

"Fortunate for you," she grumbled.

"It is, indeed." Far too many didn't survive their early years. "Any chance you could find work that didn't put you in the open like this?"

"None," she said firmly. "And I ain't no one's burden." She turned in the direction of a dog being walked by what appeared to be a maid.

The bullyboys would snatch her up in an instant, if not today then tomorrow.

"Would you consider at least tucking yourself away for the day?" Brogan asked. "Give those fellas the shake for now?"

For now. There would be others. There were always others.

"You know somewhere I could hide myself?"

"A shop in Soho. And I'd wager m' eyeteeth the shop-keeper'd give you bit to do today, let you earn a coin or two." He'd pay her *his* wages for the day if need be. He couldn't simply leave her here.

She watched him warily. "Eyeteeth'd fetch a fair bit."

He nodded. "For sure."

Her eyes darted to the approaching bullyboys.

"Let's go see if I'm keeping m'teeth, lass." Brogan tried to hide his growing concern behind a tone of teasing.

"If you're wrong, I'll miss all the best dogs."

"I'll repay any losses," he said. "My word of honor."

"What's your name?" she asked.

He'd only just given his word on the matter of her income, and here he was about to lie to her about his own name. "Ganor O'Donnell. What's yours?"

"Licorice."

The street children had interesting names, no one'd argue otherwise. Hers, he'd wager, had been given her on account of her unique hair.

"I suppose I could go see this shop in Soho," Licorice said.

Thank the heavens. He motioned her onward, relief filling him from his toes to the top of his head.

She walked alongside him—head high, eyes wary—away from the park. He didn't for a moment think she actually trusted him. More likely than not, she was merely leaving before the ruffians got too close.

As he'd promised, he kept a distance between them and made certain she could see him at all times. She had ample reason to be wary of anyone and everyone. He didn't want to scare her beyond what was avoidable, while still getting her to safety.

Not more than a half-dozen steps from Hyde Park, Brogan took note of one of the men he'd been watching following them.

If Brogan took Licorice directly back to the shop, these roughs would know where to find her. They might simply wait and follow her to wherever she laid her head at night. He wasn't about to let that happen. Móirín wasn't home, so he didn't particularly want to take Licorice to their flat. DPS Headquarters was entirely out of the question—the Dreadfuls would never turn their back on a child in danger, but revealing the location was a violation of the oath they took when they joined. Besides, he wasn't considered one of them any longer.

He could hail a hansom cab and be out of sight of the bullyboy in no time, but that'd only delay the danger if the driver happened to know the man following them.

"How do we mean to shake 'im?" Licorice, of course, had noticed. Nothing got past the urchins.

"I don't think we can, lass."

She didn't look shaken or afraid, but there was no doubt her every sense was on alert. "So what comes next?"

He rolled his neck a little. "What comes next is you learning a bit more about me than I'd figured you'd learn." Brogan stopped on the spot. "You make certain I am always between you and that man; move about, run if you're needing to."

"What're you gonna do, Mr. O'Donnell?"

"I'll be offering the man a 'Liberties greeting.'" The Liberties was the area of Dublin he'd called home. A lad growing up there learned to wield fists of diplomacy and wield them well.

Brogan turned about, his eyes meeting those of their pursuer.

He must've been able to tell Brogan hadn't turned to him in a gesture of goodwill. "Don't ruffle up, mate. We can share."

Brogan didn't wait, didn't hold back. With a quickness and precision borne of far too many street altercations, he delivered a fist to the scoundrel's gut just below the ribs. The man bent forward with the impact. Brogan took a half step back, cocked his fist once more and landed it solidly on the man's nose. He grabbed his neckcloth and twisted so it pulled tight around the would-be-assailant's neck, then pulled him up close.

"This wee one's protected," Brogan growled. "You leave her be. Understand?"

The man made a motion that likely would have been a nod if not for his quickly swelling nose and Brogan's grip on his neckcloth.

"Say it," Brogan growled out. "Convince me you mean it."

"She's protected." The strangled whisper emerged nearly as broken as the man's nose.

"And?" Brogan pressed.

"I'll leave her be."

"Not just you." Brogan pulled the neckcloth tighter. "You get the word out."

Another jerking and graceless nod.

"And, just to make certain you don't forget . . ." Brogan slammed his knee into the man's groin, sending him crumpled to the ground.

Then, calm as a saint in church, he turned about, wiping imaginary dirt from his hands as well as a very real trickle of blood from one knuckle. "Shall we, then?" He motioned Licorice forward.

"Where'd you learn to fight like that, Mr. O'Donnell?"

"Like what?"

"Like a criminal."

He likely ought to have been offended, but he found himself laughing. "I was taught to fight by a criminal."

"Were *you* a criminal?"

"I've been poor and desperate, and there's bits of m' past that don't bear scrutiny," he said.

"Seems you and I ain't that different," Licorice said.

"I think most of us are more alike than we realize."

She hadn't much to say as they walked; Brogan kept a bit closer to her than he might've otherwise but still let her have space enough to feel safe. They reached Sorokin's Print Shop and he still hadn't the first idea how she felt about much of anything.

He led the way inside. It was busy, as it often was.

Vera looked over as he stepped inside and, to his amused delight, looked immediately curious. He liked that she seemed pulled in by mysteries, no doubt from having read so many penny dreadfuls.

"Miss Vera," he said, dipping at the waist.

"So formal?" She laughed a little.

Licorice spoke before Brogan had a chance to reply. "You're Miss Vera?"

"I am."

"Olly works for you and your papa sometimes." Licorice took over the conversation, not needing an invitation. "And Burnt Ricky and Bob's Your Knuckle."

Vera motioned to the children in the shop at the moment. "Among a few others."

Licorice popped her fists on her hips, not a posture of defiance but determination. "I'm needing a spot of work, and I know you hire on urchins like me now and then."

Brogan blinked at her boldness. What a grand trick the girl had played on him.

"You didn't tell me you knew Miss Vera when I suggested we come to this shop," he said.

With a look of impatient superiority, Licorice said, "I ain't required to tell you everythin' I know. Besides, you only said a shop in Soho. You never said which one."

Vera smiled at the girl. "What do they call you, love?"

"Licorice."

"And do you need the occasional spot of work, or regular employment?" Vera asked.

"I'm a pure finder just now, but I cain't keep doing that."

"I can give you a spot," Vera said. "You'd earn a few coins at the end of the week. Cain't promise you anything beyond that."

Licorice nodded firmly. "Maybe I'll twig something else I can do before the week's out."

"Something safer than you've been doing," Brogan requested.

She tossed him a cheeky smile. "I thought 'this lass is protected.'"

He laughed; he couldn't help himself. "That'll offer you some buffer, girl, but pure finding ought to be something in the past for *you*."

Licorice set her shoulders and turned back to Vera. "Tell me what you're wanting from me first."

Vera pointed behind herself. "Dip into the back room. Wash your hands, then come back out and I'll give you work to do."

"Your papa's back there, is he?" Licorice eyed the door with misgiving.

"Not just now. He's popped off to the papermill." Vera motioned her away with a jerk of her head.

After the girl had slipped away, Vera turned to Brogan. Her eyes darted to his hand. "You're bleeding."

He couldn't tell if the observation was disapproving or not. "Had to give a bloke a warning."

"Something you've done before."

His scars testified to that. He slipped his hands behind himself, not wanting to see disapproval in her eyes. "There's always someone needing saving. At times that someone's been me."

She pulled a dust rag from a low shelf behind the counter. It was still folded, meaning it was clean. Vera held out her hand as if expecting him to give her something. "Your hand, if you will. The bleeding one."

Hesitantly, he set his injured hand in hers. "It ain't badly hurt. A little slip skin is all."

Her small hand all but disappeared under his. Their size might've seen them labeled dainty if not for her firm, strong grip, and the callouses that told of a life spent working. Vera bent over his hand, dabbing at the small bit of blood. There was a determination to her efforts, a fierceness, and yet her efforts were also inarguably gentle.

She held herself with confidence and spoke with authority. She ran her shop with precision and a keen mind for business. But she also showed compassion to the urchins who crossed her threshold. She knew their names, their situations, their worries.

She began each day dressed with precision, but always ended it with a dusty apron, a smudge or two on her cheek, and her once-neat knot of hair on the verge of chaotic. The contrasts in her were utterly captivating.

"Why is it Licorice needs to sack off the pure finding?" Vera asked as she dabbed carefully with the cloth.

"She's starting to draw attention from the town bulls." Saints, he'd nearly choked on the words as he opened his mouth. Vera had him more than a little upended.

Keep your wits about you, man.

"Well, they'll not snatch her here." Something gave Vera pause. "This *is* Soho, though. We've a number of brothels hereabout. She'll not be in danger from any of them, but the reminder of her thinly escaped net might make her a touch nervous to be in this corner of London."

"We'll keep our ears perked for other options should they be needed," he said.

"*We?*" she repeated.

"I didn't figure you'd toss the girl out with nowhere to go and nothing to do."

"You have me sorted, it seems."

"More than you realize." He pulled a small bag from his pocket. "They're not as hot as they were, but I think you'll like them just the same."

She accepted the offering and peeked into the bag. "Roasted chestnuts. You remembered."

Vera smiled at him, and the sight did odd things to his heart. Very odd indeed.

THE MERCHANT
AND THE ROGUE

by Mr. King

Installment II
in which an Unkind Deed causes sorrow in
Innocent and Roguish hearts alike!

Royston Prescott could not understand why he was so very bothered that the local confectionery merchant didn't seem to care much for him. He'd heard talk of Miss Tallulah O'Doyle and had been intrigued over the weeks since her arrival. At long last, his curiosity had gotten the better of him, and he had slipped in to discover for himself if what he'd heard of it was true.

The children in the village adored her, proclaiming her the kindest lady of their acquaintance. Many throughout the area applauded her generosity. A few expressed some concerns that her tender heart would make it more difficult to turn a profit, but overall, she was declared an excellent addition to the shops at the market cross.

He had seen her about town, always from a distance. She was lovely, animated, and seemed a decidedly happy sort of person. He also saw in her something he recognized:

loneliness. There was a certain melancholy resting deep in her eyes that spoke of someone who felt out of place, longed for someone to recognize what she struggled with.

She had taken up his banter readily and had thrown back as many quips as he had tossed at her. She was funny and clever, and he appreciated that. But it had become quickly obvious that she saw him as everyone else did—as he made certain everyone else did—dismissing him as little more than a hopeless scoundrel bent on shallow and meaningless interactions.

It shouldn't have bothered him, but it did.

He stepped inside her shop two days after his initial visit and found the place quite busy. She, of course, had children inside staring longingly at the jars of colorful candies and displays of petits fours. This was a place of dreams for young, poor children. How easily she could have made it torturous for them, but she didn't. When a child produced a ha'penny or, if they were particularly blessed, a pence, she helped them select the very best assortment of candies.

"You're very kind to our little ones," Mrs. Morris said. "We've never before had a confectionary shop in town. Your corner of Chippingwich has become a place of dreams."

"*My* dreams as much as anyone else's," Miss O'Doyle said. "I like the baking and making, and the children are a delight to have about. And the town is proving right friendly, which I'm needing being so far from m' home."

"Perhaps this'll become a home to you." Mrs. Morris echoed the words of the squire from two days earlier, but *she* sounded sincere.

"Miss Tallulah." Georgie Kent, one of many children in

Chippingwich seen pouring in and out of the shop, held a ha'penny up to her. "Anise candy, please, Miss Tallulah."

She accepted the coin. "You are in luck, Georgie. Anise candy is reduced in price today. You'll get an extra piece."

Georgie bounced in place, his eyes pulling nearly as wide as his grin. He left, as so many did, utterly delighted with their local confectioner.

"Mr. Prescott," Miss O'Doyle greeted, his turn having arrived. "What may I do for you?"

"I have heard quite a lot of praise for your petits fours." He offered what he knew was a very winning smile. "I simply must judge for myself."

"You realize, of course, I will charge *you* the full price."

He pretended to be affronted. "Am I not endearing enough to be granted the Adorable Village Youngster price?"

She made quite a show of regretting the necessary answer. "Even were you endearing, you would be disqualified on account of your advanced age."

Oh, she was a delight!

"Do you not offer generous pricing to the exceptionally aged?"

"The shock might send you into your somewhat early grave."

He tipped her a flirtatious glance. "I'd be willing to take the risk."

She quoted him the usual price, but with a laugh in her eyes he felt certain was answered in his. He purchased two petits fours and sat at one of the two dainty tables in the establishment set there for the use of the customers. He would enjoy watching her interact with the villagers as he ate the tiny cakes. There was something very calming and pleasant about Miss Tallulah O'Doyle. Even one such as him could appreciate that.

Before any of the little ones or their parents could request their preferred sweet or baked good, Squire Carman slid inside, making his way directly to the counter. He was not one to wait his turn. Neither was he one for any variety in his clothing. Always the red hat and cape. At times, like this day, he wore a crimson waistcoat as well.

"I've come for the cake I commissioned," he said.

"Of course."

Miss O'Doyle turned to the curtained cooling cabinet in the corner and pulled from a low shelf a queen cake, dusted liberally with confectioners' sugar and decorated with candied fruit. Sugar came dear. This offering, elegant and no doubt delicious, would not be inexpensive. Of all the people in Chippingwich, only Clancy Carman could afford such an indulgence.

The cake was set on the counter before him. The other customers looked on in awe. It was a beautiful creation, one sure to inspire envy in the hearts of everyone not permitted to partake. The squire's lofty guests would be duly impressed.

Was Miss O'Doyle? Or did she see the squire for what he truly was?

"This is not what I asked for." Mr. Carman eyed the baked marvel in much the way one would a decaying corpse.

"It *is* what you asked for," Miss O'Doyle replied, calm yet firm.

Mr. Carman raised his chin to an authoritatively arrogant angle. "I remember my requirements precisely."

She opened the drawer directly beside her and pulled out a slip of paper. "And *I* wrote down your requirements." She held the paper so he could see the writing thereon. "Which of these demands does the cake fail to meet?"

The shop had gone quite still and as near to silent as two children and four adults could be. The squire was not known to be a generous man, and many people whispered a warning about his temper. Miss O'Doyle might not have known that.

"If your list"—he sneered out the word—"matches what you have just placed on this counter, then you wrote down my requirements incorrectly."

"I did not."

"Are you calling me a liar?"

The snap in his tone silenced Miss O'Doyle. She watched him, brows drawn, expression both confused and concerned.

"The cake is a disappointment," Mr. Carman said, an infuriating veneer of satisfaction touching every inch of his face, "but I haven't time to obtain a replacement. I'll pay you half."

"Half?" Miss O'Doyle's eyes opened so wide one would not have been surprised if they simply fell from her head. "I paid more than that just for the ingredients."

Carman was unmoved. "You are fortunate I am willing to pay you *at all*."

Miss O'Doyle's eyes darted about the room, clearly searching for someone who could help her make sense of this turn of events. Royston left his petits fours on the table and moved with feigned disinterest to the counter, stopping behind it, beside her, and addressed the baffled woman in a low voice.

"He has done this before. I doubt we've a merchant in the entire market cross that hasn't had him balk at some purchase or another."

She kept her voice to a whisper like his. "He's claimed disappointment at your haberdashery? I find that difficult to believe; you do have a reputation."

A corner of his mouth tugged in an unfeigned show of amused pleasure. "Let us simply say he has saved a great deal of money in my shop."

"And no one ever fights him on it?" she asked.

"He is powerful. It has generally seemed best not to rock the boat."

"Until the boat capsizes," she said.

"What are you two whispering about?" Squire Carman demanded.

Royston looked over his shoulder at the weaselly man. "I was telling Miss O'Doyle that I am enjoying the tiny cakes I just bought from her."

The squire's gaze narrowed on him, and a chill washed through the room. Mr. Carman had that effect. The people of Chippingwich could not say precisely why, but he made everyone uncomfortable in eerie and disconcerting ways.

"Does he ever grow violent?" Tallulah asked in an even quieter whisper than they'd been employing.

"No one doubts him capable of it," Royston said.

She released a small, heavy breath. "I suppose some

payment for the cake is better than none. And it would afford me time to decide what I mean to do moving forward."

He nodded, not necessarily to give approval of that particular course of action over any other but as a means of acknowledging that she had chosen a path.

Miss O'Doyle looked once more to the squire; Royston got out of the way.

"Have you come to your senses?" Mr. Carman asked.

"I have come to the realization that I am neglecting my other customers by prolonging this transaction." Miss O'Doyle held her hand out for the meager coins she had been offered.

The squire dropped the coins not in her upturned palm but on the counter before taking up his ill-gotten cake and leaving with a smug air.

The other villagers present in the shop stood frozen on the spot. Carman held enough sway to inspire wariness, and he was enough of a fiend to inspire fear. He was not missed when he left a place and gained few friends by arriving.

How would their relatively newly arrived confectioner respond to the man who'd been making life miserable in Chippingwich for years? Would she rant and rage? Weep and crumble? Loudly decry the unfairness of it all? They were reasonable reactions, each and every one.

She did none of those, however. She simply looked out over the gathered customers, her dignity firmly in place, and said, "Next, please."

CHAPTER 8

Licorice proved an absolute banger of a shop assistant. The girl was a hard worker and a quick study. When given a task, she didn't muck about. She was also stubborn and unafraid to talk *at* the customers, her language a touch too colorful at times.

"You ain't s'pposed to say things like that in here, Licorice." Olly stood facing his fellow urchin, with his hands on his hips and a disapproving glare worthy of a monarch. "Miss Vera ain't running a boozing ken!"

"I've heard you say worse and more," Licorice tossed back. She had at least six years on the boy but didn't always act that way when he began pricking at her.

"Not in here, you haven't. Miss Vera lets me earn coins, and she gives me food sometimes, so I wash m' hands and keep m' words clean too. Iffen you don't do the same, she'll toss you out, and you'll be back chasing dogs and looking over your shoulder."

Licorice paled a little. Time to intervene.

"Don't let him gnaw you, love," Vera said, turning the

girl back toward the chair she'd been polishing. "You'll twig what you're meant to say and do soon enough."

"I'm not trying to make trouble for you, Miss Vera."

"I know." She nudged her on, then turned back to Olly. "Quit kicking off at her. She's new to our shop. You made a few missteps yourself when you first started working here."

"I ain't bungling things so much now," he said almost plaintively.

"You're a right legend," she said a touch dryly. "Now hop to it, *zaychik*."

He grinned before snapping a cheeky salute and spun around to continue his dusting. Vera caught sight of Licorice out of the corner of her eye and saw a fond gleam in the girl's expression as she looked at the little boy, very much the way one looked at a younger brother.

"I hope you'll not let his sauciness put you off working here," Vera said in a low voice. "I've appreciated your help, especially on the days Mr. O'Donnell's not here."

"Let me know what days *Olly* ain't here. Those'll be my favorites."

Vera clicked her tongue. "Don't feed me any of that flim-flam, Licorice. He picks at you, but you're fond of him."

Licorice shrugged a little and focused on her work once more. She wasn't likely to admit her fondness for the boy, but it was obvious. Olly didn't always spend his days in the shop; Vera suspected Licorice wouldn't either. But she liked having the two around. Between them and Ganor, she didn't feel nearly as lonely.

Papa stood in the doorway of the back room, where he was spending his day. Though there were penny dreadfuls on display in the shop front—there always were—it was not a delivery day, so the number of tales was low. On those days, he was a little more willing to take a step or two inside.

He had his coat on.

"Are you going somewhere?" she asked.

He nodded as he buttoned the front, still hovering in the back doorway. "I heard of someone who might be looking for a new printer. Thought I'd go make myself known to the man."

"Who is whispering to you about print work?" She couldn't think of anyone he chatted with regularly.

"I may not have a lot of friends, *kotik*, but I am not entirely without acquaintances."

She'd set his back up, and she'd not meant to. "I hope you get the job, Papa. You'd do a fine job of it. Whoever this man is, he'd be fortunate to have you doing work for him."

He gave an almost regal dip of the head. Her papa had never been a person of high standing or importance, but he had always carried himself with dignity.

"What sort of printing does this person need done?" Vera asked.

"Political broadsides." Papa pushed his spectacles back; they'd slipped when he'd nodded to her.

"You don't care for politicians." She knew that perfectly well.

"I also don't care for writers, but as you see, that has made little difference." As he put on his hat, he motioned with his beard toward the display of stories.

"Only the stories, *pápochka*. Not the ones who create them."

"And I'll print the broadsides," he said, "without thinking too hard on 'the ones who create them.'"

"Then will you stop growling at me like a bear with a sore paw every time new stories are delivered? Seeing as you understand the need to sometimes hold your nose and make a living."

He did not appear the least convinced by her logic. "Writers are not to be trusted. How is it I have not given you enough understanding of that after all these years?"

She lowered her voice. "I'm well clued to our history, Papa. I've no intention of opening our doors to people who'd as soon destroy us as look at us."

His shoulders drooped. "The Petrashevsky Circle ruined our lives. I will not let that happen a second time." They only ever spoke of this in whispers.

"There is no Petrashevsky Circle in London, Papa. We're safe from that here." She'd told herself that ever since she was tiny. Many children grew up fearful of otherworldly creatures and fairy tale villains. The Petrashevsky Circle had been her terrifying hobgoblin.

"We're not safe from it anywhere. Not ever." He adjusted his hat for good measure and moved into the shop, weaving through the customers milling there, and stepped out onto the street.

His words echoed in her mind: *"We're not safe from it anywhere."* A lifetime of remembered fear surged up in her. She had no recollection of the years they'd lived in St. Petersburg. She remembered nothing before South London. But she'd heard her parents whisper of the threat they'd fled from. She'd heard "Petrashevsky" muttered often enough that its syllables were worryingly familiar.

But that Circle was a lifetime ago.

They had avoided writers, had even kept little company with their fellow Russian immigrants. Surely the threat was behind them.

"We're not safe from it anywhere."

No. She refused to believe that. They had to take care. They had to keep a safe distance from writers. But they didn't need to live in the degree of fear Papa seemed to.

Peter dropped into the shop. He did so often, but not always in the middle of the day. "I'm liking that 'Dead Zoo' tale."

"It's a beaut, i'n'it?"

"Right plummy." Peter eyed the display. "Got anything like it?"

"Dr. Milligan writes tales that are suspenseful like Mr. Donnelly's." She motioned for Olly to fetch a copy.

Peter nodded and accepted Olly's offer.

Vera helped a few others choose stories. She sold a small handful of pen nibs. George, the bookkeeper's clerk, turned up for his usual order. She filled it quickly with pen nibs and parchment, blotting paper and a bottle of black ink, and sent him on his way.

She was managing the shop, juggling the various areas of it. The children were helpful, in their own way. She should have been content with the day but, oddly enough, she wished Ganor was there. She'd not known him long, but she missed him when he was away. And not merely because he helped shoulder the burden.

She liked him. She liked having him around.

Upon returning to the counter after chatting over a penny dreadful, she found a note addressed to her. Though she wasn't entirely certain, she thought the handwriting looked like the same that had been used on the mysterious letter she'd received the previous week.

This week's quid will be collected in the morning.
—The Protector

This week's quid? Nothing in the previous note had indicated the payment for extra eyes on the shop would be a weekly one. For how long would that be asked? She couldn't afford £52 a year.

The previous payment had been collected by a brawny man she'd not seen before or since. He'd certainly not been in the shop that day. Who, then, had left the note? She'd liked to have asked for more information, but of whom?

Lowering herself onto the stool behind the counter, she set her mind to twigging the scheme. No one unusual had been in. No one had been the least out of place.

She rubbed at her temples. Someone had to have left the notes.

"Are you unwell, Miss Vera? You look stomped on." Licorice's voice managed to penetrate her thoughts.

"Only thinking," she said.

"A person can get into trouble that way."

Vera forced a bit of lightness. "Don't I know it."

Licorice shrugged a shoulder and made her way to the back.

The shop door chimed. Ganor O'Donnell stepped inside. Relief slid over her on the instant. He'd talk her through the mystery, help her think her way through it.

"Miss Vera." He tipped his hat to her.

"I'd not figured on seeing you today," she said.

"I brought some scarves for the children." He held up two thick scarves. "Winter's nearly upon us, and they're needing a bit more protection from the cold." He glanced around the shop. "Where are the wee saplings?"

"Olly's hunched on the other side of the display table, sweeping up a bit of dust. Licorice is doing a bit of work in the back room," Vera said.

Ganor dropped his voice. "Is having her here a burden to you? I dropped her on you without warning."

Vera shook her head. "She's a hard worker and well fit to the shop. These street children don't tend to stay in one place for long. She'll likely grow bored of the shop before too long and scout out something else more to her liking."

"Smart as a whip, from what I saw of her," Ganor said. "She'll sort herself out as often as need be, I'd wager."

So few had kind words for London's street children. It reflected well on him. A lot of things did. His kindnesses. His friendliness. The more she knew of him, the more she liked.

"And if she doesn't sort herself, Olly will," Vera said. "The two snip at each other like brother and sister."

He laughed. "I have an older sister. She's been poking at me my entire life."

Olly had spotted Ganor and rushed over to him. "I earned a penny and bought the next bit of the story."

"And which story's that?" Ganor hunched a bit, enough to talk more directly to the scamp. "We've discussed a few."

"'The Dead Zoo.'"

Ganor nodded solemnly. "What did you think of it, then?"

"I think Jonty's the one stealing the animals. Do you?"

"I think it's a possibility." Ganor ruffled Olly's hair as he stood tall once more.

Olly smoothed his hair with a disgruntled swipe of his hand. "Miss Vera does that too. Makes me wash my hands then messes my hair."

Ganor's eyes darted to her.

She shrugged. "I think I improve his look when I fuss with his hair."

"I got a reputation." Olly's salute held more defiance than usual but hadn't lost an ounce of its cheek. He spun about and marched off, resuming his work.

Vera rested her elbows on the counter and her chin against her hands. "He's a handful. But he's been here every day this week. Likely, he'll disappear for a while now. Never do know what they get up to."

"I've been a street urchin," Ganor said. "'Tis likely for the best you don't know what they do when they're away from here." He motioned toward Licorice. "I'm going to gab a bit with the girl. But I won't keep her from her work. Swear to it."

"I ain't worried," she said. "And it'll do Licorice good to have a moment free of Olly's pestering."

Ganor laughed and crossed the shop. His laughter

warmed her through and through. It was little wonder she missed him when he wasn't at the shop.

Vera stepped onto the pavement out front. The place wasn't overly busy, but the flow of customers into the shop was steady. Either of the children could nip out and grab her if she was needed. Peter was at his cart as usual, near enough for a quick gab.

She stood under the front overhang, watching the comings and goings on Old Compton Street. This was not the area of London where she'd grown up, but it had come to feel like home. She knew her neighbors and fellow merchants, knew the street sellers, knew the urchins who lingered in corners, and the workers who passed by on their way to and from employment, knew those many pretended not to see. The area was not the most affluent, but it was generally peaceful and calm. In this little corner of Soho, people felt a bit of hope, a bit of peace. She wanted it to stay that way. But £52 a year was more than she could pay.

Across the way, Mr. Overton stood outside the door of his barbershop.

"Mr. Overton seems burdened," she said to Peter. He spent his days on the street, so hardly anything happened that he didn't know about. "Is the barbershop struggling?"

Peter shook his head. "Plenty come in and out. But his shoulders are always slumped. His mouth ain't ever nothing but a frown. Something's fretting him."

She understood that all too well.

"Something's fretting a good many people," Peter added.

"Including you?"

"Two merchants didn't buy their usual bundles. Mr.

Overton"—he motioned across the street— "said he'd an unexpected expense. Couldn't spare even a quid."

"I find myself struggling with that amount as well," Vera said with a sigh.

"Seems the debt of the day. Mr. Bianchi mentioned needing an extra £1."

Odd. "Anyone else toss out that as a sum?"

Peter's brow dipped in thought. "Come to swirl on it, yeah. Been hearing that amount the last day or two from near everyone. And heard it a week ago as well."

That couldn't be a coincidence. "Do you remember all the locals who mentioned the £1 expense?"

"Aye."

"How many would you say there was?"

His lips moved silently. Then, "At least a dozen. All right here in this stretch."

A dozen. Someone in that group must have some idea who the Protector was and how often they were meant to be paying. A little more information would make a difference.

"If you dropped a word in their ears, do you suppose they'd come to the shop and help me sort this?"

Peter shrugged. "Couldn't hurt to ask."

She didn't mean to bother Papa with it all. He'd lived for years looking over his shoulder, expecting danger at every turn. The last thing he needed was to be alarmed at this business enterprise if there was no need. She'd sort it out, and he'd be none the wiser. If she asked, Ganor would help her.

"Ask those you know of to come by the shop at eight o'clock."

"Will do, Miss Vera." Peter pulled his cap.

With luck, they'd have some answers tonight. But she suspected those answers would prove more complicated than she'd prefer.

CHAPTER 9

Vera stepped back inside the shop just as Ganor was approaching the door.

He dipped his head to her. "I'll see you come Tuesday, Miss Vera."

"Actually, do you have a minute more?"

He eyed her a moment, brows angled low. "Something amiss?"

The shop was full with customers milling about. That made for a whole heap of perked ears and open eyes.

"Why don't I hover about the place for a time?" he suggested. "Then we can talk when the shop is quieter."

"I'd appreciate it," she said. "But I can't pay you for an extra day of—"

"Vera." He took her hand, sending a bolt of lightning straight through her. "I'm here today as a friend."

A friend. That somehow weighed on her heart and brought a smile to her face all at the same time. "I can't remember the last time I had a friend, unless you count the characters in Mr. King's stories. They start to feel like friends by the time he finishes a tale."

"What of the characters in Mr. Donnelly's stories?"

"I'm usually terrified of them by the time I'm done."

Ganor laughed quietly. He still held her hand, and he walked with her the rest of the way into the shop. Though she had work enough to do, she wished they could remain just as they were. "Why is it you think authors are so crooked?" he asked.

"We've known enough of them and suffered enough because of them." Vera sighed. "Devious lot, the whole of them. But, then, they spend their days writing falsehoods; only stands to reason they'd have false *lives* as well."

It was a damning evaluation, to be sure. Did she not see any redeeming value in writers?

"Their writing has given you friends," he said. "That's at least something in their favor."

She regretfully slipped her hand from his, taking up a stack of papers that needed to be put away. "I don't know how to make sense of it all. And I've a heap too much on my mind at the moment to try twigging so big a question."

He motioned with his head toward the browsing customers. "You see to your work. When the shop's not so busy, you can tell me a little of what's weighing on you."

Ganor was as good as his word. He wandered about the shop, talking with customers, teasing Olly, encouraging Licorice. And he smiled at her. Often. Beyond the way it flipped her heart about in her chest, it was a comforting connection she needed more than she'd realized.

She'd not been lying when she told him she had few

friends. She couldn't really say she had any since coming to Soho. The shop kept her too busy. Papa's wariness of new people kept her too isolated.

But Ganor had found his way past all of that. He'd shown himself to be kind and thoughtful. He'd brought the children scarves and had more than once supplied her with roasted chestnuts simply because he knew she liked them. He was funny and personable. She enjoyed talking with him and was certain he felt the same way. If only he could be in the shop every day.

The afternoon passed. The children collected their day's coins and went on their way, Olly with a salute and Licorice with a quiet word of parting. Soon enough, the shop was empty except for Vera and Ganor.

He joined her at the counter. "Why don't you spill your thoughts while I help you close up?"

She nodded. "But don't lock up. I've people coming later."

"Do you, now?"

She began moving prints and pens and parchment from the displays to the drawers where they were kept. Ganor saw to the end-of-day sweeping.

"Do you remember the note I got last week offering to keep an eye on the shop and see to our safety?"

"For a quid, if I recall rightly."

"Exactly." She glanced over her shoulder at him. "There was another note from the Protector today, telling me *this week's* payment would be collected tomorrow."

His head tipped to the side, the way one often did when

pondering on something surprising. "I didn't realize 'twas more than the one payment."

"Neither did I. And I haven't the first idea who's behind it, so I cain't even ask questions." She pulled the money box from the cash drawer. "Will he be asking £1 every week? And what's he doing, exactly, for that quid? And if he's made this promise to so many of the businesses on the street, can he promise to have enough eyes and ears hereabout to keep all safe who're paying for it?"

"Hold, hold, hold." He stood with the broom in one hand, but his attention fully on her. "Others in the area have received the same offer?"

She nodded. "Peter said he's heard of it from quite a few. I'm having as many as'll come to the shop tonight to see if we can't twig the thing."

"Twig, meaning 'sort out,' if I remember."

She smiled. "I'll have you sounding South London before too long."

"Not if I have you sounding Irish first."

She did enjoy when he flirted. "You'd have to spend a heap more time here for me to work that miracle."

"Is that an invitation?" he asked, his voice low and warm. Quick as anything, his dashing expression dissolved into laughter. "I shouldn't enjoy making you blush, lass. It ain't charitable of me."

Her heart leapt about, something it often did when he was nearby. "I don't mind."

"So, you don't know who's leaving the notes, but do you at least know who's collecting the payment?" he said.

"Oi, but it ain't anyone I've seen before, and he ain't been in here since."

He took up his sweeping. "You're hoping someone else knows more."

"I'm probably making an ocean out of a puddle," she said. "But this ain't the sort of mystery I like. It has me a bit unsettled."

"Would you mind terribly if I hover about for your meeting tonight?" Ganor asked.

"I'd appreciate if you did." And not merely because it'd mean spending some extra time with him, something she enjoyed even more than she'd let on. Having another mind spinning over the mystery would increase their odds of solving it.

Vera stood in the shop that night looking over the familiar and worried faces of her neighbors. The window shades were pulled down, giving them a whisper of privacy. Papa had returned from his errand a bit pensive, focused to the point of near silence. She wasn't certain what that meant, but it was keeping him in the flat above the shop, making this meeting far less complicated.

Having called for the gathering, Vera was the evening's foreman of the jury. Best get to it.

"Two weeks ago, I received a note," she said, "promising to watch over this shop, in light of the burglary at the tobacconists, for the price of £1. Today, I found another note—"

"—about the *next* payment," Mr. Overton tossed in, understanding dawning in his face and tone.

Vera nodded. "And I'll confess, I'm more than a touch confused. The first note said nothing about any more payments."

Murmurs of acknowledgment hummed around the room.

Peter spoke up from the back, surrounded by a few street sellers. "Ours is a touch different. This 'Protector' must know we ain't got a quid to hand over. We're being asked a sixpence."

"Have any of you seen who's leaving these notes?" she asked the group.

"I haven't," Mr. Okeke said.

"Me either." Mr. Bianchi, whose misfortune had led to all this, was present as well. Apparently, he was being offered protection too.

Heads were shaking all around.

Vera looked at Ganor, sitting amongst her neighbors. He was jotting notes on a small writing pad. He truly meant to help her make sense of this, and he'd managed to do so without shoving her to the side.

"Has anyone made a second payment?" she asked the group.

"We have," Mrs. Murphy said.

"Same bloke collected as last time?" Vera pressed.

Mr. Murphy shook his head.

"It's curious." Vera couldn't make heads nor tails of any of it.

"May be strange methods," Mr. Bianchi said, "but the

street's been peaceful this past week. That's worth having a few unanswered questions."

"I'd still like to know who the Protector is," Mr. Okeke said. "I need to know how many payments we're meant to make, and if we can bring the cost down a touch if we can't afford it."

"I agree," Mr. Overton said.

"So do I." Vera leaned against the counter. "How many of you, if you tossed it around your brain box a bit, could draft a list of the people who'd been in your shop or business the days you found your notes?" Seeing worry enter the faces of the two misses—the sort Soho was known for—and, knowing their profession made saying too much a dangerous thing, she quickly added, "Memories can be patchy, obviously. It wouldn't need to be a full list."

"The street sellers'll never remember everyone," Peter said. "Hundreds pass by our carts every day."

She nodded. "You'd likely do better to set your mind to anything or anyone *unusual*."

Peter turned to his fellow mongers and a low conversation began.

Vera looked over to the merchants and neighbors gathered as well. "What say the lot of you, then?"

They all agreed to do what they could. The group milled about, bemoaning their troubles and tallying their odds. Gemma, one of the misses, approached, concern in her eyes.

"Something else weighing on you?" Vera asked in a low voice.

She nodded quickly.

"Are you in danger?" Clare, who stood nearby, asked.

Though Vera didn't know her line of work, she didn't think Clare belonged to Gemma's profession.

"We're all of us always in some danger." Gemma turned back to Vera. "But leading this charge, as you are, could be the Protector won't appreciate it. Might be you'll rue trying to identify him."

"Could be." She'd not deny it were risky. "Bein' afraid ain't reason enough to not do things that are important."

"You're either very brave or very foolish," Gemma said.

She was likely a little of both. But she also wasn't alone. She could depend on Ganor; she knew she could. Vera pasted an unbothered smile on her face. "I suppose time'll tell, won't it?"

"It always does," Clare said. "Always."

CHAPTER 10

Móirín cleaned buildings in a few different areas of London, but Brogan hadn't known her to do so in Drury Lane. Yet, that was where she was headed this time. And in the evening, which was odd. She generally did her cleaning during the day. Brogan walked with her part of the way since it was on his way to the print shop.

"Did one of your other jobs fall through?" he asked her. She shook her head.

"Then why this new arrangement?"

"I'm wanting a little extra change in m'pocket. Is that so terrible a thing?"

"We ain't hurting for funds now that I've an extra spot of work."

"You aren't the only one of us who can add to the coffers." He recognized that unyielding tone from years of experience with it. Móirín was about to saddle her high horse and go for a bruising ride. "We're living in a comfortable corner of London with enough for our needs, which I won't risk undermining. And we're helping the poor of this dirty old town, which I won't stop doing. So if we're to have enough for set-ting up our own homes, living independent like we've talked of, we *both* need to bring in more."

He was grateful he'd settled on that explanation for tak-ing up the job at the shop. It wasn't entirely untrue, and he was heartily tired of lying to his sister. "You do know I've no wish to toss you out. I simply thought we'd both like having an option."

"I know it," she said. "And I think 'tis high time we cut these apron strings."

He laughed. "I don't consider m'self tied to your apron springs, Móirín."

"'Tisn't *my* apron strings I'm hoping to sever."

"Are you calling me a mother hen?" he asked with a laugh.

"For not the first time."

She *had* made similar accusations before.

"I made a vow to our parents," he said. "I'll not break it."

"*We* made that vow, Brog. Only you have taken it to extremes." She hooked her arm through his, something she didn't often do. "I can't tell you how grateful I am to have you in m'life. And I'm not unaware of all you've done—and do—for me."

"But you've complaints to make?" He tucked his free hand in his coat pocket and didn't look at her as they walked. He didn't like the idea of having disappointed his sister. "I've not been neglectful."

"Of *me*," she said. "Before we left Dublin, you used to talk about having a family of your own someday, and a home that was yours. You never mention that now."

He had once rambled a great deal about such things. "I've too much on my mind for fretting over that."

"And I mean to see to it that I am not one of those things on your mind."

"You always will be, Móirín. We've been through far too much together."

She squeezed his arm. "We have at that. But maybe, Brogan, it's time you started spending as many worries on your own welfare as you're always spending on others."

"You're trying to wrangle me into being selfish?" He shook his head in disagreement with her notion.

"Reclaiming some dreams isn't selfish," she said. "Making your life what you want it to be isn't selfish."

"Do you have dreams you're hoping to recapture?" he asked.

"My dreams are of returning to Dublin," she said. "But we both know that can't happen."

"I wish it could," he said.

"So do I."

Móirín tossed him a light, quick smile. She always grew more somber when they spoke of home. They both missed it, but neither of them could return. There was no life for them in a city where they weren't likely to remain free, perhaps even alive, for a single day after their arrival.

They went their separate ways, but her words continued to weigh on him. *"Maybe it's time you started spending as many worries on your own welfare as you're always spending on others."* Looking out for people, caring about them, supporting them—these weren't bad things. He found a lot of fulfillment from those efforts. It was his favorite thing about being part of the Dread Penny Society, with his friendships there being a close second.

Why, then, did her criticism hit too close to the mark?

Perhaps because his efforts with the DPS had left him even more alone than he'd been before.

Perhaps because his current efforts were placing him in the uncomfortable position of investigating a woman he was coming to like more and more. A woman who, if she realized he was one of the dishonest writers she so despised, would want nothing to do with him.

Perhaps because there was part of him that hadn't entirely given up on the hope of building his own life, of settling somewhere, having a family of his own. He still wanted that future, but he'd not allowed himself to dream of it in years. Friendship and doing good for as many people as possible, especially his sister, had plastered over that emptiness.

"Reclaiming some dreams isn't selfish." Móirín might've been quite sure of that, but he wasn't. He could've turned down the Dread Master's request that he leave the society in order to investigate a mystery, but that would've left the Russian ambassador vulnerable. He could've saved the time and money he and his sister spent helping the poor of London and gained the house and future he'd dreamed of, but that would've left far too many people suffering without any relief. He could've ignored Móirín's troubles in Dublin and remained there in his homeland instead of living as a fugitive in London, but she'd've been left in a horrific situation.

Sometimes dreams had to be sacrificed. Sometimes

keeping hold of them was *absolutely* selfish. And selfish was one thing he refused to be.

The print shop was only open half the day on Monday. Vera's heart-wrenching admission, "I can't remember the last time I had a friend," had sat as a painful weight on his heart. She said she'd found friendship in the characters she read about. She enjoyed discussing them, but worried about doing so too much while her father was nearby.

An idea had occurred to Brogan, and he'd not been able to empty his mind of it.

He knocked at the locked shop door, his excitement growing as he waited for her to answer. Not only did he sincerely believe she'd enjoy what he'd come to propose, but if she agreed to it, he'd be granted an entire afternoon of her company. He would treasure that.

Vera opened the door. The surprise in her expression was delightful. "Ganor. This isn't one of your work days. We ain't even open."

"I know." He was well aware his grin was unrepentant. "I've come to suggest an outing."

"Of what sort?"

He leaned a shoulder against the door frame, hooking one boot around the other. "I know how much you enjoy discussing the penny dreadfuls but doing so here is something of a walk in a snake pit."

She smiled a bit crookedly. "Are you calling my papa a snake?"

"It isn't the pit I'm calling him."

She laughed almost silently but with every indication of sincerity.

A couple stepped up behind him.

Vera shifted her attention. "May I help you?"

"You are a print shop, yes?" To Brogan's untrained ear, the man sounded Russian.

"We are, yeah," Vera said. "But we're closed just now."

The two looked inarguably disappointed.

"We'll be open first thing in the morning," Vera said. "You're welcome to—"

"Let them in, *kotik*." Mr. Sorokin had arrived at some point.

Vera stepped aside and motioned the new arrivals in. Mr. Sorokin showed them to the table near the back where he discussed printing jobs with customers. He did so fairly often, though the shop was still struggling. He likely wasn't taking on terribly profitable jobs.

For a moment, Brogan was distracted watching the couple. The man kept an arm about his wife, keeping her tucked up tenderly beside him. She glanced up at her husband, and not a soul seeing her expression would doubt the love that existed between them.

Móirín's voice echoed in his thoughts. *"Reclaiming some dreams isn't selfish."*

But dreams were a distraction, especially ones that were out of reach. He'd do far better to keep his feet planted firmly on the ground.

"I thought you didn't have a lot of connections with the Russian community." Brogan motioned to the couple.

"We don't," Vera said, "though we do have customers who're Russian."

Ah.

"What is it that brought you to the shop today? You mentioned an outing of some sort?" she asked.

"I know an older gentleman, lonely but sharp as a freshly made nail, who reads the penny dreadfuls as faithfully as you do," Brogan said. "He longs for company, but doesn't ever leave his home, so he has little of it. You'd get to discuss the stories you love while doing a world of good for a very lonely man."

"Truly?" She stood taller, her attention fully captured. Her lips parted in small circle of interest.

"He has a daughter about your age, though I don't know if she'll be there. And he has a soon-to-be son-in-law who is there now and then. But it might land as only the two of us visiting with him."

Her expression was both compassionate and intrigued. "I would like that."

"I'd hoped you would."

A quick moment later, she had the shop locked up, and they were walking down Old Compton Street side-by-side.

"Where does this man live?" Vera asked.

She'd agreed to go with him without knowing their destination. 'Twas a fine thing being trusted that much.

"Warwick Square," he said.

Vera looked abruptly at him. "Warwick Square? That's a rum-bung area of Town."

"Rum-bung?" He laughed. "I thought I knew London cant. Then I met you and found I don't understand a word of it."

"You might know London," she said. "That don't mean you know *South* London."

"'Tis that different, is it?"

Her smile remained. "Likely not, actually. But my papa is convinced I speak a language other than English."

"You mean *Russian*?"

"I don't speak Russian as well as he does." She hooked her arm through his. He liked that far more than he probably should. "It frustrates Papa. He mentions now and then how *un*Russian I am. But I've not had much connection to Russia growing up here. I only know a bit of the language because, when my mum still lived with us, the two of them spoke it. We don't spend time with many others from our home country, not even with the few who stop by the shop."

"Does he not have friends from his homeland here?" Their conversation had veered directly into the topic he needed to cover: Mr. Sorokin's connection to Russians in London. She'd mentioned it vaguely before, but he needed a few details.

She nodded. "There're plenty in London who hail from Russia, but he has hardly anything to do with any of them. Adamant about it, in fact."

So, Russians and writers were on his list of people he intentionally avoided. "I tremble to think what he'd do if he crossed paths with a Russian writer."

He actually felt her stiffen.

"What do you mean by that?"

Not only had his jest fallen flat, he'd somehow managed to worry her. "I'd meant to be funny. You've said he doesn't like writers, and now you're saying he doesn't care to rub elbows with his fellow Russians. I hadn't meant any insult."

She nodded. "I'm sensitive about it, I guess. Papa is sad

that I'm so much London and so little Russian. But he's the reason I'm not. It's a weight I can't seem to shake off."

They walked along in silence for a while. He had hit upon something, there was no denying that. Her father's distance from his homeland community was connected in some way to his distaste for writers. But what, if anything did that have to do with him lingering near the Russian embassy? And why was it such a point of contradiction with his daughter?

"M'sister and I haven't a great many connections in the Irish community here in London," Brogan said. "I'd wager your da misses that tie to his homeland as much as we miss ours."

"He never fails to notice any news about the ambassador or some of the prominent Russians in London, but he talks with only a couple of his countrymen, and even then not often." There was something of a sigh in her words. "He never speaks of going back, but my mum did almost constantly."

"Do *you* long to go back?" he asked.

"I was a tiny child when we came here. Going back there wouldn't be returning home; it would be leaving the only home I've ever known."

Vera felt no real connection to Russia, but her da had a complicated one and an established interest in the ambassador. Something was odd there. The Dread Master hadn't been entirely misguided in his suspicions.

Brogan stopped at a roasted nut cart and purchased two bags of hot chestnuts.

Vera bumped him with her shoulder. "You spoil me with these, you know."

"You deserve a spot of spoiling. Besides that, the Newports aren't wealthy people, no matter that they've an impressive address. I can't say we'll be offered anything to eat while we're there, and I've no wish for you to be hungry."

She accepted the offering with a grateful smile. "Very thoughtful of you."

He dipped his head in an overdone impersonation of a fine society gentleman. "I *am* terribly gallant."

"Or just terribly hungry."

He laughed as they walked along. Lands, he enjoyed spending time with her. How easily he could imagine them spending every afternoon this way, growing ever more acquainted, ever more fond.

As soon as they finished their nuts, he hailed a hansom cab. It'd take an hour each direction to walk to Pimlico, and while he *did* enjoy her company, that felt drastic. During the drive, their conversation ranged from penny dreadfuls to pastries to entertaining stories from their childhoods.

How easy it was to forget he was investigating her father's possible connection to an infamous criminal enterprise.

The Newports' home was in finer feather than when Brogan had first seen it. He'd come before on DPS business and had assumed a false name—the very name, in fact, he was using at the print shop. Mr. Newport's daughter knew Brogan's actual identity, but they'd not told her father. That would only lead to questions that could not be safely answered.

"Mr. O'Donnell, what brings you by?" Mr. Newport

greeted him in the humbly furnished sitting room, which had been entirely empty mere weeks earlier. Ana's engagement to Hollis Darby, Brogan's colleague at the DPS, had improved their situation.

"I've found someone who loves the penny dreadfuls as much as you do." Brogan motioned to Vera. "Miss Vera Sorokina, this is Mr. Newport. Mr. Newport, Miss Sorokina."

"A pleasure."

Vera dipped her head. "Likewise."

In the length of a breath, they were deep in conversation about the various penny serials and the storylines. Mr. Newport was as excited about the visit as Brogan had hoped. And Vera was as sincerely friendly with the often-lonely man as he'd known she would be.

Brogan sat beside her on the faded settee, adding to the conversation as needed, but mostly enjoying watching her eyes dance with excitement. Her entire face lit when she was enthusiastic about something. And that something, more often than not, was characters and stories and tales of adventure.

Her father's opposition to her interests robbed her of that. Why such a deeply ingrained distrust of writers, one so solidified that he'd deny his own daughter such obvious happiness? Vera had indicated she, too, shared his misgivings.

Thank the heavens neither of them knew Brogan's actual vocation.

Or the real reason he'd come to their shop.

Or the way he was evaluating everything he learned about them.

As the weight of that settled on his mind, his heart grew

heavy with it. He was being shockingly dishonest with them. He, who had made so many speeches at DPS meetings about wanting to be a more honest man.

If this kept up, he would quickly be in deep, deep water.

THE MERCHANT AND THE ROGUE

by Mr. King

Installment III
in which our Heroine makes a most shocking
Discovery about the Town in which she lives!

The squire's refusal to pay for his cake put Tallulah's ledgers in tremendous jeopardy. Two nights in a row she spent hours searching for a means of recovering from the financial blow he'd dealt her. If she was quite careful, she could manage it, but she could not endure another swindling from the man. And yet, Mr. Royston Prescott had indicated this was a common practice for the local squire.

Under normal circumstances, she would not have selected a known tease as a primary source of information on such serious matters, but Mr. Prescott had shown her a degree of support that had surprised her. He'd not told her what to do, neither had he defended the squire. He was the closest thing to an ally she had.

She closed up her shop a little early, two days after the incident with the cake, and made her way down the road to the haberdashery shop where she knew she would find him.

She stepped inside and found the establishment empty, though she knew he did excellent business. But Fate was smiling on her. She'd found him at a time when he was not overly busy.

He looked up as she entered. A flirtatious smile spread across his face. "Miss O'Doyle. Have you come to purchase a waistcoat?"

"Wouldn't I be quite the sight? Walking up and down the market cross while dressed in men's clothing?"

The twinkle in his eye told her the possibility did not, in fact, horrify him. Why this brought her pleasure, she couldn't say. Most any other man would have offered words, however hollow, of horror at the idea, accompanied by lofty praises of her femininity. He simply looked more roguish.

Her first impressions of him were proving accurate: he was a rogue, but not the threatening or dangerous variety. In fact, she found herself sorely tempted to smile along with him.

"I've come to ask you a question," she said.

"As I'm not currently inundated with customers, this would be an excellent time to ask any and every question you might have."

"You say that as if you hope my question will be something overbold."

He shrugged elegantly and walked with careful and graceful strides to where she stood. He leaned a hand on the table, tipping his posture ever so slightly askew, granting him a casual connectedness to her that might've been a touch too familiar for an ordinary man. It seemed almost subdued for a rascal.

"What is your question, Miss Tallulah O'Doyle?" He even said her name in a way that was a touch scandalous. And, heaven help her, she liked it.

Forcing herself to focus on the business at hand, she asked, "Why is it that the squire has been permitted to mistreat so many for so long? Why has no one tried to stop him?"

His eyes narrowed, and his head tilted. "Why do you assume no one has ever tried?"

How *had* she come to that conclusion? "At my shop when the squire declared he meant to cheat me, not a single person looked surprised or outraged. And you said he'd done this before. I suppose I assumed it'd been ongoing long enough that it would've been stopped by now if enough effort had been made."

Royston shrugged. His posture and expression remained quite casual for one discussing a tortured town. "Your assessment, then, is that Chippingwich hasn't tried hard enough."

"Or that even the best efforts haven't managed the thing."

"Well sorted," he said.

She folded her arms, not in a show of defiance but in a match to his playful posture. "I believe you will find I'm terribly clever."

"Are you?"

She took the slightest step closer to him, lowering her voice a bit. "Clever enough to know that you're not telling me everything."

The smile he offered was playful. Was he ever anything other than devil-may-care? He'd shown her concern in her shop while the squire was there, but that had been fleeting and not without a heavy hint of impishness.

He motioned her toward the table not too far distant. It was where he, no doubt, took orders from his customers and offered his customers' companions a place to rest while they waited.

She took the seat he offered her. He sat beside her, sitting with as much swagger as he employed when on his feet. "What would you like to know? Your every wish is my cherished command." Had her hand been within reach, he likely would have kissed it. The man never stopped flirting. Tallulah hoped he'd be serious long enough to explain a few things about Chippingwich.

"Am I the only one who finds the squire's company . . . rattling?" She wasn't explaining her feelings very well. "He makes me feel as though I'm about to crawl out of m' skin."

"I don't know a soul who doesn't find his presence uncomfortable," Royston said.

"And not merely on account of his odor?"

That brought confusion to the man's expression. "Does he smell strange to you?"

"Doesn't he to *you*?"

Royston didn't answer, but narrowed his gaze further, as if trying to make sense of her confusion. She didn't dare ask if he heard noises when the squire was about. Tallulah did quite regularly. Mostly, it was a gurgling sound, but sometimes, though, she heard a distant, echoing laughter that sent chills down her spine.

"Someone has obviously tried to stop the squire, but

hasn't succeeded," she said. "What was tried? And who did the trying?"

"I've been here two years now, and there's only been one attempt I know of to thwart Mr. Carman," he said. "His reign of terror was a well-known and well-established thing by the time I arrived."

"And who was the person who stood up to him?"

"The man who owned the shop that you now claim as your own."

A weight settled on her heart. Her shop had become available, she knew, not because the previous owner had grown too old for running it, nor because he had moved to a larger or different location. It had been available because it had been empty.

"Was his opposition to the squire the reason he lost his shop?"

"Not exactly."

Not exactly. "What happened to him?"

Mr. Prescott released a breath before he answered. "No one knows."

"He disappeared?"

A slow nod answered her quavering question.

Cheating the local merchants was not, then, the true threat they all faced. 'Twas little wonder Squire Carman held such power over them all.

"I'd not realized how difficult the situation was."

"I did tell you that day in your shop that he's believed to be violent."

She rubbed at her forehead. "I didn't take your warning entirely seriously." She felt her cheeks flush at that admission. She did try not to judge people too quickly, yet she'd done precisely that with him. He seemed to be a rather shallow, swaggering blatherskite, so she'd assumed everything he said was somewhat empty.

The shop door opened, pulling both their eyes in that direction. Kirby Padmore, the proprietor of the local pub, shuffled inside, his expression as weary as ever yet still maintaining kindness and welcome. He was the reason his pub was so popular a destination.

Mr. Prescott rose and crossed to the new arrival, strutting as always. "How may I help you, Kirby?"

"I'm in need of new shirtsleeves," he said. "I've ruined my last."

Mr. Prescott crossed to the ceiling-tall shelves along the back wall, shelves that held a tremendous amount of fabric, but he did not pull out a bolt. Instead, he reached behind one particularly wobbly pile and removed an already sewn shirt.

Kirby accepted it.

"What did he toss at you this time?" Royston asked.

"Guinness."

Mr. Prescott looked to Tallulah. "I hope that doesn't pain you too much, hearing of this senseless waste of a drink your country holds in such esteem."

"I might be pained, were I not so confused."

Kirby sighed. "The squire's temper can run a touch hot. When he's put out with me, he has a tendency to douse me with whatever happens to be in his glass."

'Twasn't difficult to imagine that scenario. "Does he grow

'put out' with you on account of you asking him to pay his bar tab?"

"That's generally the trigger."

A plague, indeed. "You must miss the years before he was the squire."

"I've never known a time when he was not," Kirby said.

The man was noticeably older than Mr. Carman. Kirby, like Mr. Prescott, must have come from elsewhere.

"How long have you been in Chippingwich?" she asked.

Kirby paid Mr. Prescott for the shirt that had been waiting for him, no doubt a longstanding arrangement between the men. "I've lived here all my life." With that, he slipped from the shop.

All his life?

Kirby was seventy if he was a day. Mr. Carman didn't look a day over forty, yet he'd been squire throughout Kirby's memory.

How was that possible?

CHAPTER 11

Brogan wasn't sleeping. He'd spent the entire afternoon and a good bit of the evening with Vera.
They'd passed two hours with Mr. Newport, talking
about stories and life and any number of interesting topics.
His daughter hadn't returned while they were there, which
was likely for the best. If she'd been there, Hollis would've
been more likely to drop in as well.

After their long chat with Mr. Newport, Brogan and Vera
had walked back to the shop. The distance took a full hour
to cover, and it had been one of the best hours he'd passed in
years. While he had kept to his false name and hadn't talked
at all about his work as a writer, he'd told her of growing up
in Dublin, of coming to London with Móirín a few years
back. He'd not told her why they'd come; that was a confes-
sion for another day.

Vera had talked of her childhood in Southwark and the
printshop they'd had there. She'd told him of her mother,
how she'd pined for Russia and had, in the end, decided
England was no place for her and had left her husband and

child behind to return home, how they'd abruptly sold the shop south of the Thames and had opened the one they were in now.

They had a surprising amount in common—similar interest in stories, in history, in people. Talking with her was easy, friendly, comforting.

Thus, he wasn't sleeping. Thoughts of her spun in his mind. He would be at the shop again in the morning, but that felt too far away. He missed her, and he'd only just seen her. Lying atop his blanket, hands threaded behind his head, eyes on the dim ceiling above, Brogan felt a very pleased smile spread over his face. Vera Sorokina was turning him to mush, and he wasn't the least unhappy about it.

The tiniest creak of the floorboards pulled his gaze to the doorway. Fletcher stood there, probably laughing at him; the light was far too dim to know for certain.

"Móirín let you in, did she?"

"Didn't need to," Fletcher said, keeping his voice low.

"You 'let yourself in,' then."

"Needed to talk to you."

"In the middle of the night?"

"Ain't that late, Brog."

They were both keeping their voices low. Fletcher, despite his insistence the hour wasn't so unreasonable, must've realized Móirín was asleep in her own room.

Brogan rolled off the bed. His feet protested the cold slap of the floor, but they'd adjust. He took hold of Fletcher's arm and swung him about, setting him walking away from the bedchamber and toward the staircase.

They moved more or less silently down to the ground

floor. Brogan wasn't the least surprised Fletcher had managed to breech the house and navigate it undetected. All the Dreadfuls were stealthy, but Fletcher made most of the rest of them look like lumbering dullards.

"I have to say I'm a little disappointed," Brogan said as they slipped into the front sitting room. "You gave yourself away with the angry floorboard. The Phantom Fox would never have been so careless."

"Yes, well, unlike her, I am not a sneak thief by trade."

The Phantom Fox—a London thief with a reputation for a shocking degree of stealth—was a friend of theirs. Brogan and Hollis, in fact, were the ones who had discovered her actual identity. The other Dreadfuls knew now who she was, though her identity remained a mystery to the rest of the world. Enough so that Vera had, unknowingly, spent hours at the Phantom Fox's house talking with the thief's father.

Brogan lit a small lamp and set it on the table, where he sat with Fletcher. "Now, what's so urgent and secret that you're needing to climb in through a levered window in the middle of the night?"

"This." Fletcher pulled from his coat pocket a folded and sealed piece of parchment, more or less identical to the one he'd handed Brogan in the Quill and Ink weeks earlier. "I was told not to delay."

"And, saints, you certainly didn't."

Fletcher tossed out one of his characteristic smirks.

Brogan flipped the note over and broke the wax seal. He unfolded the note.

Donnelly,

Mr. Sorokin was confirmed to have been in a shadowy corner of London, visiting a place rumored to be a hiding place for questionable people. That he is likely also connected to the Russian ambassador's troubles strengthens our suspicions regarding him. Learn what you can of where he goes when not at his shop. Worry inside the embassy is growing.

DM

Brogan's heart dropped. "Sorokin's acting suspicious."

"Apparently."

Mr. Sorokin was out and about often, but Vera had always said he was at the paper mill or seeking out new print orders. And the people he interacted with at the shop were customers and neighbors.

Brogan pushed out a breath and leaned back in his chair. "Would you think me a coward if I told you I'd rather not dig into any of this?"

"That'd depend on your reason."

"A simple one," Brogan said. "I don't want to find out that Mr. Sorokin is a criminal or connected to anything that has to do with Four-Finger Mike or the Mastiff."

"I didn't realize you were so fond of Mr. Sorokin," Fletcher said.

"I'm not." Brogan didn't dislike Vera's father, but 'twasn't him Brogan was most worried about.

"Ah," Fletcher said with a nod. "But you have grown rather fond of his daughter."

Brogan had no intention of denying it.

"I think you need to be ready for the possibility that Miss Vera might be involved in this as well." Fletcher's gaze was both sympathetic and unyielding.

"'Tis easier said than done, Fletch."

"Difficulty don't matter either direction. It has to be done. If she's in this, and it proves something truly nefarious, you have to be prepared for that."

'Twas a very real complication he'd not thought of while daydreaming in his bed and reminiscing fondly of the afternoon he'd spent with her. He'd been sent to the print shop to investigate. Instead, he'd begun losing his heart. He needed to regain his perspective and his distance. He needed to be ready, as Fletcher said, for whatever answers presented themselves.

He might be able to convince his mind to be, but his heart was a different story altogether.

CHAPTER 12

Vera was as perplexed as a mare with a foal that won't walk. Ganor was behaving oddly. He kept his own company, today—did his work in near silence. Something was clearly worrying him, but he seemed entirely unwilling to talk. And that was not at all like him.

"He's grumpy," Olly muttered, watching Ganor with frustration.

"Any inkling why?"

Olly shook his head. His brows pulled down a bit. "Ain't like him though."

"If you sort any of it, drop a word in my ear," she said. "I miss the Mr. O'Donnell who makes us laugh."

His mouth tipped a bit. "Do I make you laugh, too, Miss Vera?"

"Laugh? You ain't nothing but trouble, boy."

He laughed. Olly never failed to catch when she was teasing. "A spot of trouble ain't a bad thing."

"No, it ain't." She ruffled his hair.

"Mr. O'Donnell does that too," Olly said as he smoothed his hair again. "You two's strange."

You two. She liked hearing them connected that way. The afternoon and evening she'd spent with Ganor had been wonderful. He was so easy to talk with and be with. They'd shared stories from their childhoods and thoughts on current matters in the country, what it was like to be an immigrant, how that varied when one had been in a country since childhood compared to arriving as an adult. She'd learned more of his sister and wanted to meet her. She'd told him a little more of her family history, though she'd veered clear of the Petrachevsky Circle. Even having to leave that out, she'd had a more personal interaction with him than she'd had with anyone in ages.

Papa stepped inside, interrupting her reverie.

"You've been away quite a spell," she said.

"And well worth it, *kotik*. I've secured a new printing order. Our largest one ever."

"What type of printing?"

"Any number of things." Papa fussed with his beard, not looking directly at her.

"Such as?" She found it odd that he was being evasive about something he seemed so pleased about.

"The printing is my area, Vera." His lips flattened in a gruff line.

His sharp tone drained every ounce of breath from her. "I'm sorry. I hadn't meant to . . . " She wasn't sure how to finish the sentence, not knowing what she'd done wrong.

"You ask too many questions," he said through tight teeth.

She hadn't a ready answer for that. He'd not ever griped this much about her being inquisitive. Why was he so guarded about this particular job?

Olly tugged at Papa's coat. "What does *kotik* mean?"

"'Kitten,'" Papa said. "I have called Vera that since she was younger than you are."

"I like when you speak Russian," Olly said, tossing his gap-toothed smile at them both.

"Russian is a beautiful and powerful language," Papa said. "You would do well to learn it, *malysh*."

"I want to learn," Olly insisted.

"The first lesson"—Papa spoke somberly, but with a twinkle in his eyes that let Vera breathe again—"'*do svidaniya.*'"

Olly popped a salute and tossed out an enthusiastic, *"Do svidaniya,"* earning him a nod of approval from Papa.

With a dip of his head, Papa said, *"Do skorovo"* and, pushing his spectacles back into place, moved with a broad stride to the back room.

"That weren't the same words," Olly said.

"No, they weren't."

His little forehead creased. "But what does it mean?"

"The words he taught you or the words he just said?"

"Both." Olly tossed his hands in the air. "He didn't tell me what either one meant."

"He did after a manner," she said. "Toss it about in your idea pot. You'll sort it."

Olly stood rooted to the spot, a mighty pout on his face. Vera looked to Ganor, expecting to exchange amused looks. But the man kept quietly at his work. Vera didn't for a moment think he was unaware of what was happening. The man was sharp, and he didn't miss anything.

He might be in a bit of a sour mood, but she was willing to risk it. She wanted his thoughts on Papa's new job. She wasn't certain whether she was overreacting. Talking with Ganor had started to help her sort the matter of the Protector's letter, and chatting about their pasts the evening before had given her a measure of peace and a sense of belonging.

Vera crossed to him. "We're to have some new printing orders."

"I heard your da say as much." He kept his eyes on the window trim he was repairing. "He seems pleased."

"Pleased and mysterious," she said. "I often ask him details of the jobs he's doing. He's never bit off my head like that before."

"Could be he's not so sure of the job as he wants you to think he is."

She shook her head. "He's not ever tiptoed around that before. He tells me if he ain't sure a client'll prove a good one."

"'Twasn't the client he refused to talk to you about," Ganor said.

That was true, though she'd not twigged that right away. "We talk about his printing regularly, what he's printing, how complicated it might be, how many pages it'll require, what type of parchment. He wouldn't even tell me the type of job this time. No clues whatsoever."

For the first time since she'd joined him there, Ganor looked up from his work. He didn't look at her, though, but at the back door where Papa had exited the shop. "Maybe he's printing something he doesn't want you to know about."

"What could that be, though? He ain't one to do anything nefarious."

He offered her a quick, half-formed smile. "Maybe he's agreed to print a book and doesn't want you knowing, since it'd make him a bit of a hypocrite."

Heavens, that could be the answer. She hesitated, then lowered her voice so as not to be overheard. "A group of writers caused some difficulty in St. Petersburg when we lived there, and my papa was accused of being part of it. That set the police on our trail, and we had to make like the waves and leave Russia behind. If he's printing books now, he'd never admit to it."

"What sort of difficulty did these writers cause?" he asked, matching her low tone.

"I've already told you more than I tell anyone." And she'd done so unprompted. She'd never trusted anyone that much before. "The history is my papa's. I'd be playing him a terrible trick to share anything more."

Beyond that, Papa thought they needed to be careful still. She'd not risk more trouble by making their history known.

"Sounds a great deal like m'sister's feelings about the blue-bottles," Ganor said.

"Your sister don't like the police?"

Ganor pounded a nail in before answering. "Not so much a matter of not likin' them as worrying over them being too nearby."

He'd said her reasons were similar to those Papa had for

worrying about writers. "The police caused her trouble at some point, did they?"

He nodded. "The both of us. We had a spot of trouble with the Peelers—that's what we call the police in Dublin—and we'd no choice but to, as you put it, make like the waves."

"What was your spot of trouble?" she asked.

He shook his head quickly and firmly. "That's a seven-magpie story, that one."

"I don't twig you."

He explained. "That old rhyme about the magpies and what it means to see a particular number of them."

"Ah." She understood now. But what was the meaning of seeing seven magpies? She'd read the latest installment of "The Dead Zoo" recently enough to remember without much thought. "'Seven for a secret, never to be told.'"

"That's the front and back of it, lass."

"A seven-magpie story," she repeated. "That's a right clever turn of phrase, that is. I've said it before, but you're something of a wordsmith at times."

"I do try," he said with a laugh.

"Fortunately for you," Vera said, "there are two magpies present just now. Two is for joy, not secrets."

His dipped-brow expression told her he'd not the first idea what she meant.

Vera took pity on him. "Sorokin is a name that comes from the Russian word for magpie."

"Miss Vera!" Olly's voice rang out from the street in tones of absolute terror. "Fire, Miss Vera! Fire!"

They ran to the door where the boy stood, frozen with

terror. Across the street, smoke poured from the front-facing windows of Overton's barbershop.

"Cricum jiminy." She looked to Olly. "Run downstairs to the printing room. Tell Papa."

He obeyed without argument.

Vera turned to Ganor. "We've buckets out behind the shop fit to purpose, and there's a pump down the street."

He nodded and rushed off to the back. Vera darted across the street, reaching the barbershop just as Peter stumbled out with Mr. Overton.

"Anyone else inside?" Vera asked.

Peter shook his head. "Everyone's out, but the fire's spreading."

"Mr. O'Donnell's fetching buckets of water. Has anyone else nipped off for water?"

Her question was answered by the arrival of the Okekes with water-laden buckets. They ducked inside to toss their loads on the flames. The scene replayed with two others. Then others. Ganor joined their ranks as well.

Vera did her best to keep curious onlookers at a distance, all the while listening to the pop of flames and the smoky coughs of her neighbors.

Several fire brigades arrived on the scene with their water pumps. Vera searched the façade of the barber shop for a fire marker. Few businesses in the area could afford to pay the insurance needed to receive the help of the brigades.

Ganor appeared out of nowhere, eyeing the building as well. "No fire marker."

Fear clung to her heart like a thornbush. "They'll let it burn if there's not a marker."

"We'll do what we can for him." Ganor accepted an empty bucket from one of the neighbors just stumbling from the building.

Buckets were nothing compared to the might of the brigades' pumps. Mr. Overton would lose everything. There'd be no salvaging his livelihood or saving his family from the poorhouse.

The barber sat on the edge of the pavement across the street, watching as his entire life was reduced to ashes. Vera crossed to him and sat at his side, without the first idea what to say to him. How did one comfort a man who was watching the destruction of everything he owned?

They sat in silence as the brigades left, not having offered the least assistance. Mr. Overton hadn't purchased fire insurance—he no doubt couldn't afford it—and so they wouldn't help. That was the horrible, tragic way of things.

"Should've paid," he said, his voice raspy.

"Not a one of us pays for the fire brigades," Vera said. "How can we? We're hardly covering our costs as it is."

He shook his head. "I don't mean the fire insurance. I didn't pay the Protector."

She pulled her eyes from the smoke and looked directly at him. "You didn't?"

He dropped his head into his hands. "I needed new razors for the shop. Long overdue. I bought them instead."

"And you think having those extra eyes would've helped prevent this?"

His posture slumped with defeat. "A man came to collect my quid. When I told him I couldn't pay this week, he said

149

that was a shame and that robberies weren't the only trouble businesses and people needed protecting from."

There was nothing untrue in that.

"Then he said it didn't take much for a life to 'go up in flames.'"

Even with the heat of the nearby fire, cold creeped over her. "You think the Protector set the fire?"

Mr. Overton nodded, his sooty fingers leaving prints along his temples. "I was meant to remember those words. Now, I'll never forget them."

Vera pulled in a breath, the ash in the air only making the effort more difficult. *Didn't take much for a life to go up in flames.*

The street, then, wasn't paying for help like they thought. They were being extorted.

Pay or suffer.

Pay or be targeted.

Pay or their lives would go up in flames.

CHAPTER 13

Brogan watched, helplessly, as Vera paced the shop, worry deepening the lines on her ash-smeared face. The fire at the barbershop was out, finally, but even the combined efforts of nearly everyone on the street hadn't been enough to save the building. Heaven knew they'd tried. He'd told himself as he'd frantically tossed bucket after bucket on the flames that they'd manage it somehow. Watching the building collapse, gutted from the inside, he'd felt that failure acutely. Overton's family would likely never recover.

Vera was understandably shaken, and Brogan didn't know how to help. He'd told himself the night before, when Fletcher had brought him the letter from the Dread Master, that it'd be for the best to keep a distance from Vera Sorokina—an emotional one, leastwise. That decision had held for all of a few hours. He was, once again, feeling drawn to her, pulled in.

Brogan stepped into the path of her pacing. She stopped and looked at him. He offered what he hoped was a reassuring expression, inviting her to share what was on her mind.

After a moment, she sighed. Her shoulders rose and fell. "He didn't pay."

Brogan nodded. "Most businesses can't afford fire insurance."

"Not that. The protection money. He didn't pay it. When the man came to collect, Mr. Overton told him he didn't have it, that he couldn't pay."

Brogan watched her more closely. "And what has that to do with this fire?"

"The man said that he ought to reconsider on account of it being easy for *a life to go up in flames.*"

Saints above. "'Twasn't an observation, then, but a threat."

"I'm beginning to think we haven't been paying for security, after all."

Lands, it certainly didn't seem that way. "Have you spoken with your neighbors about this?"

"What would I even say?" She spread her hands and shrugged. "I don't know how to help. It wouldn't do a lick of good to meet with them if I haven't any hope to offer."

'Twas one of the things he'd come to admire most about Vera. She never wanted to cause people pain. She had a good heart and a compassionate nature. But he also knew from first-hand experience that spending one's days trying to help everyone with every problem they had was exhausting.

"We can spin this question about our brains. And if you haven't yet told your da about it, I think you ought to. And if you've no objections, I'd suggest we pull m'sister into the question as well. Móirín is one of the cleverest people I know."

She clasped her hands together. Her eyes pulled wide. "I would finally get to meet your famous sister?"

"What do you mean 'famous'?" He was never more nervous about Móirín's welfare than when someone indicated they knew her.

"Only that you've mentioned her a few times, and I can tell that you two are close. I'd very much like to meet her."

That was a relief.

"Why don't you and your da come to my flat? The two of you could stay there tonight. It'll give you a bit of distance from the ash and smoke. I think you'll rest better away from here. And you and I and Móirín—and your da, if you decide—can see what we can sort out about all this. You've created unity among your neighbors already. If you could decide on a path forward, I think they'll take it with you."

Vera rubbed at her forehead, weariness filling every inch of her posture. "I'm not a leader of uprisings, Ganor. I'm not a general strategizing in battle. I'm nothing but a shop girl."

He closed the distance between them and set his hands on her arms. His pulse picked up a bit. "Vera."

She didn't look up at him. Her head hung. Her shoulders bent, heavy and burdened.

"Being a shop girl doesn't make someone 'nothing.' And I watched you during your meeting with your neighbors. You're a leader and a general whether or not you think you are."

She shook her head. "That was when we thought this was merely a mystery. Now we know it's a threat. The consequences of failing are far bigger."

"Come spend the evening with my sister and me," he suggested again. "Your mind needs time to wrap around this change. Once it's not so new, it'll feel less overwhelming."

"You've a lot of faith in me," she said.

"And I think you've more faith in yourself than you realize in this moment."

Her shoulders rose and fell with a deep breath. When she spoke again, she sounded more composed. "I cain't promise my papa will take you up on your offer."

"I vow not to be offended."

A little smile touched her lips. "And your sister?"

"She'll at least vow not to toss anyone out of the flat."

That brought her eyes up to him, surprise in her gray eyes.

He laughed. "That'll make a lot more sense once you've met Móirín."

"You make me wonder if I even want to." She didn't sound in earnest. Vera, it seemed, had come to know him well enough to realize he was jesting.

"Trust me, love. You do."

Looking lighter than she had all day, Vera stepped back. "I'll ask Papa. Either way, give me a moment and I'll be ready to jaunt."

Left by himself in the shop, Brogan took a moment to do some pacing of his own. He was certainly not "keeping his distance," but who could blame him? Vera had passed a horrific day. She'd learned she and her father and her neighbors were in danger. She was tired and likely afraid. He couldn't just abandon her.

And, he couldn't abandon *this* difficulty simply because he was also investigating another one. The DPS regularly tackled multiple troubles at once. Of course, the DPS had the benefit of more than one person shouldering the load.

He, alone, was tackling the investigation of Mr. Sorokin's potential connection with the ambassador, but he was in a supporting role in the mystery Vera was sorting. He was far more comfortable as the aide-de-camp than the commander.

Some people were heroes. Some people were . . . him.

Vera returned after a few minutes. Alone. She carried a small valise in her hand.

"Your da?" he asked.

"Ain't coming." She spoke swift and firm, clearly unwilling to elaborate. He wouldn't press for more. "You're certain your sister won't mind me arriving unannounced?"

"She really won't. I should warn you, though, she'll tease you mercilessly. It's what she does."

Vera didn't look the least bit uneasy about that. "Between the urchins who drop by and a certain cheeky Irishman, I think I've learned well how to endure a bit of teasing."

"Well then." Brogan held out his arm for her.

She hooked her arm through his, and together they walked out of the shop. Brogan hailed a hansom cab, and they rode all the way to Sackville Street. Just as they had the evening before, they conversed easily on any number of topics. Though he was certain her mind was still spinning on the question of the Protector and the fire, they didn't discuss any of that. He'd let her bring it up when she was ready.

He could see as they stepped inside the flat that she was nervous. "I swear to you, m'sister won't mind at all. In fact, I'd be very much surprised if she doesn't try to convince you to stay longer than just one night. She's fond of company."

And, fortunately for Brogan, she also had a keen memory and a quick mind. He was depending on Móirín to remember that he was using a false name and call him "Ganor" when he introduced her to Vera. Of course, that meant he was requiring yet another person to lie to Vera. If she didn't already believe writers were deceptive by nature, she would the moment she realized his dishonesty.

What a muck he was treading through.

Móirín emerged from the kitchen, likely having heard them come in.

"This is my sister, Móirín. Móirín, this is Vera Sorokina."

Móirín's grin was welcoming, which set Brogan's mind at ease, but it was also filled with ample mischief.

"*Zdrastvuyte*, Miss Sorokina," Móirín said. "*Ochen' priyanto.*"

"You speak Russian?"

Móirín dipped her head. "Only a little."

Móirín spoke another language, and he'd had no idea.

Vera looked to him. "You didn't tell me that."

Brogan held his hands up in a show of innocence. "I didn't know." He turned to Móirín. "Why did you never tell me you spoke Russian?"

"You never asked, Ganor."

Ganor. She'd remembered. Thank the heavens.

Móirín eyed Vera's bag. "Are you movin' in?"

"For the night," Brogan said. "There was a fire across the street from the shop, and it weren't an accident."

"Saints alive," Móirín muttered. "Of course, you'll stay here. Arson, was it?"

Vera nodded. "Among other things."

"I have stew on the stove." Móirín motioned them back toward the kitchen. "Come, sit and fill your belly, then tell me what's been happening."

Brogan put an arm around Vera's shoulder and gave her

a quick, friendly squeeze. "We'll get to the bottom of it, I'm certain we will."

She leaned into his one-armed embrace, tucking herself up against him. "I hope so."

He likely ought to have dropped his arm away. He ought to have reclaimed as much of the space between them as he could. She might very well prove to be part of the trouble he was investigating. But he found, walking side-by-side, with his arm around her, he hadn't the strength to pull away.

"You've a tangled knot there, Vera." Móirín had listened closely as Vera explained the situation on Old Compton Street. "How do you mean to untie it?"

"I haven't the first idea," Vera said.

"I take leave to doubt that."

Brogan hoped his sister's directness wouldn't push Vera away. Móirín was also funny and personable. And she was sometimes terrifying. He never knew how people would react to her.

"I don't have a *good* idea," Vera corrected.

"So tell us your middling idea." Móirín laughed a bit, and it seemed to help.

Vera's posture relaxed. "Before the fire, I asked my neighbors to think back on the days their notes have been delivered and twig who was there."

"'Twig' is London for 'sort out,'" Brogan said for his sister's benefit.

"I know," she said.

"How is it you know that?"

"Perhaps I'm smarter than you are," Móirín said with a grin.

"He was smart enough to warn me you'd be a merciless tease," Vera said.

"A regular genius, he is." Móirín offered the dry agreement before returning to the topic at hand. "Have any of your neighbors thought of anyone knocking about on the days the notes were delivered?"

"I've not collected their lists," she said. "And I'm not sure it'd be of much help now. I suggested the strategy when we thought we were trying to identify a benefactor not an oppressor."

"You don't think knowing who's behind this would make a difference?" Brogan asked.

"I don't think we can stop whoever's behind it no matter if we know who he is."

"Secrecy is power, Vera," Móirín said. "It adds potency to any weapon and danger to any scheme. Unmasking your villain shrinks the threat into something definable."

"Secrecy is power," Vera repeated on a sigh. "It's also a burden."

"You carry a few of those burdens, do you?" Móirín asked.

"More than a few," was the answer.

Móirín met Brogan's eye with a look of empathy. They had a lot of secrets as well.

Brogan reached over and took Vera's hand. She threaded her fingers through his. Oh, how easily he could let himself start dreaming of this connection between them growing more permanent.

"What if I cain't twig a solution?" Vera addressed the question to him.

"Meet with your neighbors again," he said. "There's no reason you have to face this alone."

"You'll help?" she pressed.

He raised their hands to his lips and gently kissed her fingers. "Of course."

In the next instant he caught Móirín's extremely curious and amused gaze. She'd never let him explain this away enough to avoid that "merciless teasing" he'd warned Vera of.

He could tell his sister that there was nothing overly fond in the gesture or that he felt nothing particular for Vera. But it wouldn't've done a bit of good. He'd done a lot of lying to her in the years since he'd joined the DPS, but that was one falsehood she'd see through in an instant.

THE DEAD ZOO

by Brogan Donnelly

Day Three

Amos had hardly slept. Such was the burden of one whose self-declared claim to fame was unparalleled intelligence but who had endured a monumental lapse in judgment. Burdened with questions of identity, Amos arrived at the Dead Zoo worse for wear yet unwilling to abandon the challenge he'd been issued.

The museum was not open every day. On this morning, no visitors would be admitted. Members of the Royal Dublin Society, however, had ready access.

If Amos were not so certain of his eventual success, he might have been ashamed to have not realized sooner the significance of thefts occurring while the museum was closed. Lord Baymount's misleading conversation had planted in Amos's mind a trail of thought he'd followed during the long sleepless hours of night.

For a collector of taxidermied, mounted, or skeletal animals, the Dead Zoo presented a treasure trove of possibilities. Someone without the preferred scruples might see in its displays a shortcut to the collection he desired. And who could wish for such a thing more than members of the society whose interest in such things had led to the Natural History Museum in the first place?

Still, he did not mean to storm into the mammal exhibit with accusations falling from his lips. He would build a case, gather proof. He would not be made the fool again.

William Sheenan was not the first to greet our unlucky detective upon his arrival. Amos's path crossed Jonty's first. The gruff man was not mopping as he had been that first day. Indeed, Amos had not seen him mopping since. On this day, he was dusting displays.

He grumbled as Amos passed, his words indiscernible but his tone unmistakable. He did not care for Amos, did not like him being there. The feeling was growing more mutual with every encounter.

William, however, was pleased at Amos's arrival. Though he'd not cared for the near run insult of the day before and had needed to patch things up with Lord Baymount, the situation at the museum required greater and quicker effort than previously.

"Our colobus monkey is missing," William told him.

"The long-haired, black and white one, yes?" Amos asked, unable to hide the hint of pleasure in his expression. Another missing specimen offered opportunity for more clues. Though he was reluctant to admit as much, he needed more information than he had if he was to avoid another embarrassing misstep.

He followed William to the display. Amos checked the now-empty display and found it just as the others had been:

a bit scratched, a bit scuffed. Whoever had undertaken the theft had done so with more care than before, but only a very little more.

He froze. That same feeling—a horrid, unnerving feeling—of being watched seized him. Even more than his failure of the day before, *this* flaw in his reasoning caused him great distress. He was not easily overset. He was not intellectually weak. Amos Cavey would not give way to illogical whimseys.

He told himself he would ignore any magpies he should see. Surely there were no more displays than the two he'd already seen.

He was wrong. The nearest shelves contained more. Ten this time.

Eight for a wish.

Nine for a kiss.

Ten for a bird you must not miss.

It is all rubbish. Nonsense. This place oversets the mind, is all. I will overcome it.

With himself firmly in hand once more, Amos stepped back from the vandalized display and set himself to a study of his surroundings. He had, of course, made a thorough inspection the day before, but that had yielded nothing but near-disaster. Today, however, would be different.

The comings and goings were fewer and focused. His primary group of suspects were present and no one else.

He could not err today. He would not!

Two members of the society entered the room, both looking quite pleased with themselves. Amos had interacted with them before and had found them unbearably arrogant.

He was not opposed to confidence of character, mind you—he possessed quite a lot of it himself, after all—but he did not approve when he saw it in those who had not fully earned it. Some members of the Royal Dublin Society had offered inarguable proof of their intelligence. Others, like Mr. McClellan and Mr. Kearney, hadn't.

They crossed paths in front of the hippopotamus, something Amos made look unintentional. "Gentlemen," he said with a dip of his head.

"You do realize the museum is closed to visitors," Mr. McClellan said. "Only members of the society have access to the collection today."

"Unless one who has chosen not to join the society has been particularly invited by the keeper of the mammals." Amos watched them for any signs of worry.

They did seem to find that odd, but not in a way that seemed to alarm them. Curiosity appeared to be the crowning response.

"Why has William asked you to be here?" Mr. Kearney asked.

Amos allowed a pitying look. "Alas, if you do not already know, then you were likely not meant to."

Far from felled by this subtle insult, Mr. McClellan and Mr. Kearney simply exchanged looks heavy with amusement and walked away. Oh, yes. The members of this haughty and insufferable society were prime suspects. Prime, indeed!

Amos meant to trail them as unobtrusively as possible. They would not suspect his efforts. If luck were with him, they would unintentionally provide him with incriminating evidence.

His pursuit brought him past Jonty, who watched him with obvious disapproval, though what he'd done to earn the man's dislike, he didn't know. Still, he could not be bothered with such things at the moment. His intellect was at work, and he would not allow himself to be distracted.

His quarry must have sensed him following them. Now and then, they stopped and glanced backward. If he were, in that moment, within view, he busied himself with studying whichever specimen was nearest at hand. If luck favored him and he were not visible, he simply tucked himself more firmly out of sight and waited.

It was during one of these moments of hiding that the sensation of being watched washed over him once more. Every time he felt the weight of eyes upon him, the feeling grew heavier and more difficult to explain away.

This time, his gaze sought out the janitor. But Jonty was nowhere to be seen. That, of course, did not preclude him being tucked away just as Amos was. The man had made clear his disdain and disapproval. It was, no doubt, his glares which Amos felt crawling up his neck.

Around the corner, Mr. McClellan, fully ignoring the card instructing otherwise, touched the skin of the moose on display. Such disregard for proper behavior. Oh, yes, these were his miscreants.

He stepped closer. Then came the sensation of someone stepping closer to *him*. He looked behind him. No one.

What was the matter with him? He never allowed his imagination to flourish, let alone run rampant.

Amos focused all his attention on the two suspicious men. They were very intent on the displays, but not in a way that spoke of true appreciation but rather amusement. They were in the Dead Zoo for entertainment, and what could be more entertaining than thievery to those inclined toward such things?

William was fast approaching. Now was Amos's opportunity. He would denounce the men, insist William check their coats and pockets for something they meant to slip off with, and leave a hero. The Royal Dublin Society would ask him *again* to join. He would refuse *again*. But he would likely be invited to lecture and present and otherwise make even more of a name for himself. His prowess would see him praised not merely in Dublin, but in London as well.

He opened his mouth to begin what he anticipated would be a very impressive denunciation, but William spoke before he could.

"We've something else missing," he said in a low voice. "I saw it was not in its display this morning but assumed it had been taken out by order of Mr. Carte. I have only just learned it was not."

Something of panic lay in William's words. That hadn't been present before when he'd spoken of missing items. This, then, was different.

"What is it?"

With a shaking breath, William said, "Our hartebeest is missing."

"Hartebeest?"

Amos quickly thought back to his previous wanderings in the Dead Zoo. He could picture the animal in his mind's eye. An antelope, two- to three-hundred pounds in life. No doubt, lighter in taxidermied preservation, but still quite large. Too large for carrying off undetected. Not without assistance, and assistance beyond a single partner. One would have to have access to a cart of some kind. And it could not be done in sight of others.

A sense of foreboding settled over him. He'd nearly lobbed another accusation that would have proved humiliating. He'd nearly made an absolute quiz of himself once again.

How had he been so wrong twice? *Twice?*

What was happening to him? What dark spell was this place of death casting over him?

CHAPTER 14

Brogan couldn't manage to write a single word. His publisher would have his neck if he was late with the next installment, but he couldn't concentrate. Vera had returned to the print shop that morning, having passed the night safely at the flat. 'Twasn't one of Brogan's days for working there. Thus he was at home, meant to be putting pen to paper.

His mind, though, was with her. A growing part of his heart was as well.

Was the shop safe? Was she planning to talk with her neighbors? Would his being there have been helpful today? He wished he knew for certain.

By midmorning, he'd accomplished exactly nothing when someone knocked at the door. Hadn't been that long ago when an interruption in the middle of his writing day was an annoyance. Today, he was grateful.

Until he opened the door.

'Twas Elizabeth Black, headmistress of a respected girls' school and writer of respectable novels. She was also secretly the author known as Mr. King, and the only female member of the Dread Penny Society. Brogan, of course, knew her well, but having her at his door now that he was considered a *former* member of the DPS had the potential to deal him as much of a blow as his encounter with Doc had.

She also knew Móirín. "M'sister's not here. She's off doing the day's cleaning."

"Perfect." With that, Elizabeth stepped inside, the click of her heeled boots echoing around the entryway. She'd never lacked for boldness.

Brogan closed the door and followed her to the sitting room. He was not left to wonder long what she'd come to discuss.

"I had a most enlightening conversation with Ana Newport yesterday." Her tone gave the declaration significance.

"How is Ana?"

"A better question is 'How is *Ganor*?'" She folded her arms, one shoulder tipping higher than the other, and skewered him with a look. "Why're you using a false name, Brogan?"

"Mr. Newport knows me as Ganor O'Donnell. Ana told me her own self not many weeks past that she thought it best we not burden his mind overly much by correcting that name now."

Elizabeth's only reaction to that explanation was the slightest tip of her head.

"Ana really did ask me not to—"

She cut him off with a lifted hand. "She said the report she received was that someone else was there with you who didn't seem at all to doubt that Ganor O'Donnell is your name.

That's an identity you used during your DPS years. Why're you using it now?"

Keeping secrets from Móirín had always been difficult; keeping them from the Dreadfuls was proving nearly impossible.

"I'd never've been hired at the shop where I'm working if they knew who I really am."

Her gaze narrowed on him. "I thought your latest story was selling well. I see it all around London."

She was too clever by half. 'Twas like having yet another Móirín. Brogan didn't like lying, but it seemed that was all he did anymore.

"A bit of extra coin in m'pocket might mean Móirín and I could begin building lives of our own. It'd mean a lot to the both of us."

Though Elizabeth didn't look convinced, she didn't press. "Why wouldn't this shop hire you as yourself?"

"The owner harbors a deep dislike of authors."

She grinned, looking as if she were barely holding back a laugh. His lack of amusement must've made a quick impression; her smile faded.

"You are in earnest."

He nodded.

"Why does this shop dislike writers so much?"

Brogan shrugged. "Something in the family's past."

"And you've fallen in love with the shop girl anyway?"

He actually sputtered, something he tried very hard not to do. "'Tis a bold assessment from Ana, considering she wasn't even there during our visit."

Laughter entered Elizabeth's eyes. "Her father offered that evaluation."

"And you've come because you're concerned I might be courting someone who hates writers and doesn't know my actual identity or profession?" Mercy, that was a discouraging summary.

"It was a convenient excuse."

"Excuse?"

She shrugged. "I've wondered how you've been doing since parting ways with the rest of us."

"Middling," he answered, matching her shrug with one of his own. The gesture tossed his thoughts to Vera. She had such an endearing way of shrugging. Was it odd of him to be so fond of a gesture? To smile inwardly when he thought of it?

"The Dreadfuls are struggling." Elizabeth broke into his wandering thoughts. "I'm told you're the first member to have left. It's thrown things into a bit of uncertainty."

He rubbed a hand across his forehead. "Doc *did* seem put out with me when I saw him a week or so ago."

"You were a hardworking part of the group. Making up the difference with you gone is not an easy thing."

"Foot soldiers like me are easy to replace," he said. "You've plenty enough captains and generals to fill that gap."

"Is that all you think you are?"

"There's nothing shameful in being the one who follows through on orders. Not everyone has to be the one *giving* the orders."

She leaned forward. "But you seem to think not being the one in charge makes you less needed or important. If you could see how the Dreadfuls are scrambling, you would know that is not true."

It was both reassuring and discouraging. "I hadn't meant to leave them in a lurch."

"You seem to be in a bit of a lurch yourself."

He shook his head. "*My* struggles aren't my biggest worry. Too many people in my life need a champion."

"So be one." Elizabeth had a tendency to go directly to the heart of a matter, but it meant she sometimes missed the complications.

"Again, I'm the reinforcements not the hero."

She rose. "Then be heroically reinforcing."

"I do not believe that is a *real* role."

Elizabeth gave him one of her well-known looks of amused annoyance as she made for the door. "Heroes come in a lot of forms, Brogan. Be the one you are best suited to being."

Best suited? What type of hero could a one-time street urchin, turned delivery boy, turned refugee, turned second-rate former member of a secret organization possibly be *best suited* to?

Thinking of Vera and the burden she was carrying, he found his usual doubt less powerful than his wish to help her in whatever way he could.

"Heroes come in a lot of forms." Perhaps it was time he figured out what form *he* came in.

"It isn't protection money." Vera ended her explanation to her neighbors with very little encouragement to offer. "It's extortion."

"What can we do?" Mr. Bianchi asked. "We can't go on like this forever."

Vera pushed out a slow, tight breath. "I wish I knew."

"Would the police help us?" Mr. Okeke asked.

"I received another note today," Mr. Murphy said. "It warned against bringing in the blue-bottles."

"I can't afford to keep paying the ransom," Gemma said. "I'll be plum outta blunt soon enough. How do we make it stop?"

"We take away their power," Vera said. "A big part of doing that is learning who the Protector is."

Gemma sighed, frustrated. "There's no way of learnin' that. It's a different rough every time what collects the money. And no one's yet seen who leaves the notes."

"Arson seems the order of the day. Can we at least protect against that?" Mr. Bianchi asked.

"Not one of us has the blunt for fire insurance," Mr. Okeke said.

"We shouldn't have to," Gemma said. "I read the papers. Parliament passed a law. The fire brigades are supposed to put out *any* fire."

"That law don't go into effect until January," Vera said. "We can't depend on the brigades. We need to depend on each other."

"Takes too long to get water here from the pump down the road." Mr. Overton spoke for the first time. He and his family had been taken in by the Bianchis, but heaven only knew how long that family could afford the extra mouths when Overton had no income.

"What if we all agree to keep an extra bucket of water in

our shops?" Vera suggested. "That'd give us a dozen buckets, at least, to get started dousing a fire while more water was run over from the pump."

It wouldn't be foolproof, and it might not be enough, but it'd be a far sight better than doing nothing.

"Word of the fire didn't reach everyone quickly enough," Mr. Okeke said. "If we had a plan for getting word to everyone, that'd speed things."

"Good suggestion," Vera said.

"I can organize that." Mr. Overton's downcast expression lifted. "I'll work up some kind of plot and let everyone know."

"Excellent." Vera gave him what she hoped was an encouraging nod. "And if everyone'd get me them lists of people who were about or anything unusual on the days the notes were left, that'd help a heap."

They began handing slips of paper to the people sitting closer to her, passing the growing stack forward.

"If we can convince this Protector fella that we're looking out for each other and can thwart his plans, he might leave us be." Gemma's declaration was optimistic, but not entirely unrealistic.

"And anyone struggling to make the payment needs to let the rest of us know," Vera said. "We've strength in our numbers, but only if we work together."

Exclamations of "hear, hear" and "Indeed" and other shows of agreement followed, as Vera collected her neighbors' handwritten recollections.

"Miss Vera, you've visitors coming." Peter had been placed at the window, charged with watching the street.

"Who is it?"

"Mr. O'Donnell and some cloddy bloke."

Ganor had endeared himself to everyone present with his tireless efforts to put out the fire at Overton's. He also never failed to offer friendly greetings all around. He remembered all their names, their professions, their worries and joys.

A moment later, the man himself stepped inside along with someone Vera didn't know, a man likely ten years his senior. The gathering grew very quiet, very attentive.

"Forgive the interruption," Ganor said, "but I've called on an acquaintance of mine who's taken an interest in your recent concerns."

"Who's this bloke?" Mr. Overton demanded, his tone as defiant as it was uncertain.

"This here's Captain Eyre Massey Shaw, head of the London Fire Engine Establishment." Ganor must've felt the same tension Vera sensed growing in the room. "I'll point out to you that your recent experiences were with *private* brigades, not with his."

That eased things a little.

"He told me in detail how you were treated by the insurance brigades." Captain Shaw was decidedly Irish, which was likely how Ganor had gotten to know him. "I've come with the reassurance that I will insist the London Fire Engine Establishment fill in the gap while we wait for the law to change. My brigades will be made aware of your troubles here. They're brave and tireless, and they aren't in the pocket of any insurer."

It weren't precisely a guarantee, but it was far more

reassurance than they'd had mere moments earlier. That was worth something.

"I mean to regularly check with the people of this street to know if you've had trouble in this matter." Captain Shaw turned to Ganor. "Who was it lost their building in this business?"

Ganor motioned with his head to Mr. Overton. "A barbershop was totally lost. The entire building fell in. Only by luck and the tenacity of a hastily formed bucket brigade did the adjacent buildings escape being engulfed as well."

To Mr. Overton, Captain Shaw said, "I'd appreciate being shown the site. It'd be good for me to be familiar with what's happened."

The barber nodded and rose, accompanying the man charged with overseeing all the firefighting efforts in the entire metropolis. A man who was now on their side and willing to prevent another tragedy.

Vera felt more hopeful than she had since the day of the fire. She saw that same hope reflected in the faces of her neighbors.

"The fire brigade'll be looking out for us," Mr. Bianchi said. "That takes some of the wind out of the threat, don't it?"

"A bit, leastwise," Vera answered.

Ganor received words of thanks and firm handshakes. He received them all with the broad smile she'd seen so often since he'd first begun working at the shop, the one she'd grown so very fond of.

The neighbors hung about for a spell, slowly wandering out now that their planning meeting had come to its natural close. After a time, only Vera and Brogan remained.

"How is it you convinced Captain Shaw to take an interest in our tiny, poor corner of London?"

"The man owed me a favor," he spoke rather mysteriously. "Seemed the right time to call it in."

"The head of the London Fire Engine Establishment owes you a personal favor?"

"Let us just say m' years in Dublin were . . . colorful."

"I'd love to hear about it some time."

The smile twinkled in his eyes, setting her heart to a pleasant sort of flutter. "Come to the flat for supper again tonight," he said. "I'll tell you a few tales, lass."

Despite the heaviness of her mind, Vera brightened at the prospect. In the midst of uncertainty and deception, worries over lies and threats, she had found a refuge, someone she could rely on.

CHAPTER 15

"Vera?" Ganor's voice seemed to come from quite a distance. "Vera?"

She shook herself into the present moment, realizing her thoughts had wandered far afield. Again. They'd left the shop after the neighborhood meeting and retreated to his flat for supper. His sister had indicated she had a few things to do in the kitchen and had shooed them out. To her embarrassment, Vera had heard very little of what Ganor had been saying since they'd settled into the sitting room.

"You're full distracted, you are." He turned to face her more fully, the two of them sitting on the settee. "I've a fair idea what's weighing on your mind, but I've also a very good ear for listening."

"You invited me here for an easy chat and some tale-telling. I cain't imagine you're yearning for troubles to be poured into your lap."

"Two make the load lighter," he said. "My parents always used to say that. 'Twas their way of reminding us that bearing a burden alone makes it heavier than it needs to be."

It was a fine sentiment, but putting it into practice wasn't so easy as one might hope. "You'd be every bit as reluctant to share troubles with me," she said.

Far from pushed off his purpose, Ganor looked even more determined. "I'll strike a deal with you, Miss Vera Sorokina. I'll tell you something I'm struggling with, something I've not shared with many people. And, in return, you let me bear a little of your burden."

Was he in earnest? Even her papa was often reluctant to share cares and concerns. She had thought only that evening what a refuge Ganor was. What a comfort. If anyone could be trusted to truly care, he could. She'd allow herself to trust this little bit more. She could do that much.

"What's your trouble?" she asked.

Ganor looked utterly relieved. He not only seemed to be willing to open up to her and be willing to listen in return, he seemed eager to do so. "My sister and I left Dublin under less-than-upstanding circumstances. I'll not go into detail, doing so's not necessary for this particular problem. But I will say this: 'tisn't safe for us to go back. And yet, Móirín misses Dublin. We talk about home sometimes, places we went and people we knew. Her eyes grow sad. Breaks m'heart."

"*Could* you go back?" Vera said. "You told me once that your troubles in Dublin involved the police."

"So I did." He laughed lightly. "I seem to tell you more than I realize. Certainly more than I tell anyone else."

She turned a bit on the settee, facing him more directly.

He leaned an arm on the back of the settee, resting his head against his upturned fist. "If Móirín thought for one moment she could go back to Dublin and be at all safe, she would. But if she went back, I would too. And we'd be in deep water soon enough."

"So, you're protecting the both of you by staying here where you're safe even though she—and *you*, I suspect—very much wish you were in Ireland."

He nodded.

"Why is it you'd go back with her if you know it'd be dangerous?"

"Because"—he took her hand and held her gaze—"'two make the burden lighter.' I'll not leave her to bear her portion of it alone."

"Instead, the two of you are here, making your *current* burden lighter."

His smile was a visible sigh of relief. "What you're tellin' me is, rather than worry I'm failing her by not bearing together the burden of returning to Dublin, I ought to lighten the burden of having to stay away."

"My papa has longed to return to St. Petersburg for sixteen years, and that yearning has eaten away at him. My mum constantly lamented being away from her homeland. There was no sharing the load. In the end, that burden tore them apart."

He took a deep breath, releasing it slowly. "So, perhaps I'm *not* ruining m'sister's life by failing to find a way of helping her go back?"

"If it ain't possible, then finding joy in what is possible is a mercy."

Ganor nodded slowly, thoughtfully. "I suspect you're right."

"I cain't help it. I'm more or less a genius."

She particularly liked how easily he laughed, that he recognized and seemed to thoroughly enjoy when she was being humorous. She liked to laugh but had done so far less often over the past years than she'd have preferred.

"Well, Madame Genius," he said, "I've shared m' worry. Now you're meant to share yours."

Vera slowly emptied her lungs. "You can likely guess my biggest worry is the threat hanging over Old Compton Street."

"I'd twigged that, yeah."

She smiled at his use of the cant phrase she'd taught him. "I'd hoped coming here would let my thoughts rest at night . . ." She let the sentence wander off. Gads, she was even too weary to finish talking.

He squeezed her hand. "Troubles don't disappear simply because we're not looking at them."

"Is that another of your parents' poetic words of wisdom?"

"I'll claim that as one of my own."

She ran her thumb over the thick scars on his knuckles. "Did you get these in Dublin?"

"Most of 'em."

"You did say you lived a colorful life there." This evidence of his rough past had worried her when she'd first met him. She saw them differently now. He was a fighter, yes, but one dedicated to fighting for those who needed a champion and for causes worth backing.

"Hideous ol' things, aren't they?"

"Not at all." She threaded her fingers through his, grateful for the strength she found in him. "Thank you again for bringing Captain Shaw around. We'll all feel safer knowing he'll answer if we raise the alarm."

"And yet it doesn't seem to have set you much at ease," he said.

"Not entirely." What a sour broth it all was. "If only we knew who the Protector is; who's leaving the notes and who set the fire. I had everyone write down what they can recollect about the days they received their notes. I'm hoping against hope there'll be a clue in there somewhere."

"Have you looked over the lists yet?" he asked.

"I was completely knackered by the time we left the shop. Even reading felt beyond me."

"Does it still?"

"If you'd go through them with me, I think I could manage it."

"Of course."

She rose and reluctantly released his hand. Until she'd had that connection, she hadn't realized how much she'd longed for a reassuring touch. For years, she'd reconciled herself to being, in many ways, alone. She'd more or less accepted that the characters she came to love in the stories she read on the sly would be her only reliable companions. Vera was pleased to be wrong.

Her coat was hanging on a hook near the front door. She reached into the pocket where she'd tucked the stack of papers.

When she returned to the sitting room, Ganor was standing beside the round table under the far windows. He'd pulled out a chair for her.

She sat, then set each paper down, the stack turning into

three neat rows. Ganor opened the drawer under the tabletop and pulled out a notebook and pencil. He sat in the chair beside hers.

They proved a good team, making quick work of the lists. When something matched between lists, Ganor made a note of it. The similarities ran from the vague to the detailed, everything from "more customers than usual" to "a man with a cane and pocket watch who didn't buy anything."

They'd been cracking on with the effort for a quarter hour when she realized a name appeared on every list. "Clare is on all of these."

"She frequents all the shops," he said. "I've seen her about quite regularly."

That was certainly true. Vera spun her mind on her gabs with Clare. There weren't anything suspicious in any of it. "She's a bit quiet—shy and fragile—but also friendly."

Ganor read over his notes. "Everyone said 'twasn't anything odd about her being there."

Vera shook her head. "It'd be stranger if she *weren't* knocking about."

He leaned back, clearly thinking. "You've doubts she'd be the one leaving the notes."

"Can you picture her being part of something like that?" Vera asked.

"'Twould be out of character, for certain. Unless . . ."

"Unless, *what?*"

"Unless she's being forced into it," he said.

Vera hadn't thought of that but couldn't deny it was possible. The entire street, after all, was being forced into paying the Protector. Stood to reason he might be forcing someone to leave the notes.

"Any notion where she lives?" Ganor asked.

"Somewhere near the shop." She stopped up short. "I suppose I don't know that for sure and certain."

"That'll complicate things." He rubbed at his mouth and chin. "If we can find her, we might manage to get to the truth of her situation, which might set us on the trail of the Protector, or at least save us a misdirection."

Vera bent her elbows on the tabletop, searching her memory for any hint Clare had given of her home neighborhood. "We can watch for Clare, but if she ain't knocking about Old Compton, watching won't be of much use. It ain't as if everyone and anyone knows what she looks like."

It wasn't Brogan who answered, but Móirín. "So describe her."

They both turned toward the doorway. How long Móirín had been there Vera hadn't the first idea.

"Do you mean to help?" Vera asked.

Móirín offered a single nod, then snatched up a stool and sat at the table with them. "We frequent nearly every poor corner of this ol' town. M'brother knows what she looks like. If I knew, the two of us might run her to ground. Better yet, if we'd a sketch of the lass we could ask around and see if anyone else has seen her."

"I don't have a drawing of her," Vera said. "And I cain't draw to save my skin."

"Móirín can," Ganor said. "She's brilliant at it."

"Give me some paper, Brog. I'll see if I can't sketch out this mysterious woman."

Brog? An Irish word, perhaps? Vera didn't dwell on it. They'd a woman to find and a drawing to get done. The urgency of the moment was more important than passing curiosity.

Móirín sketched as Vera described Clare. Their efforts went on for long minutes, stretching into at least an hour.

Through it, Ganor gathered up the neighbors' accounts and neatly stacked them. He fetched them both glasses of water. He brought Vera a blanket, apparently noticing she was shivering. And he sat beside her, patient and supportive. He was showing himself thoughtful. Again.

At last, fickle fate seemed to be smiling on her.

THE MERCHANT
AND THE ROGUE

by Mr. King

Installment IV
in which the Threat to the village
reveals itself in Terrifying ways!

Tallulah watched for the squire as the days passed. She hadn't the least doubt he would return, and she needed to decide how she meant to respond. Knowing he was, by all estimations, at least eighty years old despite appearing to be only half that, she knew there was something otherworldly about him. That explained the putrid air that hung about him, and the unnerving noises that seemed to follow him about.

Her gran had told her stories of the Fae, of monsters and fairies and mysterious beings. If the squire belonged to *that* world, then he was dangerous in a way no one comprehended. And yet, refusing to stand up to him simply allowed him to hurt the village all the more. He would continue his reign of terror if he was left unchecked.

"You must know what it is you're facing," Gran had said.

"To unknowingly cross paths with the Fae is a danger greater than any human can imagine."

But what was he? She wasn't at all certain, and saints knew she needed to be.

Belinda and Marty stepped inside, their eyes immediately on the colorful displays of candies.

She adored the children of Chippingwich. "What's it to be today, loves?"

"We want to try anise candies," Belinda announced. "Georgie likes them."

"He does, indeed." She set a ha'penny's worth of anise candies on a slip of paper and folded it up, trading the sweets for their coin.

"Do you have any new candies, Miss Tallulah?" Marty seldom spoke, and when he did so, he was very quiet.

Tallulah kept her own voice gentle and calm when answering. "I have chocolate-covered almonds. They come very dear, though, so we'll have to save those for a very special treat."

Marty nodded, eagerly eyeing the folded paper in his friend's hand. The two little ones would most likely have the anise candy eaten long before reaching either of their homes.

A flurry of red announced the squire's arrival. He slid into the shop with all the arrogance of someone who knows he will not be challenged or denied what he wishes for. Tallulah didn't know what he had come to demand this time, but it was clear he believed he had won already.

The children inched quickly away from the counter, watching the squire's approach with a deep-seated wariness. They were, no doubt, all too familiar with the sort of person he was. Tallulah kept her posture straight and her demeanor sure.

The squire likely did not know she had pieced together that he belonged to the world of the Fae. She hid her discomfort with his smell; she ignored the distant laughter.

"What can I do for you, sir?" she asked in a tone that was as neutral as she could make it.

"I have decided to give you the opportunity to redeem yourself," he said.

He meant to humble and humiliate her before making his demands, did he? Well, she didn't mean to allow him.

"Whatever do you mean by that?" she asked.

"I was referring to the cake," he said.

"I do recall the cake, but I do not understand the reference you're making." She understood completely, but giving him the impression that it was of so little consequence that she had already forgotten might take a bit of the wind out of his sails.

"The cake you produced was a failure," he said. "I am certain you remember that muddle."

She pursed her lips in a confused frown. "I do not recall a failed cake."

He eyed her more closely. The man, no doubt, wasn't certain what to make of her. Good. If he were upended, he might not be quite so sure of himself. Lack of confidence might render him less dangerous. Perhaps he'd even offer a clue as to who or *what* he truly was.

"I'm here to place another order," he said. "I have decided to be generous since you are new in the village, and it is the job of a squire to see to the good of his people, even if it means risking another disaster."

"I don't understand," she said, still feigning innocence.

His narrowed gaze grew bewildered and increasingly annoyed. She would do well to tread lightly.

"That ridiculous haberdasher said that your petits fours were well done. I should like to place an order for enough of those to impress visitors who are coming to Chippingwich. I will be hosting them in two days' time, and I should warn you they are not easily impressed."

"I'm afraid that will not be possible," she said.

For a moment, he said nothing. Then, in a bit of irony she struggled not to smile at, he repeated the same words that, coming from her, had so frustrated him a moment earlier. "I don't understand."

"You've declared my cake was a failure. I'd not see you disappointed again."

"I have told you I am generously willing to allow you another opportunity."

She shook her head. "I have learned my lesson, Squire Carman. I am simply not talented enough to provide someone of your eminence with confectioneries for your exalted guests. You had best ride to the nearest village with its own confectionery shop."

The entire shop fell silent. She wasn't certain the children were even breathing.

"You would rather not make money?" he asked through a tight jaw.

"On the contrary." The last time, he had paid her only a portion of what he'd promised for the cake. It would not surprise her in the least if he decided that the petits fours ought to be complementary. He would find some reason to argue that they were not worth paying for. She refused to be swindled again.

"As I said, there will be no confectioneries for you to pay for. You will simply have to go elsewhere."

"You are refusing?" The squire asked the question in so tense a tone that she felt some of her courage flee. But no. Someone had to stand up to him.

"It appears I *am* refusing." The declaration emerged firmer and surer than she had anticipated. She was proud of the steadiness of her voice. The children, however, did not seem to feel quite so much confidence. They bolted for the door and out onto the street.

"No one in this village has the audacity to oppose me," the squire said.

Something in the air changed. Literally. It was colder, heavier. Her very breath sounded different. Her voice likely would as well, but she refused to stay silent.

"I've not improved as a baker in the last few days. Nothing I make is likely to meet with your approval, so it makes no sense for me to bake you anything else. It's for your own good, and for the good of the impression you hope to make on your distinguished guests, that you obtain what you wish for from a shop that you trust."

"I am not the one who ought to be concerned with what is in my best interest."

Tallulah set her hands on the counter, feeling the shift in the balance of things. She had the oddest sensation of not being entirely stable on the ground.

"Now," the squire said in a tone that could never be mistaken for patience, "do you intend to take the order I have come to place?"

The fear she felt growing inside insisted she bow to his demands. He was frightening, and powerful. If she didn't stand up to him, she doubted anyone ever would.

She swallowed. Breathed. And pushed on. "You will have to place your order elsewhere."

The displeasure in his eyes grew quickly to fury. The very ground beneath them began to shake. Items on shelves shifted and moved, jumping dangerously about. A glass bowl of candies fell to the floor and shattered. Confections flew from shelves and boxes, landing in ruined heaps on the floor.

All the while, the squire watched her, unblinking. The hatred in his eyes gave them an unholy glow. One she was nearly certain was literal. Literal and heated and radiating red.

The glass in the window wobbled, an unnerving rolling motion she knew glass was not meant to make.

The squire's expression twisted with hatred. And with it, his face changed. It seemed to pull, elongate, grow misshapen.

Faster and faster the window shook and waved. More and more grotesque grew the squire's face.

Then—a cracking sound.

Tallulah dove to the ground, her head tucked in and her arms covering herself as much as she could manage. In the very next instant, a blast of air shook the space and the window gave, showering her and the shop with shards of wood and glass.

"You, Tallulah O'Doyle, have made a very grave error."

From her position ducked behind the counter, she heard the sound of the squire's exiting footfalls, crunching on the bits of glass and candies and debris strewn about the floor.

She remained there, curled in a ball, shaken more than she cared to admit. He had done this. He had done it while standing in place, and without causing himself the least harm. Though she was uninjured, she suspected he could have hurt her if he'd wish to. It was a warning, an easier consequence than what he would likely inflict the next time.

All was quiet in the shop. She could hear nothing beyond the sound of her breathing and the wind whistling in through the broken window. She was grateful the children had already left the shop. How many others in town would know soon enough what had happened? Her determination to help them by standing firm might simply have made them more afraid, put them in more danger.

"Tallulah?" Someone was calling her name. The sound of glass crunching beneath heavy footsteps told her the speaker was in the shop. "Tallulah, are you hurt?"

Royston Prescott. She recognized his voice now. And she felt better.

Slowly, carefully, she stood once more. Glass and bits of cake and biscuits and candies rolled off her as she straightened.

"All the market cross saw your window shatter," he said. "And even before the squire stepped out, we knew what had happened."

"You knew he had this power?" She tried not to let her fear show, but she was not at all certain she'd succeeded.

He nodded. "None of us knows where his abilities come from, but we have all had our own experience with them. He is a dangerous man."

"He is *not* a man. I know enough of the Fae to know he is some variety of monster."

Royston brushed bits of debris from her shoulders with his gloved hands. "Whatever he is, he's dangerous."

"All the more reason none of us can face him alone."

He looked her in the eyes. "This has not scared you off? Hasn't convinced you to stop trying?"

"If the children had still been in here when he did this, they might have been hurt or worse. I cannot shrug and walk away simply because I'm afraid. It's time this village escaped the grip of whatever the squire truly is."

A smile spread across Royston's handsome face. "Kirby said he was certain you wouldn't flinch. I'm happy he was right. Chippingwich has been waiting a long time for someone like you."

CHAPTER 16

óirín dropped into the shop at the end of Brogan's workday. She wore the slightly tattered cloak and bonnet she always chose when they were bound for the poorer corners of London. Blending in was a helpful thing. So was being armed. Móirín had likely brought him his pistol. She *always* had hers.

"We're for Somers Town today," Móirín said. "Frank sent word they're having troubles."

"He did?" Brogan hadn't seen any note arrive.

She eyed him sidelong. "You've been a wee bit distracted. I'd be surprised to hear you'd noticed a single thing beyond a certain gray-eyed lass from Russia."

Thank the heavens Vera wasn't in the room at the moment. Her da was seated at the printing-order table in conversation with a customer who'd only just arrived. They were too focused on their transaction to be paying Brogan and Móirín any heed.

"Vera and I have struck up a friendship between us," he said. "I'll grant you that."

"Lie to yourself all you want, Brog. It'll not change the truth of the thing."

"And what truth is that?"

"Firstly, that you talk about her constantly. Secondly"—she counted off on her fingers—"that the two of you are forever holding hands. Thirdly, I've eyes in m'head and can see for my own self how you look at her."

"I surrender." He held his hands up. "Give me a moment to let Vera know I'm nipping off."

"Go give her a kiss goodbye. I'll be right here waiting."

Kiss goodbye. Móirín was not going to stop teasing him about this. If only he truly knew what "this" was. He knew he was far more than fond of Vera, and he was well aware he felt a vast deal more than friendship for her. He thought the feeling might be mutual, but he'd no guarantee.

The woman herself arrived in the room in the next moment, having been up in the flat above the shop.

"Zdrastvui," Móirín greeted.

"What brings you 'round?" Vera stopped directly in front of them both.

"M'brother and I are jaunting out to Somers Town to look in on some people who're struggling." After the briefest look of absolute mischief tossed Brogan's way, Móirín again addressed Vera. "We'd love for you to join us."

Vera's expression brightened. "I'd like that. Neither of the children is working here today, so I'm not needing to see them off."

Brogan might've pointed out that their errands could be dangerous and that the people they were looking in on didn't know Vera and might be uncomfortable with her seeing them in their difficulties. He might've. But she set her hand gently on his arm, and he was entirely undone.

In no time, they had the shop set to rights: the various items back in drawers, a cloth set over the penny dreadful display to save it from dust and make it less tempting to anyone passing by the window.

"This is the first I've seen your da up here today," Brogan said as they pulled their coats on. "Whatever job he secured a bit ago must be quite a large one."

"It ain't a heap of printing," Vera said. "He says it's complicated, and he's worried he won't get it right. Must be important."

"Enough that you'd not be selling the penny dreadfuls any longer?" That might let him finally tell her who he really was. Except, of course, that she and her da both distrusted writers and telling them he'd been lying about being one wouldn't improve their opinion of them.

"He'd need a string of important print jobs. Until that happens, we'll be selling the stories, and he'll be put out about it."

The three of them stepped out of the shop. Vera tucked her scarf more securely around her neck.

"Perhaps we'll find Clare while we're out," she said, walking alongside them. "She's not been in the shop in ages, it seems."

"Makes the lass a bit more suspicious, yeah?" Móirín said.

"She didn't strike me as the type to be part of anything like this." Brogan had spoken with Clare a few times in the past. "Quiet, a bit withdrawn, personable."

Móirín didn't look put off the idea. "It may be she's a fine actress. Or it may be she's being forced into it."

"Plenty enough women in Soho haven't choices in how they live their lives or keep the roof over their heads," Vera said. "Some fare better than others. I suppose that's true of most everyone on Old Compton, i'n'it?"

Brogan knew the street wasn't faring too well just now. "Have you heard anything from Mr. Overton?"

"Peter said he was in the area this morning, picking through the ashes of his business. He's ruined. Won't be long before the bailiffs come from King's Bench Prison."

"He has a lot of debts, then?"

She nodded. "He could make good on 'em if he had his business, but that's no more than soot now."

Brogan reached over and took her hand as they walked. "'Tis moments like this when I wish I had the resources of a lord. Breaks m' heart not to be able to help people who're needing it. There're far too many suffering people in this world, and I've far too little ability to help them."

She moved closer to him, walking so near that their shoulders brushed. Vera was almost exactly his same height, making holding her hand and walking in-stride a far simpler thing than it would be otherwise.

"I'm feeling proper guilty myself," she said. "I told my neighbors I'd help. Don't seem I've done much."

Brogan slipped his hand free and, instead, set his arm around her. She rested against him, still walking along. He'd assumed the arrangement simply to offer her comfort but found his heart pounding in a most disconcerting way. He didn't drop his arm away. He couldn't. Walking with her as he was, enjoying their conversation and her nearness, he felt more at home than he had in ages.

Home. A future. Love. They were dreams he'd not let himself have in years. This remarkable woman was stirring them up in him again. His heart insisted he fully embrace the possibility; his mind argued that it wasn't wise.

He was still waging that internal war when they reached Somers Town.

Vera took up the efforts there without hesitation, distributing food and medicines and listening to people share their stories. He wasn't surprised—she'd shown herself compassionate time and again—but he was grateful to see it extended far beyond her own neighbors and customers.

They'd been there a full quarter-hour when Brogan finally had a moment to talk with Frank. "Móirín says you're having difficulties."

The man looked torn down. "We'd a fire not long past. No one was hurt, and we managed to put it out quickly."

"Fires seem the threat of choice lately," Brogan muttered.

"A note's been left at a few flats saying more fires could be prevented if—"

"If the note-leaver gets paid a small bit each week?"

"Oi." Frank eyed him, confused and clearly more than a bit worried.

"The same thing's happening in Soho," Brogan explained.

"I've heard whispers from Covent Garden, Vauxhall, Globe Town." Frank shook his head, the gesture one of weariness. "Someone's turning a fine profit, but on the backs of the poor."

"And does that someone have a name of sorts?" Brogan asked.

"Oi. Calls 'imself the Protector."

"Same villain that's causing trouble in Soho," Brogan said. "We think there's a woman by the name of Clare, who might know something about him." He pulled out the drawing Móirín had made and showed it to Frank. "Have you seen her?"

Frank studied the sketch but shook his head. "Cain't say I have."

"Study it a spell," Brogan said. "If you see her, send word to Móirín or me. We're needing to find her without her knowing we're looking."

He made an obvious study of the face in front of him. "I'll send word."

"We'd appreciate it."

Ganor served the poor people of London as naturally as most people breathed. Vera enjoyed watching him every bit as much as she appreciated being helpful herself. He'd told her that he was disappointed at not being able to do more for people in need and that his heart was heavy at not having a means of taking his sister back to Dublin. She'd known his was a kind heart, but seeing such ample evidence of it endeared him ever more to her.

Her efforts with the O'Donnell siblings took them to a few different corners of Town. At each spot, the brother and sister knew the people they worked with by name and remembered without prompting what was weighing on each of them. Ganor was precisely that way with the people of Old Compton. He cared, and he worked tirelessly on behalf of others. When she had been torn to bits with exhaustion, he'd buoyed her.

But who, she found herself wondering, buoyed him?

Either Móirín or Ganor showed the sketch of Clare to people in the various corners they visited. Two thought her face looked familiar. The others didn't recognize her. But all promised to consider the matter and send word if they twigged any clues.

"Do you always do so much walking in an afternoon?" Vera asked as they made their way from yet another stop, the streetlamps having been long since lit. Darkness came early in the winter.

"We don't usually make so many stops in one day," Móirín said. "But we're needing as many eyes peeled as possible looking for your mysterious Clare."

"But you're not doing only that," Vera said. "You're helping people too."

"They've enough to worry about without us interrupting their day for something that'll be of no help to them," Ganor said.

The O'Donnells paused at a vegetable cart near Covent Garden, though whether doing their own grocering or gathering food for others, Vera didn't know.

A harsh "psst" caught her attention. She looked about, searching. A moment later, she heard it again. On the third go, she spotted the woman making the noise and waving her over.

Vera closed the distance, which wasn't far. "Are you needing something?"

"Only a word." The woman sounded Irish. "I've seen who you're here with."

Vera tilted her head. "The O'Donnells?"

Frowning, the woman shook her head.

"You've confused them, it seems," Vera said, kindly. "That's Ganor and Móirín O'Donnell."

"'Tisn't, though. Móirín she is, but his name's Brogan. And they're the Donnellys. They're too well known in Dublin to be mistaken for anyone else."

Brogan Donnelly? The writer of "The Dead Zoo"? No, it couldn't be.

But at the sibling's flat the night before, Móirín had called him "Brog." Vera had assumed at the time it was an Irish word. What if, instead, it was a nickname tossed out by habit?

Brogan Donnelly. No. He'd told her his name was Ganor. Ganor O'Donnell. He answered to it. People who knew him called him that. He'd not have perpetuated so large a ruse. He'd not have lied to her so much and for so long.

"I'd not pour rumor broth in your ear if I didn't think you ought to be warned. I can't imagine you know or you'd not—" The woman clamped her mouth shut and shook her head fast and furious.

"Cain't leave it there," Vera said. "Spill your budget."

The Irishwoman's eyes darted in the direction of the brother and sister, worry and something like fear tugging at her expression. "Donnelly is a name well known in Dublin. *These* Donnellys."

Ganor had said he and his sister had fled their hometown with the blue-bottles close on their tails.

"They can't go back, they can't," the woman added.

"I've heard that." Ganor had said the two of them would be in danger if they returned to Ireland. That this woman was saying the same about him while calling him by a different name was too great a coincidence to be a coincidence.

"And do you know why they can't go back?" the Irishwoman pressed.

"I'm beginning to doubt I know anything," Vera muttered.

"'Twasn't a small thing that triggered their run from the Peelers," the woman said. "'Tis why I had to talk to you, why I had to warn you."

Vera's heart dropped ever further. What else had he lied about? "What was it that sent them fleeing from Dublin?"

Another darting look at Ganor—*Brogan*—and Móirín delayed the woman's answer. But when it came, Vera wasn't the least prepared for it.

"Murder."

CHAPTER 17

It had been two days since Vera had accompanied him and Móirín on their mission to Somers Town, and Vera had been very quiet toward him ever since. She'd not been herself, and it was fretting Brogan. Though he'd not give Móirín the satisfaction of knowing she'd read him right, he'd admitted to himself that he'd begun falling in love with Vera. He thanked his lucky stars every time they were together, and he missed her when they were apart.

He, who had long ago given up on his once-cherished dream of a family and home of his own, was letting himself imagine that again. They could teach each other bits of the languages of their homelands. They could fill their home with reminders of where they'd come from, of family members they'd lost. They'd continue on with the work he and Móirín undertook in the struggling corners of London. He'd read her his stories before sending them to—

That caught him up short. She didn't know who he really was. She didn't know he was a writer, a member of the profession she distrusted and despised. He'd do best not to build castles in the clouds until he knew how likely they were to come tumbling to the ground.

When Brogan reached the print shop, Peter was at his cart beneath the overhang, calling out to passersby, telling them he had "fine fruit" and "perfect pippins."

"How's today's apples?" Brogan asked, pausing in front of the shop door.

"Perfect," Peter said.

"That *is* the word on the street."

Peter perked up. "Who's been talking 'bout my apples?"

"You have." In a decent imitation of the man's monger shout, Brogan repeated, "Perfect pippins!"

The fruit seller laughed and waved him off.

The pause had allowed Brogan to regain a bit of his footing. He knew he would eventually need to tell Vera his real name and profession. But he was being honest with her in most other respects. He'd told her of fleeing Dublin, of being unable to return. He'd told her of struggling with his sister's unhappiness. She'd gone along with him as he'd looked in on the struggling people he tried to help. They were working together to solve the mystery of the Protector. No matter that she didn't know Brogan's name, she knew him better than most of the people in his life.

He simply had to trust that, in the end, it would be enough to give her some faith in him.

Vera was standing near the display of penny dreadfuls, giving instructions to Olly and Licorice. It'd been ages since both children had been working there on the same day. Olly popped him a salute. Licorice offered a quick nod.

Not wishing to interrupt, Brogan slipped quickly to the

back and hung his hat and coat on the nail he always did. Mr. Sorokin must've been nearly finished with his latest printing order. The table in the back room was strewn with samples, several marked with changes to be made. He'd left the room in disarray, something neither father nor daughter ever did. The man, it seemed, was overwhelmed by the job he'd taken on. He likely wouldn't be if he confided in his daughter more.

Brogan hoped the job proved as lucrative as Mr. Sorokin believed it would be; Vera had spoken many times about the struggle they'd had to make the shop profitable.

He stepped back into the main room, excited to start the day. Working at a shop would not have been his first choice, but he found he thoroughly enjoyed it. That, he suspected, had far more to do with Vera than with the work he did there.

Vera nudged the children on to do their work. Brogan smiled at her when she turned to face him. She, however, did not smile back.

Odd.

"Good morning, Vera."

"A minute of your time, please." She pointed toward the back. Her tone was too formal, too unemotional. Something was decidedly wrong. Whatever had been bothering her when they'd last been together seemed to be troubling her still.

"Of course."

He followed her to the back of the room, but not through the back door. She looked him in the eye, her shoulders back, her chin at a confident angle.

"Is something the matter, Vera?" he asked. "You seem upset."

"I'm not upset." But she wasn't terribly convincing. "I

pulled you aside to inform you that your employment here has come to an end."

'Twas little she might have said that would've surprised him more than hearing that. It'd come without warning. There'd been no indication she was unhappy with his work. He'd always done his best, gone beyond what was asked of him. He was, he'd thought, an asset to the shop.

He'd thought he was more than that.

"If this is a jest of some kind, I'm struggling to find the humor in it."

Vera gave a firm shake of her head. "No jest."

He watched her closely, searching for some kind of clue as to what was happening. She was as unreadable as an empty page.

"You're truly giving me the sack?"

"You'll be paid the wages that are due you."

He quickly eyed the children. "Is the trouble that you can't pay me and the wee'ns both? I'd give the children my pay if need be. I'm certain they need it more than I do."

Nothing in her demeanor softened. "It's precisely what I told you: you're no longer needed here."

He folded his arms across his chest. "No longer *needed*, or no longer *wanted*?"

"No longer either." The coldness of her response sent a shiver down his spine.

It made no sense. "You're the one I work for, so I've no ability to override your decision here, but I do think I'm entitled to some explanation."

"I gave you one already." With that, she turned about and made to walk back to the heart of the shop.

To her retreating back, he said, "You said I wasn't needed or wanted, but you didn't tell me why."

Vera half-turned, enough to look at him over her shoulder. "I do not employ people I cain't trust."

Her words were piercing. Hadn't he been thinking on his way to Soho how much he disliked the dishonesty between them? She had declared she couldn't trust him. That was truer than he would prefer.

"Why is it you don't think you can trust me?" He could hear the worry in his voice.

"Why is it you think I *can*?" Then she added in a hard and unyielding tone, "Brogan."

Brogan. She had found out somehow. Learning his actual name told her more than merely *that* lie. It told her he'd lied about his profession. He'd lied about his need for employment. He'd heard her explain more than once her family's feelings about writers, and he hadn't said anything, hadn't kept a distance when he'd known that was what they'd prefer.

He'd been open with her about so many other things that he'd hoped it would be enough to overcome this . . . eventually. Seeing her walk away, back ramrod straight, he knew it wasn't.

Stomach firmly in the soles of his boots, he stepped into the back room. No more than a minute had passed since he'd been there, but he felt decades older. He pulled his coat off the nail he'd only just hung it on. His mind refused to make the least sense of all that had just happened.

He swallowed. He tried to breathe. His mind was so befuddled that his body didn't seem to know how to function without it.

There must be a way of fixing this. There has to be.

But even as the desperate thought spun in his mind, he knew it was futile. He himself had argued that this would eventually be the result for all the Dreadfuls and the lies they told. The secrecy allowed them to save lives, but he'd always known it would eventually exact a steep, terrible price. And he was paying it now.

He'd sacrificed the friendships he'd made in the DPS. He was still telling half-truths to his sister. He'd lost Vera, lost all the dreams he'd begun having of the two of them. And for what? He wasn't any closer to solving the mystery he'd been sent to Soho to investigate.

His eyes took in the back room while his mind attempted to find a way of moving forward. A name on the papers scattered across the desk caught his attention: Lord Chelmsford. That was the gentleman the Dread Master had mentioned was on the outs with the Russian ambassador.

Brogan looked around, making absolutely certain he was alone, then stepped closer and carefully slid the paper out from underneath the ones nearly hiding it, making note of its position so he could return it with no one the wiser.

It was a handwritten letter, which was odd for a print shop, and addressed to the Russian ambassador. A quick glance at the bottom showed it was signed by Chelmsford. In it, the baron spoke of a document that he implored the ambassador not to share. He mentioned their long-standing friendship, the trust that bound them. The letter spoke of damage to Chelmsford's reputation should the document be found.

Strange.

On the table, directly below where the letter had been, was a stack of nearly identical documents, ones with only the slightest changes made between them. He took them up as well, careful not to disturb the papers that had been hiding them. Here was a solid connection between Mr. Sorokin and the ambassador. 'Twas what he'd come to the shop to search for. Weeks earlier, he'd've been excited by the discovery, but now he felt no joy, so sense of accomplishment.

Rather, he felt lost.

Brogan tucked the papers carefully into the inner pocket of his coat, then pulled it on, followed by his hat. Determined not to make a scene, he slipped back out, making his exit as quietly as possible. Though he wanted to leave unnoticed, it hurt a little how easily it was managed.

No one offered a goodbye. No one seemed to care that he was leaving for good. The ache in his heart turned to a piercing stab of pain. He'd let himself dream again, as Móirín had suggested. Those dreams had seemed to be nearly within reach, only to be snatched away.

Reclaiming dreams might not have been selfish, but it had proven foolish in the extreme.

Brogan stopped at Soho Square, an unassuming green in the midst of this rough area of town. He stopped beneath an obliging tree and looked over the papers he'd nipped off with. Perhaps focusing on the mystery he'd been tasked to solve would prove enough of a distraction to ease the pain in his chest.

The letter was covered with notes about adjusting the formation of certain letters, of keeping aspects of the handwriting consistent. A great many things were noted about the signature in particular.

The document printed on a press rather than written by hand was a list of names, money amounts, and phrases such as "evidence" and "verbatim testimony" and "will offer no information." Despite the fact that these documents must've been printed in the last day or two, they were dated 1824.

Among the nearly identical lists, he found a paper containing nothing but Baron Chelmsford's signature, written again and again, only the slightest differences between them all.

In a flash of understanding, Brogan knew what he was holding.

Forgeries.

This was the print job, the lucrative opportunity Mr. Sorokin had been so excited—and so secretive—about. Vera had been confused by her father's refusal to discuss any part of this job, but that made perfect sense now. It also explained why Mr. Sorokin had been hanging about the embassy and the concern the ambassador had.

Sorokin *was* involved. And it seemed he was keeping the truth of it from Vera. Brogan wanted to be relieved at that, but he wasn't. Forgeries were a dangerous business, and ambassadors made powerful enemies.

Brogan kept his posture as casual as he could manage. The green wasn't empty, and 'twouldn't do to draw attention while he was in possession of forged documents. The people behind the deception wouldn't be happy with the arrangement, and the police would never believe he hadn't had a hand in making them.

He tucked the papers in his coat once more and leaned back against the wide tree trunk. Fletcher needed to be told about the papers, but rushing off would only make Brogan more conspicuous. Time slowed as he stood there, pretending all was right in the world when absolutely nothing was. There was something painfully fitting about being required to lie even to himself now.

When time enough had passed for him to appear to be lazily wandering away, Brogan made his way to Fleet Street. He searched the faces he passed, looking for one bootblack in particular. Henry, Fletcher's most active and helpful urchin informant, always knew how to get a message to him without drawing the least notice.

The moment he spotted the boy he was looking for, Brogan pulled from his watch pocket an etched penny. All of the Dreadfuls used these precise calling cards. Some of them were given to their contacts to use when getting them messages. They each possessed one penny that granted them access to headquarters; Brogan had been required to turn that one over. But this penny was one he'd marked with his own symbol. The Dreadfuls used those to send word to a fellow Dreadful when they needed to discreetly discuss something.

Brogan leaned up against the wall beside Henry. He spun his penny around in his fingers. Henry gave only the tiniest indication that he noticed.

"Think you could get this to a mutual friend of ours?" Brogan asked.

Henry made a noise of agreement. Brogan tossed the penny to him, and he caught it easily. Henry pocketed it but didn't move. Brogan had done this often enough to understand the rest. He would walk on. When enough time had passed to not draw notice, Henry would do the same.

Brogan pointed himself in the direction of his flat. Perhaps working on the next installment for his publisher would give him something to think about other than the shattered remains of his heart and the echo in his mind of Vera spitting out his name in disgust. He'd lost her, and with her, every hope and dream he'd kept in his heart.

THE DEAD ZOO

by Brogan Donnelly

Day Four

William watched from the first-story windows of the museum the next morning as Amos paced the grounds below. The man had arrived nearly three-quarters of an hour earlier but had not come inside. The calm air with which he had taken on the task of solving the mystery William had presented to him was growing thin. His once-tidy appearance had given way to a haphazard one. A frantic detective was, he supposed, better than no detective at all.

Unaware he was being observed, Amos made yet another circuit of the wide expanse of lawn situated outside the Dead Zoo. How was a simple matter of thievery baffling him so entirely? He couldn't wrap his powerful brain around it. It wasn't even a sophisticated scheme. Displays were hastily opened. Specimens were made off with while no attempt was made to cover up the effort.

This was hardly a complicated matter, and he was not a simpleton. On and on he paced. The tension in his shoulders grew by the moment. He'd not slept more than a few moments here and there. Though he'd not passed anyone upon his entrance to the grounds, he felt certain the Royal Dublin Society members stood about somewhere, laughing at him. Mocking him.

"That's why I feel eyes on me," he muttered to himself, pushing his mess of hair away from his face. "That's why I feel followed."

He eyed the museum. He remained on the grounds, not out of fear of going in but as a means of watching delivery persons coming and going. Who else could arrive regularly with a cart and haul items in and out without arousing suspicion?

That was who he was looking for. It had to be. He could not be wrong again. He was Amos Cavey, an intellectual and a logician. He would not be felled by so simple a mystery.

Yet half the day passed without a single workman coming onto the grounds. Nothing entered or exited the museum beyond a few members of the society. Even William Sheenan didn't make an appearance outside of the building.

The two men's eyes met in midafternoon, Amos standing in the grass, William standing inside at a window. Long minutes passed with them simply watching each other. Neither knew what the other was thinking but would, no doubt, be surprised if he knew.

William was holding out hope that the man he'd selected to undertake this difficult task did not mean to abandon it.

Amos's frustration was turning to anger. He, who prided himself on his logic, on his unflappable intellect, stormed toward the building, his movements angular and stilted.

Mere steps from the door, he froze. More magpies—living this time—sat perched in a line on the branch of a tree. Twelve. All watching him.

Eleven is worse.

Twelve for a dastardly curse.

For the length of a breath, his heart froze. *Twelve. Twelve.*

No, he would not be undone by this. He would not give way to childish superstitions.

He pushed onward and through the museum doors. Amos stormed into the large display hall so forcefully that he nearly tripped over Jonty's push broom.

"Watchya," Jonty grumbled.

Amos might normally have pointed out the preposterousness of telling someone who had nearly tripped over a broom stretched across a doorway that he was the one needing to show greater care, rather than the one who had put the broom in the doorway in the first place. But he had larger fish to fry, as the saying went.

"What day are your deliveries?" he demanded the moment he reached William at the very window where he'd spotted him from the grounds below.

"We do not have a specific day." William turned to him as he spoke. He was a patient man, as calm as Amos prided himself on being, but even his endurance was wearing thin. His frustration did not stem from thinking the mystery was taking overly long to solve—only four days had passed, after all, since he had recruited Amos Cavey—but rather the fact that he was finding himself the aim of Amos's angry darts.

"How often have deliveries been made over the past fortnight?" Amos demanded more than asked. "How many were made by the same people? By people *employed* by the same people? Did they deliver with carts? Or wagons?" His questions came rapidly, almost without breath between. His wide eyes darted about.

"Are you unwell, Mr. Cavey?"

"Am I not permitted to be anxious in the solving of these thefts? Would you rather I shrug and leave you to face Mr. Carte's wrath?" Had he been less overwhelmed, perhaps Amos would have recognized the unwarranted intensity in his questioning. He could not recall the last time he had failed in an intellectual endeavor. He hadn't the least ability to endure it.

"A mere four days have passed since I first told you of our situation," William countered. "That we do not yet have the answers is not a failure."

"I do not fail," Amos said. "Not ever."

The man seemed horribly on edge. William judged it best to give the man room to breathe and calm himself. In a tone he hoped was soothing without being patronizing, he answered the earlier questions. "We had one delivery of note. It was a replacement pane of glass for a display case. That was brought almost exactly a fortnight ago, before these disappearances began. The courier did bring it on a wagon, but he and his wagon have not returned since."

"Was anything taken from the case that needed the glass replaced?" Amos asked.

"No. Not a thing." William had truly begun to worry about the man. He appeared quite rattled. "Perhaps you ought to return home for the remainder of the day. Rest a spell."

"I am not unwell." He took a breath, his jaw still taut. "The thefts are not occurring during the day. They must be the work of someone here at night."

"No one is here at night," William countered.

Amos pointed a finger in his direction. "No one *you know of.*"

"You suspect someone is sneaking in?"

"I am nearly certain of it." Amos paced a few steps away before returning to where William yet stood. "I will stay here after closing tonight and watch. By morning, your mystery will be solved."

"You sound very confident."

Amos raised up to his full height. "By morning, you will have your answer."

Not quite as sure of himself as he wanted to appear, Amos returned to his own home long enough to have a bite to eat and a cup of tea. His appearance, he knew, had grown haggard. In his eagerness to resume his investigation that morning, he had not stopped to shave, nor had he invested any effort into his appearance save running a comb quickly through his hair and remembering to change out of his nightclothes. He did not bother addressing the state of himself before returning to the Dead Zoo.

Mr. Carte was leaving the museum as Amos approached. The director was not meant to know about their situation, so Amos slipped behind some tall shrubs, shielding himself from discovery. Once the path was clear and he was no longer likely to be caught, Amos stealthily moved to the doors of the Dead Zoo.

William awaited him there. "Mr. Carte is beginning to

ask questions. Please take care not to disturb any displays or leave behind any indication you have been here overnight. I would struggle to explain that without digging quite a pit for myself."

"I am not entirely inept." Amos's defensiveness came as naturally now as his arrogance once had.

With a barely withheld sigh, William motioned him to the door, which he held open. "Best of luck, Mr. Cavey."

"I do not need luck. I will use my mind."

"Such as it is," William muttered not quite loud enough to be overheard.

As soon as Amos was inside, William pulled the door closed and locked it.

Night had not entirely fallen. Dim light spilled through the windows, illuminating the rows of displays and glass cabinets. The galleries, though, were in complete shadow.

Amos lit the lantern he'd brought in anticipation of this difficulty. He climbed the stairs to the lower gallery and placed himself in a corner he had specifically chosen for its view of the museum. The vantage point wasn't perfect, but he could see enough to spot someone making off with an animal or a skeleton. And he could see the doors.

He would catch the no-good thief. He would!

For more than an hour, he stood rooted to the spot, studying every shadow, every still form. His eyes darted about, quick to examine any movement, though his mind told him there was none. He was the one doing the watching, and yet he couldn't shake the all-too-familiar sensation of the situation being reversed.

The museum was empty. He was the only living thing

inside, and yet he didn't feel alone. The Dead Zoo had an unnerving effect on the senses. Surrounded by death, by animals captured in lifelike poses but with empty glass eyes, even the strongest of minds would struggle—did struggle.

His eyes might have been playing him for a fool, but he trusted his ears still. And his ears heard something below.

The lantern cast quivering light as he made his way down the stairs to the mammal exhibit. The sound was clearer now.

Scraping. Scratching.

Someone, he felt certain, was attempting to jimmy open a display or loosen fastenings as had been done before. He was about to find his culprit.

The sound echoed off the walls and three-story high ceiling, bouncing off glass and huddling around taxidermied animals. The muffled confusion, nevertheless, grew more distinct as he grew nearer to it. Past the warthogs, past the goats. He'd studied the Dead Zoo enough to know what lay around each corner, which species was housed where. He passed beneath the suspended skeleton of the giant whale and approached the seals.

Suddenly, the sound stopped, and silence fell heavy around him. He held the lantern aloft as he circled the seal display. The light scratches he'd seen in the wood frame were not the only signs of wear he spotted now. Deep gouges marred the surface. New gouges. A powder of wood bits made a light coating on the floor below.

Someone meant to make off with a seal. How in heaven's name did the miscreant intend to do that? Such a thing would require multiple people and a large wagon with a strong team. Seals were enormous, their only natural predator being the massive polar bear.

Amos glanced over his shoulder at the creature in question. But it was gone.

The polar bear was gone.

How had someone made off with such a large item without making noise, without being seen? It was impossible. Utterly impossible!

He studied the stand on which the bear was—or *ought to have been*—displayed. There was absolutely no sign of tampering. None at all. There was not even the tiniest speck of dust. It was almost as if the polar bear had simply walked away.

His mind insisted that was impossible even as his eyes darted frantically around.

Something heavy and soft, by the sound of it, landed upon the floor somewhere out of sight. The same sound again. Then again.

It sounded not unlike the pad of a dog's feet on the floor. A rolling paw, soft enough to muffle the noise but made loud by the weight it bore.

Paws. Against the floor.

An empty polar bear display.

An inelegant attempt to gain access to a seal, the polar bear's natural diet.

Amos shook his head, insisting the theory forming in his mind was too ridiculous to be true. There had to be another explanation. There simply had to be.

Heavier and quicker came the sounds of paws on stone.

Amos's heart rate rose. He backed up, watching and holding his breath.

He could hear breathing—heavy, deep-throated breathing.

The wide expanse of the museum, its columns and high ceiling, turned even the tiniest sound into a cacophony, and nothing about these sounds were tiny. Fast, heavy paws and threatening growls came at him from every direction.

He did all he could think to do. He ran. Every turn he made, the sounds followed him. He swore he could feel hot breath on his neck, though he did not turn back long enough to look. He ran. Ran. Ran.

The door to the museum was locked. It would not give at his frantic pulling. He pounded and shouted, his own voice bouncing off the walls and attacking him anew. Perhaps another door? A window?

He raced back into the enormous room. Where were the windows? Why could he not find them? He knew there were windows. He'd seen William standing at one, looking at him. There were windows. There were! But where?

He could find nothing. His mind refused to identify anything. The shapes around him shifted and contorted, monstrous collections of limbs and heads. They moved. He swore they did. They turned and watched him as he ran past, and he never felt their eyes leave him.

He was running in circles, passing the same skeletons, the same animals, over and over again. But they were positioned differently, facing him no matter where he was. And all the while the fall of heavy paws continued.

Out of the corner of his eye, he saw a flash of white. He dove behind the glass-sided display of deer.

A roar split the darkness. The display shook. Glass shattered.

Amos tried to scramble to his feet, but he couldn't rise.

Closer came the sound of paws on the stone floor. Closer. Louder. Slower.

Deep, growling breaths.

A shadow fell across him. A shadow despite the darkness.

And then a face.

CHAPTER 18

As it was morning still, Móirín wasn't at home. That simplified things. How Brogan would've explained Fletcher's visit without giving away secrets, he didn't know. And the complication of it proved bigger than he'd expected.

Fletcher arrived, but not alone. Stone, another of the Dreadfuls, was with him.

"Lower the eyebrows, mate," Fletcher said, stepping past Brogan and making himself at home in the sitting room. "Stone was sent here by a higher power."

"Divine direction?" Brogan asked dryly.

Stone didn't take the bait, but Fletcher most certainly did.

"Not quite that high." Fletcher tossed him a tightly folded note with a familiar wax seal.

Brogan opened the note and read quickly.

> *Stone is being brought into this. Tell him what you know.*
>
> *DM*

He looked to Stone. "Did you know I was still working on behalf of the DPS?"

"Not 'til right now," Stone said.

Brogan had never known anyone else from America's South and didn't know if his friend's manner of speaking was common to everyone who lived there. The man didn't talk often. And he never appeared the least upended. He was the sort of person one was lucky to call a friend but would fear having as an enemy.

"Henry tossed me your coin," Fletcher said. "What do you have for me?"

"Slipped these out of Sorokin's shop this morning." Brogan pulled the stack of papers from the table drawer where he'd hidden them. "Took me a blessed minute to sort out what I was seeing."

He dropped them on the table. Stone began studying them immediately. Fletcher moved from the settee to the table and did the same.

"The letter mentions a document?" Fletcher looked back at him. "What document?"

Brogan motioned with his head. "The rest of the stack."

The men looked them over.

"These are all the same," Fletcher said.

"No, they ain't." Stone was, of course, fully correct.

"Near as I can tell," Brogan said, "they're *versions* of the same document. Mr. Sorokin was refining it, trying to get it right."

"This is dated more than forty years ago," Fletcher said. "That don't make a lick of sense."

Stone snatched up the paper containing nothing but

dozens of versions of Baron Chelmsford's signature, each a little different from the others. Some shaky with uncertainty, some more sure and flowing.

"Someone's been practicing mimicking the fella's hand." The flavor of America sat heavy in Stone's words though he'd escaped the inhumanity of slavery years earlier.

"The Dread Master wondered what Ambassador von Brunnow was so nervous over," Brogan said. "Being tied to forged documents'd do it, I'd say."

Fletcher dropped the papers on the table, jaw tight and eyes narrowed with pondering. "But is the ambassador part of the scheme or a victim of it?"

"I've not the first idea." Brogan had pondered the puzzle ever since snatching the papers, and he hadn't any answers yet.

"We have to wonder the same thing about Mr. Sorokin," Stone said. "Participant or victim?"

"And is Miss Sorokina aware of any of it?" Fletcher tossed in.

Both men looked at Brogan. "She tossed me out on m'head this morning. I'll be getting no more information from that quarter."

"Why'd she toss you out?" Fletcher asked.

"Somehow or another, she discovered my real identity. And she hasn't a very high opinion of writers, which means neither of you two could simply waltz in and ask questions."

"Being unfairly disliked wouldn't be anything new, Donnelly," Stone said with his usual direct, matter-of-fact tone.

Someone pounded on the front door.

"Móirín, maybe?" Fletcher guessed.

"She has a key." Brogan stood and moved to the door.

Though he'd no real guesses as to who he'd see on the other side, when he pulled it open, he was so shocked it took him a moment to speak.

"Mr. Sorokin."

"You were in my back room." The man was boiling as blazes.

Fletcher stepped into the entryway.

Sorokin looked at him for only a moment. "I don't have business with you."

Fletcher shook his head, as if it were a great shame. "Hate to bob you, chum, but you do, whether you know it or not." He pulled Mr. Sorokin inside. To Brogan he said, "Shut the door. It's time we gabbed a spell with our resident printer."

Without taking his eyes off Mr. Sorokin, Brogan reached back and pulled the door shut.

"I will not be handled this way," the man spat, his salt-and-pepper beard shaking as he spoke.

"Before you run your mouth, spin on this," Fletcher said. "We already know what you're looking for."

Mr. Sorokin paled.

Brogan took advantage of the momentary silence. "You've a daughter and two little ones at your shop. Whatever muck you're wading in will splatter them too."

"I don't—I don't know what you're—what you're talking about."

Fletcher set a hand on Mr. Sorokin's back and guided him into the sitting room. Stone remained at the table, watching their return, quite at his leisure. The forged documents had been tucked away again. Stone never missed a thing.

Fletcher saw Mr. Sorokin to the table and "invited" him to sit. Fletcher grabbed a stool and sat as well. Brogan leaned against the nearby windowsill.

"What I can't sort," Fletcher said, clearly addressing everyone *except* Mr. Sorokin, "is why a forty-year-old document would be so important."

"The past can chase a person," Stone said.

"Oi." Fletcher threaded his fingers and tucked his hands behind his head. "But which person is it chasing *now*?"

Brogan recognized Fletcher's familiar approach to getting information: giving the impression of near-indifference and having a conversation between each other that was absolutely meant to be overheard.

"There's risk, for certain," Brogan said. "The reward'd have to be significant."

"I'd wager an ambassador is well able to make the danger palatable," Fletcher tossed in.

Slowly, and in perfect unison, they turned their heads to look at Mr. Sorokin. He swallowed audibly in the silence that followed. They didn't look away, didn't speak, didn't give any indication they were anything but relaxed and perfectly satisfied. Stone had long ago mastered that posture and expression; Brogan wasn't the least certain how much of it was an act.

"You stole them," Mr. Sorokin whispered after a moment, the accusation in his tone subdued by the quietness of his words.

"Stole *what*?" Fletcher asked, the picture of innocence.

"You know what."

"Cain't be certain that I do, now can I?"

"Give them back."

Brogan took the same approach. "Give *what* back?" It'd help them out if Mr. Sorokin offered his own description of the papers; doing so would tell them a load more about the nature of his involvement and the scheme behind it all.

"I can't cut you in for any profit, if that's what you're holding out for." Mr. Sorokin's spectacles slid down his nose.

Fletcher looked away from the man and resumed the intentionally overheard conversation. "I'm not looking to risk being tossed in Old Bailey, are either of you?"

"Not a bit of it, Fletch," Brogan said. "In fact, I do m' best to steer clear of any scheme involving someone who holds the ear of *two* governments. Too much opportunity for being double-crossed."

"I'm not afraid of Ambassador von Brunnow," Mr. Sorokin said, shoving his glasses back in place.

Stone didn't flinch. "He ain't insignificant."

"I'm not afraid of *him*." Mr. Sorokin's repeated declaration came, this time, with just enough emphasis on the final word to send Brogan's mind in a new direction.

Brogan held up a hand to forestall Fletcher's next comment. To Mr. Sorokin, he said, "Who *are* you afraid of?"

"Give me back my papers. It's our only hope."

Brogan shook his head. "We're not meaning to turn you over to the police. We're far more worried about your daughter, those little urchins, even the ambassador, who'll all be burned if you keep playin' with fire."

The man's face, alternately defiant and angry, held an

unwavering note of what looked like fear. "Give me back what you took."

Fletcher stood. "Don't think we will."

"Tell us what's goin' on, and we might be able to help," Brogan said.

Mr. Sorokin shook his head. "Without those papers, we're all dead."

"You think the ambassador will kill you?" Fletcher asked.

"No."

Fletcher leaned forward, elbows on the table. "Lord Chelmsford, then?"

"I'm not afraid of *him*, either."

Mercy. How many people were involved in this?

"Bung your eye," Fletcher muttered.

Mr. Sorokin stood. He gave the three of them a quick glance. "You have no idea what you are dealing with."

"We would if you'd tell us." Stone had spoken more during this interrogation than Brogan had just about ever heard from him.

Mr. Sorokin only shook his head. He left without another word, without any explanation.

Stone pulled out the forged papers and spread them on the tabletop again.

"The letter's a fake," he said, "and the document it references is as well. There ain't no doubting that. We know the two names in the letter. What we need to find is this other person Sorokin's worried about."

"How do we do that?" Brogan asked.

From the sitting room doorway, the last voice Brogan expected to hear answered. "With help."

CHAPTER 19

Only with effort did Vera keep herself calm and collected. In a twenty-four-hour period, she had learned the man she'd been falling in love with was lying to her, had tossed him from her shop, and had then followed her papa directly to the home of that same man. She'd slipped inside after her papa—the door hadn't been locked—and had been quiet enough to not be detected over the conversation occurring in the sitting room. While she'd tucked herself out of sight around the kitchen doorway, they'd been discussing her papa's involvement in something apparently dangerous and illegal involving very important and influential people.

The world around her was spinning, and she was struggling to keep her footing. She was tempted to simply slip back out again after Papa had stormed out—she knew the flat well enough by now to navigate it quickly—but she needed answers.

The men in the room jumped to their feet, clearly surprised to see her.

"Miss Sorokina," Brogan said. "How long've you been here?"

"Long enough to have a vast many questions." She walked with as much confidence as she could muster to the table where they were gathered. "My first is"—she looked at the two strangers—"who are you? And don't lie to me. This one"—she hooked a thumb in Brogan's direction—"already took that approach."

The man standing nearest her, his entire demeanor filled with amused swagger, dipped his head in greeting and said, "Fletcher Walker, Miss Sorokina. A pleasure."

Fletcher Walker. That was the author who wrote the "Urchins of London" penny dreadful series. Not a great omen.

Vera looked to the third man in the room. He was taller than his companions, and larger. His deep brown eyes studied her in a way that told her he was not one to miss any detail, large or small. Was he also a writer of penny dreadfuls? She knew of two among that fraternity who were Black: Martin Afola and Stone.

He didn't leave her in suspense. "Stone," he said.

She was surrounded by members of the very profession she'd been taught all her life to avoid.

She eyed Brogan out of the corner of her eye. "Let me guess, Lafayette Jones and Barnabus Milligan are in the kitchen, preparing tea?"

Brogan actually looked guilty, though whether that was because other writers *were* in the flat or because he felt bad about lying to her, she wasn't certain.

Though she didn't know the other two men, she suspected

Stone was the most forthright of them all. So she directed her question to him. "Are there any others here?"

He shook his head. "No, miss. We do know them other fellas, but they ain't here."

Hearing him talk, she could tell Stone wasn't from England.

"How long've you been in England?" she asked.

"Eight years," was his quick reply. "From America."

There was a story there, but she wouldn't press for it. A person ought to be entitled to choose when and if he talked about his past.

For her part, Vera needed to talk about the present. She took the empty seat at the table. "What papers of my papa's do you have? What do they have to do with Ambassador von Brunnow and Lord Chelmsford? And why are you concerning yourselves with it?"

"Wanna take these questions, Brog?" Fletcher tossed out.

Vera shook her head. "Not him. He might lie to me."

"We're talking about Brogan Donnelly, are we?" Fletcher shook his head, eyes dancing with apparent amusement. "Brogan, who despises lying?"

"He's gained a liking for it of late," Vera said dryly. "I haven't a heap of time. What are these papers, and why did you say they were putting myself and the urchins that work at my shop in danger?"

Brogan paced away. While she'd said she didn't want him explaining, she found herself disappointed that he was so readily leaving his associates to give her the details.

"The papers are a letter and a few versions of a printed

document," Fletcher said. "The letter is from Lord Chelmsford to the ambassador talking about the document."

Nothing in that was alarming.

In three words, Stone turned everything on its head. "They're all forgeries."

"We've every reason to believe your papa created them," Fletcher continued. "But we couldn't get the bloke to tell us why or who hired him to do the job."

There had to be a mistake. "Papa abhors falsehoods. He'd not be involved in anything that'd risk an innocent person being hurt by lies."

"The man he wouldn't identify might be strong-arming him," Brogan said as he continued to pace. "He and Clare could likely compare experiences."

Strong-armed. That made more sense than voluntarily participating. Except . . . "He was happy at snatching this print job. He'd not've thought it the cat's whiskers if it were something underhanded."

"Might not've known at the time," Stone said.

"And if the whole thing falls to bits, Papa's likely to get bashed up for it." Endangered by someone else's scheme. Again.

"Depending on how these papers are used," Brogan said, "he'll find himself far more than bashed up. He'll be locked up."

"My papa's fled from wrongful imprisonment once already. I'll not sit back and simply wait for it to happen again."

Brogan's brows shot upward at that revelation, but Vera didn't intend to dive into tales of the past.

She squared her shoulders. "What do we know, and how do we fix this?"

"*We?*" Brogan shook his head. "Everyone in this room, aside from you, are writers. And everyone we associate with are as well. That's a 'we' you'd not be best pleased with."

"You'd be surprised who and what I'll endure to protect my papa. And Olly and Licorice. And Burnt Ricky and Bob's Your Knuckle. And my neighbors."

"And all of London?" Fletcher added with a laugh. "Banging on about rescuing everybody, you sound like Brogan."

"That's a comparison you'd do best not to make," Brogan said. "You'll insult the lady."

At least he was being honest about *that*. And yet, Fletcher wasn't entirely off the mark. No matter that Brogan was a liar, he did do a tremendous lot for a great many struggling people. He'd helped the urchins at the shop, the frightened people on Old Compton, the destitute families in the hidden corners of London.

"You still haven't told me how any of this involves the lot of you."

Fletcher answered. "A friend heard whispers that there was concern among the ambassador's staff. To set the bloke's mind at ease, I said I'd see if I could learn anything. I assumed I wouldn't, but there was something to it after all. And that something proved to be connected to your father."

"But why bother yourself with it to begin with?"

"Has Brogan, while you've known him, ever done things for people he didn't know or helped with troubles that weren't his?"

She couldn't deny that he had.

"We've that in common, the three of us," Fletcher said. "We when see suffering, we can't simply turn away."

That surprised her. "And all three of you are writers?"

"Why is it you think so poorly of writers?" Stone asked.

"They've shown themselves untrustworthy. Repeatedly."

That didn't appear to satisfy any of them. Brogan continued to pace, but she suspected he was every bit as curious.

She didn't generally share any details of her family's past, but learning Papa was in a similar scrape to the one that'd taught them all to be wary made her wonder if there might be solutions lying in the past.

"Are any of you familiar with the Petrashevsky Circle?" she asked them.

All three indicated they weren't. She wasn't surprised. There was a reason Papa had chosen England as a place of refuge from that horrific chapter in their lives.

Vera told them what she knew of the Petrashevsky Circle, though it wasn't much, as her father typically refused to discuss the matter whenever she brought it up. "In the late 1840s, a group in St. Petersburg began writing of things considered treasonous and rabble-rousing," she said. "They'd been meeting in secret, plotting things beyond the publication of incendiary tracts and pamphlets. They were called the Petrashevsky Circle. They called for improvements in the lives of ordinary Russians, but Tsar Nicholas and his ministers didn't care for that."

"I'd imagine not," Stone said.

"Someone betrayed the Circle," she continued, "and they were rounded up, arrested, and sentenced to death, though the Tsar himself intervened at the last minute and sent the Circle's leaders to Siberia instead."

"Was your father part of the Circle?" Fletcher asked.

"No, he weren't."

"He didn't—He didn't betray them, did he?" The idea clearly sat uncomfortably on Brogan's mind, and well it might, he being a writer who kept a number of secrets himself.

"The Circle betrayed *him*." She breathed against the flood of remembered retellings and the pain that always filled her papa's face when he spoke of it. "He weren't one of them, but he'd done a spot of printing for them. He was an innocent, a provider of a service was all. They named him as part of their group, though they knew he had as much to do with them as those who served up tea at their weekly meetings."

"What happened to him?" Fletcher asked.

"We fled St. Petersburg," she said. "Dozens of men were arrested. How he escaped the raids, I don't know. He rushed us from the house in the middle of the night. I was a very small child, too young to remember anything else about our flight. We've been in London ever since."

"Is he still in danger of being arrested?" Stone asked.

"Russia may have a different Tsar than when all this happened, but Alexander is unlikely to shrug off a fugitive from the law. If Papa returns, he'll be arrested. If he makes too many waves, even here, they'll find him."

"And all on account of a group of writers turning on an innocent man." Brogan sighed. He met her eye. "I'd say you have ample reason for not trusting members of our profession."

Stone's expression was one of deep thought. "Maybe whoever's twisted your papa into making these forgeries knows about this Circle and is threatening him with it."

The possibility had occurred to her. "It'd be a powerful threat. Though I cain't say how the person behind it all learned of Papa's connection to the Petrashevsky Circle."

"Does the ambassador know?" Fletcher asked.

Vera shrugged. She hadn't the first idea.

"Perhaps we'd do well to find out." Fletcher exchanged looks with his companions. He, it seemed, took a leadership role in this group.

"None of us knows von Brunnow," Brogan said. "Even if we could invent a reason for seeing the man, we've no guarantee he'd allow it."

Vera leaned back in her chair, hope warring with wariness in her chest. "I know someone on his staff. If I asked, she might be able to get me in to see the ambassador. But if it proves true that he knows Papa's history and is using it against him, I don't know that I'd be wise to visit him alone."

"One of us can go with you," Fletcher said. "Who that ought to be will depend on what reason you give for calling on the man."

What reason could she give? "I could say I've some worries about the immigrant communities in London. I spend time with enough."

"That'd do it, I'd wager." Fletcher hooked a crooked smile. "You'd do best, though, to bring with you a fellow immigrant. That eliminates me."

Stone tossed in his thoughts. "And there's too great a risk

that I'd prove . . . let's just say, too much of an immigrant for the fella's comfort."

"I wish that weren't as true as it is," Vera said.

His mouth tightened. "As do I."

Fletcher stood. "We'll leave you and Brog to sort out how you mean to make this call and do your digging." He dipped his head. "A pleasure meeting you, Miss Sorokina."

She rose at the same time Stone did.

He also nodded in her direction. "Hope your efforts are successful."

"Thank you."

While Brogan saw his friends to the door, Vera took long, deep breaths, trying to release some of her tension. Only a couple of hours earlier she'd tossed Brogan firmly from the shop, and now she needed to plan a risk-filled mission to un-cover information, one that required they trust each other. At the moment, that felt impossible. *Everything* felt impossible.

When he returned to the room, he had his hands stuffed in his trouser pockets, watching her with a look of wary un-certainty. "If you'd rather, I'm certain we can find someone else to go with you to the embassy. Móirín would, I'd wager. And she speaks a spot of Russian. That might prove handy."

She shook her head. "I'd rather not have anyone else know about my papa's entanglements."

"Then it seems you're stuck with me."

"Seems that way."

He lingered in the sitting room doorway, hovering with palpable awkwardness. "I know you're enduring this out of love for your da and the people you feel responsible for. I'm sorry that it'll be a misery for you."

Heaven help her, he looked sincere. But how could she believe him?

"Why did you lie to me about your name?" she asked.

"Would you've hired me if I hadn't?"

She held her hand up to stop him. "This won't be pegged on me. I ain't the one who lied."

"Fair." He stepped into the room but watched her with clear discomfort. "I needed the job. But you sell stories I wrote in m'own name right there in the shop. I wasn't expecting that. I feared it'd make things complicated. Ganor O'Donnell's a name I used in Ireland. It popped in m' mind, and I tossed it out."

"Why'd you use a false name in Ireland?" She'd been told truths about his life there that he wasn't aware she knew. How honest would he be about that?

"I'm not able to tell you *all* the history of that, lass. It ain't my place to."

"I am so weary of secrets, Brogan Donnelly. I need a moment's honesty from you."

He came closer, not in a threatening way, but quiet and considerate. "I'll tell you the bits of it that're mine to tell, like you did with your da's history."

She nodded.

He motioned her to the settee. She sat at one end. He took a seat on the opposite side. "Móirín and I grew up in County Offaly, the countryside of Ireland. The Hunger came when I was eight, and Móirín was nine, and our parents starved to death, like millions of our countrymen. Móirín and I made the harrowing walk to Dublin, a week's journey. We lived on the streets for a time until we could begin scraping together money. I took up running messages for people—I was fast and agile, and I could read, which not many Irish children can do. Móirín took up as a crossing sweep.

"In time, we'd money enough to be off the street. Then enough to eat regularly and replace our ragged clothes. By the time we were approaching adulthood, we had a humble flat in the Liberties. She worked at the Guinness factory, like most people did in our neighborhood. I was working as a courier and messenger still, but also writing columns for local papers. Life wasn't easy, and that corner of Dublin was rough to say the least. 'Twas a fight to survive, often literally."

Unbidden to her thoughts came the memory of sitting in this very room, brushing her fingers over his scars, and, later, tending his bleeding knuckles in the shop the day he'd rescued Licorice. She'd been utterly fascinated by the touch of his rough but gentle hands.

"A short few years back, someone started making trouble for m'sister," Brogan continued. "She's a fetching thing, though she would disagree. Her fiery personality adds something to her striking looks. Men have often found her intriguing and alluring, often too much so."

Vera began to suspect where this was headed.

"I'll not betray *her* secrets by telling everything connected to that," Brogan said, "but suffice it to say, the situation grew more than merely annoying. The confrontations were frequent and increasingly combative. This bloke pushed the boundaries, threatened, endangered, and eventually did physical injury to her. He made clear he didn't mean to stop."

Vera listened, heart aching, mind spinning.

"Again, without details, I'll say only that the man's dead,

not of natural causes, and I'm not sorry he's gone." Brogan pushed out a breath. "If that makes you think poorly of me, I'll have to endure that, but she's not the only woman he . . . Had there been another way . . ."

"Were you still in Dublin, the blue-bottles would round both of you up for the man's death?"

"They would," he said. "The charges are murder and harboring a murderer."

"And the Peelers don't care that the man's death came about as a result of saving your sister from him?" Vera was growing increasingly angry on his and Móirín's behalf.

He met her eyes. "How often does the law care when women are persecuted by men?"

Every woman who'd lived even a day in Soho knew the answer to that question. "Not often at all."

He slumped on the settee. "I can't tell you more than that, Vera—it ain't m'story to tell in full—but that's more than I've shared with anyone. 'Tis possible you think even less of me now, knowing the axe that hangs over my family, but that's the truth of it."

"You realize I could hand you over to people who could force you back to Dublin."

"I know it," he said quietly. "You may have no faith in me, but I have faith in you."

Despite herself, that declaration touched her. It shouldn't have. She wished it didn't. But it did.

"You'll help me sort out a means of helping my papa?" she asked.

His smile was soft and a little uncertain. "I'll do anything I can for you, Vera Sorokina. You need only say the word."

The fluttering of her heart triggered warning bells in her mind. She was not at all indifferent to this man she was struggling to trust. It'd be best to keep a distance until she knew if she'd be better off stepping closer or running the other way.

CHAPTER 20

Brogan received a note from Vera two days after the discovery of Mr. Sorokin's forged papers. Waiting to hear from her had stretched Brogan's patience thinner than the parchment he now held in his hands. 'Twas more than worrying over whether she'd managed to secure a bit of the ambassador's time, more than wondering how her da was behaving in light of everything. He wanted to hear from *her*. He wanted to know if he'd undone any of the damage his lies had inflicted. He wanted a reason to hope.

The note instructed him to meet her at Chesham Place at four o'clock that evening and to come dressed as he did when working at the print shop. That had struck him as odd. Gabbing with an ambassador called for one's finest togs. Still, he trusted her and followed her instructions to the letter.

At four o'clock precisely, he stood within visual distance of the Russian Embassy. Vera peeked around the corner of Lyall Street.

"The servants' entrance is this way," she said.

Servants' entrance. He caught up to her, not asking any of the questions flowing through his thoughts.

"I did try to secure a meeting with the ambassador, but nothing came of it," Vera said. "Our best approach is to gab with the staff. I've an acquaintance among them, and few things happen in a house that the servants don't know about."

"Excellent." Concerns expressed by the staff had first grabbed the attention of the Dread Master. Speaking with them would be wise.

"You're not disappointed?" she asked, eyeing him through slightly narrowed eyes.

"I'm here to help," he said.

Her brows pulled low. "You're meaning to still follow my lead?"

"Following is what I do best."

Vera's head tilted, and she studied him closely. Trying to safely explain his vast history of "following" would set him firmly back in the same frustrating position of dishonesty he longed to leave behind.

They reached the servants' entrance—modest door and no portico to protect arrivals from the elements. Yet, Brogan found it reassuringly familiar. He'd spent all his years in Dublin making deliveries to the humble back doors of that city. While he had occasion now to pass through fine entryways at times, he still felt more comfortable at the backs than the fronts.

Vera knocked, and they waited in awkward silence. How he wished they could reclaim the easy comradery they'd once shared.

A woman, likely the housekeeper, ushered them inside. She and Vera spoke in what he guessed was Russian, though Vera's efforts were noticeably more stilted. When both women looked at him in the same brief moment, he kept his expression both pleasant and unobtrusive, knowing Vera was likely attempting to gain him entry into the gab she'd arranged.

After a moment, they were ushered down the narrow corridor to the servants' hall. The room was in a state of ebbing chaos, the staff's meal likely having only just come to a close. Vera searched the faces; Brogan mostly kept out of the way.

Soon enough, the bustling room, with its two long tables and mismatched benches, emptied of all its occupants other than Vera, Brogan, and a maid near in age to them.

"Katya," Vera said to the maid, "this is Brogan Donnelly, the man I told you was helping me sort all this. Brogan, this is Katya Volkov."

"Zdravstvuyte," Brogan said, earning looks of surprise from them both. To Vera, he explained, "I asked Móirín to teach me a couple words."

"I've never heard Russian spoken with an Irish accent," Katya said with a broad smile. Her accent actually was Russian, unlike Vera's, which sounded utterly London. "An odd combination, that."

"I hope not one that offends your ears."

Katya shook her head, then waved them both over to the nearest table. She sat on the end of one bench. Brogan sat beside Vera on the bench opposite.

"I'll not muck about," Vera said, "but jump right to the

heart of things. I've reason to believe my papa is eyeballs' deep in something he oughtn't to be, and that something is connected somehow to the ambassador. What can you tell me?"

Katya leaned forward and lowered her voice. "The ambassador is upended, walking about with worry on his brow. He is seeing to his official duties but participating in little else."

"Does he have callers?" Vera asked.

Katya shook her head. "Almost none. He turned Lord Chelmsford away only a few days ago. He used to call on the regular."

"I heard the ambassador and Lord Chelmsford's friendship has been strained of late," Brogan said.

"The ambassador won't see him, warns him to keep away." Katya shrugged, her shoulders lifting, her hand spread wide beside her. It was precisely the same way Vera shrugged. Seemed it was a Russian gesture. "It's an odd thing between the two gentlemen, as they've always gotten on well."

The ambassador was keeping Chelmsford at bay. Perhaps Chelmsford was involved in the forgeries, meaning to do his one-time friend a bad turn.

"What could that have to do with my papa? He don't know either man."

"I'd say 'nothing,'" Katya replied, "but Albie, our little knife-boy, saw your papa knocking about out by the mews about a week ago."

"How did Albie know who he was?" Vera asked.

"Tugged me over there near the horses. Worried about

something he saw. I knew it was your papa, seeing as I've met the both of you."

"What worried the lad?" Brogan felt certain *that* answer was important.

"Can't rightly say." Katya hopped to her feet and moved to the door of the servants' hall. She beckoned another maid closer. "Fetch Albie, would you?" She returned to the table and took a deep breath. "Near all the lower servants have been whispering about the change in the ambassador, how odd he's being."

"Is he tossing all callers out?" Brogan asked. "Or only Lord Chelmsford?"

Katya gave it a moment's thought. "The ambassador hasn't had many social callers, but the only one he's told not ever to come 'round is Lord Chelmsford. There've been a couple others he didn't seem too pleased to see."

"Who?" Vera asked.

"Don't know who they were. Didn't seem like the fine-and-fancy sort. All the staff noted what a mismatch they were to someone of the ambassador's standing."

Unusual callers. The ambassador on edge. Forgeries and an interrupted friendship. Perhaps von Brunnow wasn't entirely innocent in the matter either.

A boy, no more than ten years old, slipped into the hall. His frame was slight, but his eyes were knowing.

"The men you saw gabbing with the ambassador and then with the stranger by the mews," Katya said. "What do you remember of that?"

The boy cast a suspicious glance at Vera and Brogan. On the off chance the child was part of the network of informers the DPS utilized, perhaps someone from whom the Dread Master had gotten his information, Brogan slipped a penny from his pocket and spun it casually in his fingers. The boy took note of it but didn't say anything.

The signal might've been the reason the boy moved ahead with his story. It might've had nothing to do with it. Either way, the child answered Katya's question.

"The two men what come 'round now and then were calling on the ambassa'or. He weren't any happier about it than ever. One of them scoundrels said to 'im 'Cooperate or your tsar'll have reason to snatch you away.' And the ambassa'or says that Tsar Alexander wouldn't believe the word of a couple of thieves and liars and no-goods. Then the other one says something about how the ambassa'or knows they can make people believe near anything. And the ambassa'or says as how they won't find anyone to print the things for them they need, especially needing some of it to be Russian. And then the both of them scoundrels just laughed." Albie shuddered. "Didn't like the sound of their laughs, so I nipped off, keeping out of sight. Weren't more'n a few minutes later, I were going out to the mews to ask the coachman if I could brush one of the horses, when I seen these two good-for-nothings was out there whispering to a man with a beard. Katya came by about then. I told her I didn't like them three men kicking about. She said not to kick up dust over it, seeing as the ambass'or was tied in knots and all."

"Did you overhear anything the three men said?" Vera asked, remaining admirably calm for a woman who'd just learned her da was consorting with questionable people.

"The one without all his fingers said to the bearded man

that they needed the papers in a hurry so they'd have time to slip them into the place they needed to be," Albie said.

The one without all his fingers. 'Twas, Brogan was certain, Four-Finger Mike.

"The bearded man says he don't like making trouble, and the other one said he didn't have a choice, because they knew something about the new man that he'd not want people to know."

Blackmail. Against the ambassador and Mr. Sorokin. And the forged documents were at the heart of it all.

"What did this other man look like?" Brogan asked. "Not the bearded man or the one with missing fingers."

Albie took a step back, though he didn't seem to realize he had. "I don't ever want to see that man again. Made me feel that frozen sort of scared deep in my middle. I didn't like him."

Brogan would wager that was the Mastiff. Mercy and mercy.

"Is there anything else that might help me twig this mess?" Vera asked.

"Molly, she's a chambermaid here, heard the ambassador mumbling to himself about how it was too late for Lord Chelmsford, that 'it' would be discovered soon enough."

Vera muttered something in Russian that earned her a nod of agreement from Katya. Both women stood, so Brogan did as well. Farewells were exchanged. In a flash, they were on the pavement outside the embassy.

"Papa really is knocking elbows with scabby blokes." Vera pushed out a forced and tense breath. "I'd hoped we'd twig it weren't true."

Brogan hated seeing her look so defeated. "He's involved, yeah, but from what Albie heard, he's doing so against his own wishes. And, based on the description Albie and Katya gave of the two men he was meeting with, I know full well who they are. Dangerous and manipulative criminals, the both of them. Your papa is being forced, threatened, and not idly. I'd wager everything I own on that."

"Do you think you nicking the forgeries from the shop has stopped the scheme?" Vera looked as if she already knew the answer.

He gave it anyway. "They were drafts, not the final version."

Vera met his eye, her expression anxious. "Where's the final version, then?"

"If I'm twigging things right—" He paused to add a tiny bit of emphasis to his use of the bit of South London cant she'd taught him, hoping it'd lift her spirits, even if just for a moment, but his efforts didn't have the effect he'd hoped for. "I'd guess those papers are already in place, waiting to be 'discovered soon enough.'"

She rubbed at her temples. "And I'd further wager they're 'in place' at Lord Chelmsford's home, meant to look as though he'd written the letter but not yet sent it. Someone'll discover it, and when he denies it's his hand, the ambassador will likely insist the letter is about something they've talked over before."

"Which'd mean Lord Chelmsford is the actual prey in this scheme, and von Brunnow and your da are simply being manipulated to that end."

He motioned for her to walk alongside him. They'd

garner too much notice if they loitered about outside the embassy.

"What can we do?" Vera asked.

We. 'Twasn't precisely a renewed vote of confidence, but he chose to see it as a good step toward repairing what he'd broken.

"Mister!" a young voice called from behind them.

They both turned back. Albie stood just outside the embassy, motioning toward himself.

"Mister," he called out again.

Brogan dipped his head to Vera. "Be back in a hop." He crossed back to Albie. "What's on your mind, lad?"

"Your penny," Albie said in a low voice. "Are you needing me to send a message to Mr. Walker?"

The lad was one of *Fletcher's* urchins. Who, then, was the Dread Master's informant at the embassy? So many secrets. 'Twas little wonder Brogan still found himself drowning in them.

"Aye, Albie," Brogan said. "See if you can't ask that overgrown urchin you work for if he'll call on 'his Irish friend.'"

Albie dipped his head and rushed back inside. No doubt Fletcher would be at Brogan's flat before day's end ready to sort through these newest revelations.

Vera stepped up next to him. Having her there, even with the difficulties between them, was a comfort.

"What did Albie jaw with you about?" she asked.

He didn't want to lie to her. Again. "The lad wanted to know if he could help." 'Twas a more honest answer than he once would have given her. It was a step in the right direction, and one that gave him hope.

Brogan didn't yet know how to save Vera's father from the mess he'd landed in, but he knew an entire group of people who could and regularly did manage the impossible. If only he could convince them to listen to a man they believed had deserted them.

THE MERCHANT AND THE ROGUE

by Mr. King

Installment V
in which terrifying Secrets are revealed about
the grave Danger facing the Village!

Bob Kent stood in the doorway, looking over the destruction. "She stood firm?"

Royston nodded.

"Is it time to try again?" Bob asked.

"I believe it might be." He looked to Tallulah. "Are you injured?"

"No, but I'll likely be a bit bruised." She watched them both, clearly confused and curious.

"We'll see to this." Bob motioned to the mess. "Best consult with ol' Kirby. This may be our best chance."

"Kirby Padmore?" Tallulah asked Royston.

"He knows more of this than any of us, and you need to understand it better as well."

Royston offered her his hand, unsure if she would accept, but there was not even a moment of hesitation on her part. She set her hand in his and walked with him through the broken glass and scattered confections and splintered wood—all that remained of her once-impressive shop.

Just outside, a crowd had gathered, looking at the blown-in window and debris with a heaviness that spoke of familiarity. Whether Tallulah realized it or not, this had happened before.

He walked with her, their fingers entwined. She was quiet, not surprising considering the harrowing experience she'd passed through.

"Are you certain you are not injured? There was a fearful amount of glass strewn about."

She nodded. "I was not hurt, but I am worried all the same."

He met her heavy gaze. "This village harbors a terrible secret, Tallulah. Kirby can explain it all far better than I can."

They stepped into the pub. Royston glanced around, wanting to make certain the squire was not present, but only Kirby was there. Someone must have whispered to the proprietor the details of all that had happened at the sweets shop because he didn't appear the least surprised at their arrival.

"Revealed himself, did he?" Kirby asked.

"Aye," Royston answered, "though how much, I'm not certain."

Kirby motioned them to a small table tucked up near the low-burning fire. Royston saw Tallulah seated, then sat himself.

"I'd already sorted out that Mr. Carman is some sort of creature." Tallulah jumped straight into the matter at hand. "When you said a few days ago that he'd been squire here for as long as you could remember, I knew there had to be something otherworldly about him. And, blessed saints, the smell of him." She grimaced. "He can toss noises around, make a body hear things that aren't there. All that confirmed my suspicions. But after what he did in my shop today . . ." She wrapped her arms around herself as a shudder shook her frame. "He is something other than a man," she whispered. "I'll not be convinced otherwise."

"Because of the damage he did?" Royston pressed. It was crucial they know precisely what the squire had revealed of himself to her.

"Yes, but more than that." Her gaze darted from Kirby to Royston and back. "His eyes glowed. I realize that sounds ridiculous, but they did. They glowed red."

Royston looked to Kirby. "She saw his eyes glow."

"So did you," Kirby reminded him.

"We tried then," Royston said. "We must try again now."

"Begging your pardon," Tallulah said with a bit of dryness in her voice, "but I'd like to be part of this conversation, especially considering it's meant to be about me."

He couldn't help a laugh no matter the heaviness of their topic. "A thousand apologies, my dear." Royston then dipped his head to Kirby. "If you'd be so good as to explain to our fair companion."

"Even in a time such as this, you flirt," she said to Royston with a smile.

"Is that a complaint?"

Her eyes twinkled as she shook her head. "Not in the least."

Oh, he did like her. Royston set his hand atop hers, and

she threaded their fingers together once more. As her fingers bent around his, small scratches pulled, tiny bubbles of blood emerging from some. He hoped she had no further injuries.

Calm as could be, Tallulah turned to Kirby. "Tell me what we are facing."

"My father first told me when I was very young about the creature. He has lived in these parts for an age, though we do not believe he originated here. Many a tale has been told of cruel tricks and dastardly doings perpetrated by him. He fools people into doing embarrassing or dangerous things. He destroys crops, buildings, belongings. As near as I've been able to tell, he began his reign as our local squire on a lark and discovered he liked it—liked the ability to do mischief and to cause terror."

"And does he play such dastardly tricks on his exalted visitors as well?" Tallulah asked.

Royston breathed a small sigh of relief. That Tallulah had not dismissed the otherworldly explanation out of hand was a good sign.

"We aren't certain what becomes of his visitors. It is whispered about that he can change people into other forms, at least temporarily. There is some worry that he might . . . eat people."

"Then why order baked confections to impress them if he means only to do them harm and—" The question halted and understanding dawned in her expression. "In order to inflict his mischief upon *me*."

Kirby nodded. "And he doesn't take well to being irritated

or ruffled. His tricks are to be endured without complaint else his ire be earned."

"The citizens hereabout, I've discovered," Royston said, "do not see his glowing red eyes, even when he is using his ability to blow open doors or break windows or such things. Only you and I have ever seen that."

"And we both come from somewhere other than this village," Tallulah said.

"That, we believe, is a clue to his origins," Kirby said. "He has remained here so long because he can do so in disguise. Only the arrival of outsiders threatens to reveal his true shape and form."

"It was not merely his eyes that changed," Tallulah said. "In his most angry moment, I felt certain his nose and face elongated, pulling out almost into a triangular snout, almost like a—"

"A rat?" Royston finished the thought in unison with her.

Her wide eyes turned on him, and she nodded.

"When angry, he also has a tail," Royston said. "It is hidden beneath his cloak and, I suspect, cannot be seen by any of the villagers."

"Rat features," she repeated in a contemplative whisper. "Does he ever *not* wear his red cap and cloak?"

"Never," Kirby said.

"He has rat-like features, plays dastardly tricks, smells of something rotten, produces unnerving noises, and, I suspect, no one has ever seen him eat."

Royston looked to Kirby, unsure of the answer.

"He's thrown back many a pint in here," Kirby said, "but never have I seen him eat so much as a crust of bread."

Tallulah tapped her free hand on the table. "He's a *fear dearg*, I'd bet m' life on it."

"A far darrig?" Royston repeated the words phonetically, not being at all certain what they meant

"'Tis a lone Fae, a solitary creature, and not one at all inclined toward friendliness. These monsters are known to play horrid, often cruel, tricks on humans. They look like humans except for their rat-like fur, face, and tail. And they always wear red: sometimes limiting themselves to a cloak and cap, sometimes wearing red from top to tail, as it were. In Irish, *fear dearg* translates to the Crimson Man, named so on account of the color they always wear."

"Any idea why it is that we, who are from here, cannot see the squire in his true monstrous form?" Kirby asked.

"The Fae are connected to their homes in strong and often mystifying ways," Tallulah said. "It could be that tucking himself in this foreign-to-him corner of the world protects him, hides him."

"Could be, could be." Kirby leaned back in his chair, stroking his chin as he pondered. "Royston could see him because he is not from here. And you could as well because your origins lie away from this village."

"Not only away from Chippingwich," Royston said, "but your origins reach back to the country of the *fear dearg*. I'd wager you can see him better than any of us. And perhaps that is why you can smell things we can't and hear things we don't. He cannot hide as entirely from you."

"Have you any idea why he doesn't eat?" Kirby asked.

"The *fear dearg* do eat," Tallulah said.

"Do I dare ask *what*?" Royston had a suspicion it wasn't anything pleasant.

"They eat carrion, carcasses."

"Human?" Kirby asked, his voice small and cracked.

She nodded. "And animal."

A heavy silence filled with uncertainty and worry settled over the all-but-empty pub.

"As far as we have been able to discover," Kirby said, "he cannot be killed. Many have tried, and all have failed."

"He can be," she said, "but only with the right weapon."

"And what weapon would that be?" Kirby sighed, his voice weighed down by years of defeats and frustrations. "We've tried everything we know."

"They can be defeated only with a blade of iron," she said. "Iron is dangerous to most Fae," she said. "'Tis the reason we hang iron horseshoes above a door; not for general luck but to protect ourselves from the Fae."

"Have you tried iron?" Royston asked Kirby.

"I can't say that we have. It isn't a common metal for weapons any longer."

"Can one be obtained?" Tallulah asked.

"I will see to it, but we must be careful about the arranging of it. Should our efforts be discovered . . ."

"I have a shipment of cloth arriving in a few days," Royston said. "We can secret the weapon in that. My disguise will go far to preventing the squire from growing suspicious."

"Your disguise?" Tallulah asked.

"We did not know how to defeat him. And, had he

known how well I can see his true form, he'd have killed me, I'm certain."

"What disguise did you assume?" she pressed.

"That of an unreliable, selfish, flirtatious—"

"Rogue," she finished in a tone of realization. "You make yourself seem too frivolous to appear to the squire to be a threat."

"Facing him would require selflessness, and he is certain I have none." A sudden, horrifying thought occurred to him. "Did you let on that you could see what he truly looked like?"

"Not intentionally," she said. "I spent most of that encounter attempting to hide from flying glass."

"You and I alone can see him for what he truly is, though only entirely when he is at his most dangerous. It is for us, then, to face him and free this village of his reign of cruelty and terror. But that is a task fraught with danger. I do not for a moment believe anyone in Chippingwich would hold you to that knowing you did not arrive here with this end in mind."

"Courage that exists only when one has a choice is not courage at all. True bravery lies in facing those dangers one did not expect and is not required to face simply because it is the right thing to do."

"Then we'll face him?"

She nodded. "Together."

CHAPTER 21

A half-dozen members of the DPS gathered in Hollis Darby's flat. 'Twould only be his home for another fortnight, after which he and Ana Newport would be married. Fletcher had answered Albie's message in precisely the way Brogan had predicted, but rather than allowing Brogan to address the Dreadfuls at headquarters, Fletcher had agreed to gather a few members at a neutral location and discuss only what the Dread Master would allow.

Stone, Doc, Hollis, Martin, and Elizabeth were tucked into Hollis's small sitting room, watching Brogan with both curiosity and uncertainty. They whispered among themselves, but he stood too far distant to overhear.

A hush fell over the room as Fletcher strolled inside. He was a commanding presence, even moving so casually. He made his way to the front. He took off his tall hat and set it on the mantelpiece. Fletcher then dropped into an empty chair with all the theatrical drama of a vagabond who'd usurped a throne.

"How's tricks?" His grin could not be mistaken for

anything other than enjoyment. Fletcher hadn't a demure bone in his body.

"Some of us have other things to see to today," Elizabeth said. "Please move directly to the matter at hand."

He gave her an undeniably flirtatious glance; their romantic attachment was well known to everyone in attendance. "You don't usually object."

"I also don't usually belt you, but I'm willing to make an exception."

With a laugh, Fletcher got down to business. "We've a certain Irishman in need of help. I've brought the lot of you here because I'd wager you're his best hope."

"He abandoned us," Doc said, pointing at Brogan. "Quite bold to then come asking for our help."

There were far more hurt feelings than actual anger in Doc's tone. Brogan had long suspected the man's history was a difficult and painful one. Something he hadn't told the DPS about drove him to spend vast amounts of his limited time rescuing people from horrid situations; he'd grow almost desperate when he wasn't able to.

Brogan moved to a spot where he could address them all. "I know 'tis the beyond of everything for me to be asking any of you to help me. I'd not be doing it were I the one in danger."

"Something the matter with Móirín?" Stone asked, somehow both doubtful and concerned.

Brogan shook his head. "Most of you likely know I've been toiling in a print shop these past weeks. While there, I've . . ." He had to tread carefully. Too many secrets were tucked into the folds of those recollections. "The entire street is being bullied into paying 'protection money,' and those who don't hand over the blunt have been robbed or had their shops set ablaze."

"That's happening in other corners, too," Martin said. His specialty among them was gathering information. How he knew so much and so quickly, none of them were sure, but he was reliable as the day was long. "I'm hearing whispers from all around."

The others didn't look at all surprised. This, likely, had been discussed at DPS meetings Brogan had missed. There were distinct disadvantages to not being among them. He hoped they'd be willing to overlook the current gap between himself and the Dreadfuls.

Fletcher jumped into the discussion once more. "Were that the only difficulty Brogan's juggling, I'd not've dragged the lot of you here."

Brogan knew the underlying message in those words: the Dread Master had given the nod to tell these few Dreadfuls about the blackmail. But unless Brogan received a letter specifically telling him to do so, he'd not reveal his assignment or the Dread Master's involvement.

"Baron Chelmsford, former Lord High Chancellor, is being blackmailed," he told the group, "and that blackmail is being perpetrated by the Mastiff."

This, clearly, *was* new information among them. Surprised and concerned glances were exchanged all around.

"The man that owns the print shop where I work has been forced to create counterfeit documents, likely by holding over his head the axe of his own difficult history. The Russian Ambassador is being forced to corroborate the forgeries, likely by means of threats. The papers that will be his downfall are assumed to already be at Chelmsford's house, tucked in a place where they will be discovered and made public."

"Any notion what the forgeries are?" Elizabeth asked.

He pulled the papers from his coat. "A letter from Lord Chelmsford"—he held it up—"asking the ambassador not to reveal the existence of this document"—he held up the marked drafts—"which is also a forgery."

"What's the document about?" Doc asked.

"A list of names, of payment amounts, and what was being paid for. Printed at the top are the words 'Securing a Verdict in the Radlett Case.' The obvious inference is that this is meant to document the bribing of witnesses and judges and such to obtain a particular verdict."

"This is to do with the Radlett murder?" Hollis let forth a low whistle. "Chelmsford's efforts in defending Joseph Hunt in that trial are quite famous. It is the stuff of folklore: songs recounting the gruesome scene, waxworks recreations, penny dreadful retellings." Hollis gave them all knowing looks. "Calling into question his role in something so well-known is a risk."

"What's the risk to Chelmsford?" Stone asked.

"That trial is one of the reasons he was made a baron. His reputation, his accomplishments, his potential future place in administrations rests in significant part on that case," Hollis said.

"It seems ruining Lord Chelmsford is the goal here," Elizabeth said. "Except, he likely can prove it false."

"Or," Fletcher jumped in, "he can likely *almost* prove it

false, but even doing that would leave lingering doubts. And the Mastiff likely has a plan for addressing those doubts . . . for a price."

"More blackmail," Brogan said.

"More 'protection payments,'" Doc tossed back. "Have you considered that maybe the two schemes might be related?"

Saints. "I'm considering it now. The extortion notes are signed by someone calling himself 'the Protector.' Might very well be yet another colleague of the Mastiff."

"It'd make sense," Fletcher said. "Threatening the street kept everyone's attention off Mr. Sorokin, including his daughter's. With their resources strapped in more than one way, they'd be that much more vulnerable."

Brogan pulled out of his pocket the sketch Móirín had made of Clare. "This is the woman we think has been leaving the notes. If the Mastiff is connected, she might be a clue to finding him. Maybe we could finally stop him."

He handed the paper to Elizabeth.

Hollis eyed it over her shoulder. A gasp escaped, apparently involuntarily. "It's her."

"You know this woman?"

He nodded. "It isn't a perfect likeness, but . . ." Hollis studied the face as he spoke, low and quick. "Do you remember when I was infiltrating the gambling house and there was a housekeeper, Serena, who helped us escape and begged that we rescue her and her children?"

The DPS had been attempting to find Serena ever since, wanting to uphold their promise and help her escape the clutches of the infamous Mastiff.

"This is her." Hollis tapped the sketch. "I'm certain of it."

Boil and blast. Serena was likely still in the employ—coerced, no doubt—of the criminal mastermind, being forced to do his dirty work for him, just as she had in the gambling den, though now she was going by a different name, likely also forced on her.

That meant the Mastiff *was* connected to the trouble on Old Compton as well as to the forgeries. There didn't seem to be a rancid pie he didn't have a finger in.

"Lives are in danger on that street," Brogan told them. "The Sorokins look after urchins; two work at the shop regularly. There're families living over the businesses there. Women who're already being exploited are now even more vulnerable. Street vendors with nowhere to hide. We have to find a means of stopping this. All of it."

No matter that the Dreadfuls likely still didn't think too well of Brogan for having abandoned the organization, they united fully and quickly under the necessity of a desperate cause.

"We need to unravel the game from the top," Fletcher said. "It's the only way to stop both efforts with one blow."

"It'd be easy enough to watch the street," Martin said. "A few extra eyes'd make a difference. Sounding the alarm when needed, stopping assaults. Keeping a weather eye out for this mort"—he tipped his head in the direction of the drawing of "Clare"—"and see if we can't thwart any roughs that come by to make trouble. We can set up a rotating watch of Dreadfuls. Might take a bit to organize it, but it can be done."

"I'd appreciate it," Brogan said.

"How do we stop the blackmail scheme when the

documents are already at Lord Chelmsford's house?" Doc asked.

"Can you warn him?" Elizabeth asked Brogan

He shook his head. "Not without implicating the other victims. And I've every reason to believe they're being watched—the other victims, I mean. If they double-cross the Mastiff . . ." He let the sentence hang unfinished. They didn't need to be told again how dangerous their greatest foe truly was.

"So steal 'em," Stone said in his usual direct manner, bringing all eyes to him. "If the papers disappear when neither fella is anywhere near Chelmsford's house, they can't be blamed for it."

"They'll likely be in the man's library." Fletcher shook his head. It was a tall ask, for certain. "None of us is that stealthy."

With a sigh, Hollis said, "Ana is."

She'd had a long, impressive, and entirely secret career as the legendary sneak thief the Phantom Fox.

"Would she help?" Brogan asked. "'Tis a risky business, this."

"I'd wager she'd be willing," Hollis said, "but giving her information about this raises the possibility that she'll sort out more of the DPS and our efforts. I'd guess she's not far off the mark as it is."

"We'll be careful," Fletcher said. "We've already lost one member over the weight of secrecy. We can't afford to lose another."

CHAPTER 22

Vera caught herself staring off into nothing at odd times as she knocked about the shop. Papa was drowning in illegal and dangerous forgeries. Her neighbors were on edge and worried. She was as confused as ever about Brogan Donnelly. She had every reason to be worried as a toad, and yet she was frustrated with herself for being so entirely distracted.

"Ye're full clutched today, Miss Vera," Olly said. "What's worrying you?"

"Nothing."

"I ain't bacon-brained." Olly popped his fists on his hips. "You're fretting, and I'd guess it's to do with Mr. Donnelly."

She'd had to explain to the children why the man they'd known as "Ganor" no longer worked at the shop. That he was, in addition to being dishonest, a murderer, she'd chosen not to spill into their ears.

"We're well rid of him, and I'm not thinking on him at all," Vera said.

"What a heap of bung," Licorice said. "Not having him

here ain't helping nothing, and you're thinking on him, sure as anything." She looked toward the back room where Papa was passing the day. "Mr. Sorokin certainly ain't in better spirits since Mr. Donnelly quit coming."

If only the little ones knew why that was.

"Mr. Donnelly lied to you lot. Don't that burn you?"

Olly shrugged. "He gave a wrong name. We've all done that."

Licorice nodded. "You really think Bob's Your Knuckle is that sprout's true name?"

"You mean to simply forgive him?" Vera eyed the urchins, unsure which answer she wanted them to give.

"He saved me from being snatched off the street," Licorice said. "And he never acted like I owed him anything for it, never held it over my head. He helped because that's what he does. He may've lied about his name, but he didn't lie about who he is."

"The mad thing is," Vera said, "I don't think the two of you are entirely wrong about him."

"Ain't nothing mad about it," Olly insisted. "Smart as whips, we are."

She couldn't help a smile. How she adored these two. On those days they spent time at the shop, they filled it with joy.

Sudden commotion out on the street pulled all their attention to the front windows. Voices shouting. What sounded like wood splintering. Thuds. Cracks. Crashes.

Outside was absolute chaos. Peter's cart had been overturned, and men with clubs were smashing it to splinters. His produce was strewn throughout the street, being crushed underfoot and under carts. Anything salvageable was snatched up.

Vera rushed out. Others were running from their businesses toward the fray. With an elbow and shoulder thrown hard against one of the assailants, Vera managed to knock him down.

Rather than fight back, he shook his head. "I'm sorry. I'm sorry." He said it again and again, his tone fearful.

"Sorry for what?"

"Didn't wanna do it." The man rolled, getting to his feet. "We don't have a choice. They make us."

Even the assailants were being forced into this. More blackmail. More extortion.

The man grabbed the arm of the other apparently unwitting ruffian. "That'll be enough. Cain't fault us for that much."

And they rushed off.

Peter was decidedly worse for wear. His lip was bleeding, and a bruise was quickly forming on his jaw. But the look on his face was more worrying than his physical state. Devastation. Absolute devastation.

"I didn't obey the last note," he whispered to Vera, looking at the shattered remains of his livelihood. "Wanted me to bust someone up. I wouldn't do it."

Mercy. "Bust 'em up like was just done to you?" Vera asked. "Instead of paying money?"

Peter sat on the pavement, slumped and defeated, the exact posture Mr. Overton had assumed when his business had burned. "We ain't never gonna shake them, Miss Vera. Not ever."

She'd done her best to help them all, including herself, and she'd failed. Again and again she'd failed.

"This has happened before?" Papa had arrived in the midst of the chaos.

"I've told you about this, *pápochka*. The money for protection. The fire. All of it is connected."

"I didn't—" He scratched at his beard. His eyes scanned the wreckage, then shifted to the ashes of the barbershop across the street. "I thought I was keeping us safe."

"How were you keeping us safe?" she asked.

But he only shook his head and wandered off.

The business owners, street vendors, and locals were there, picking through the piles of broken wood and finding, to Vera's relief, some salvageable fruits and veg. Even with that unforeseen bit of good luck, their faces made clear how quickly they were losing hope.

She couldn't fail them again. She wouldn't.

"Neighbors," she called out to them. "This is no time to abandon ship. The men what did this were victims of extortion, just as we are. They didn't want to be part of this. But the Protector, I'm full certain, required it of them."

"How does that give us hope?" Mrs. Bianchi asked.

"All of this—*all* of it—depends on the strong-arming and threats working. We loosen even a few links in that chain, and the scheme falls to bits."

"It's too big," Mr. Overton said. "There're too many links."

"But most of those links are *us*." She spoke with as much firmness and confidence as she could. They needed to be reassured. She needed to find the strength to offer them that. "We can break the chain."

"Not if they break us first," Mr. Okeke said.

"If we don't fight back," Peter said from where he sat on the pavement, "then they've broken us already." He took an audible breath and stood. "We can't abandon each other."

"But we're just small folks." Burnt Ricky's little voice trembled. He crushed the sides of his coat in his tight fists. Few things fretted a child of the streets.

"These big men, with their notes and their threats, cain't follow through without us," she said.

Interest flickered.

"If enough of us refuse, their schemes fail."

"She's bang up to the mark on this." Brogan emerged from the crowd and stood beside her. "Breaking the chain is the best chance we have."

Heaven help her, that *we* warmed her through. He'd helped with Papa's trouble. He was still helping her neighbors. He was standing beside her.

"How do we do it?" Mr. Bianchi asked.

Brogan, rather than seizing the reins as so many men would do, deferred to her as naturally as if they'd decided on the arrangement ahead of time. She hadn't a plan but was formulating one as she spoke. Still, she weren't entirely without ideas.

"London is a large city," she said, "and, yet, its boroughs and corners are connected by the people. I was brought up in Southwark and know people there still. We've customers in Charing Cross and Westminster I could call on. Peter, I'm certain you know other street vendors who sell in other areas."

"I do," he confirmed.

She looked to Brogan. "You and your sister know a few vendors in Covent Garden."

"That we do."

Turning back to the crowd, she continued. "Our Olly knows urchins who know every corner and seemingly every person in London. Licorice, Bob's Your Knuckle, and Burnt Ricky likely know all the rest."

"We know people in Clerkenwell," Mr. Bianchi said.

"And I've plenty of friends and family in the Rookery," Mrs. Murphy said.

Mrs. Okeke added her voice. "I've people in Bethnal Green and Wapping."

"We've connections," Vera said. "Those connections have connections. If everyone—or at least *enough* of everyone—stands their ground against our tormentor, he'll lose his footing."

"We can do this," Brogan said. "I've watched as you've helped each other. I've seen this strength in other corners of London. This challenge can be met. I know it can."

"We're fit to this purpose," Peter said to them all. "I don't want this"—he motioned to his shattered cart—"to happen again. But if we don't do something, it will for certain."

"We all know people outside of Soho," Mr. Overton said. "If we begin today, we can gather people to the cause in the parishes of London, the poor, the tradesmen, the merchants. We can free ourselves."

Discussions immediately began among them, comparisons of who they knew and where, decisions about going

together or dividing the efforts. They were focused and determined and convinced. They weren't giving up.

"Do you think we can truly do this?" she asked Brogan
out of the side of her mouth.

"You won't be doing it alone," he said. "All your neighbors are rallying. And I've a few friends who'll help as well.
I'd actually hoped they'd be watching this street already, but
organizing takes time."

"And experience." Vera sighed. "I haven't got much of
either."

"You've spread hope here today. That's a powerful thing."

A familiar and unexpected voice replied, "Not powerful
enough."

She turned at the sound. For the length of a breath, she
couldn't speak. *Clare.* The one likely delivering the notes. The
only undeniable link they had to the Protector.

Clare held out a folded bit of paper. "You might stop this
part of his plan, but it's bigger than you know. It's bigger than
anyone knows."

"Help us stop him," Vera pleaded.

She shook her head, still holding out the paper. "I ain't
got a death wish."

"But you said we could stop this part," Brogan said.
"How?"

"Please take the note. I'm risking too much even talking
to you. If he finds out—"

"He?" Brogan repeated. "The Mastiff?"

The Mastiff? Vera thought they'd been talking about the
Protector.

"He times me. If I return late—" Clare visibly shuttered. "Take the note. Please."

"We can protect you," Vera said.

Clare shook her head. "No one can be protected from a storm this large." Apparently giving up on Vera taking the note, she shoved it awkwardly into Brogan's outercoat pocket, and rushed off.

"Who is the Mastiff?" Vera asked.

"Explaining that requires I tell you what I've discovered about Clare."

"What did you discover?"

"I've a friend who knows her, but as 'Serena.'"

Another person with a false name?

"Serena works—or *worked*—as a housekeeper for a man known as the Mastiff, a criminal mastermind with connections throughout London. He's beyond dangerous. Even the police are afraid of him."

That was not the sort of discovery to put a person's mind at ease.

"She might very well work for him still," Brogan continued. "One of the Mastiff's cronies, Four-Finger Mike, has a taste for arson."

"Four-Finger Mike?" Mercy. "Albie, at the embassy, mentioned one of the men didn't have all his fingers."

Brogan nodded. "I'm certain it's the same man. The same *men*. The Protector is likely part of their criminal circle."

"Laws," she muttered. "The extortion here is connected to the forgeries and blackmail."

"Seems that way."

Vera pressed her fingertips against her temples. "I may have just sent my neighbors into a battle we cannot win."

Brogan set a hand gently on her arm. "I think Clare is right about one important thing: we've a good chance of beating him in *this*. 'Twon't solve every problem in London, not even all the ones he's causing. But you will have assembled an army of eyes and ears on the streets. That is the best defense."

With a sigh, she motioned to Brogan's pocket. Though she weren't eager to hear the latest demand, she knew better than to ignore it. "What's the note say?"

Brogan pulled it out and unfolded it. "The children are too often alone," he read aloud. His brow jumped skyward just as the reality of what the note meant struck her with horror.

They both turned toward the shop in near-perfect unison. He called out "Licorice!" just as she shouted "Olly!" They rushed inside.

Both children were huddled over a copy of Mr. King's latest installment and looked up with confusion and a touch of annoyance at the interruption. Even seeing them safe didn't set Vera's heart at ease. They were in danger. There was no doubt they were. Even if she vowed never to take her eyes off them, that wouldn't guarantee they'd not momentarily slip from view. Another mess like they'd had that day would create enough confusion that she'd easily lose sight of them. What if more ruffians came around? Maybe even armed?

"We can hide them," Brogan said.

"They're born and raised on the streets." Vera pushed out a breath. "They'd shrivel up if forced into hiding."

"It'd only be temporary. And it'd safeguard them."

"No one can be protected from a storm this large."

Papa stepped up beside Brogan. He didn't speak a word, but simply snatched the note from Brogan's hand and silently read it. Papa'd shown himself all-too-willing to relent in matters of the Mastiff's blackmail. He might regret the children being pulled into the trouble, but she weren't at all certain he'd intervene.

He readjusted his glasses, then placed the paper back in Brogan's hand. He looked only at the children. "Licorice. Olly. Fetch your coats and scarves."

His was not a tone that allowed for debate. The children didn't attempt any.

"Pápochka?"

With little ears out of earshot, he spoke quickly and forcefully. "Lead your army, *kotik*." To Brogan he said, "Help her." To them both, "I will keep the children safe. The sender of these notes will have no idea where we are."

"You can disappear so quickly? So entirely?" Brogan asked.

With set jaw, he said, "I've done it before. The tsar himself couldn't find the people I've hidden, people who are living full lives, not cowering in corners or caves. The children will be safe. I swear to you."

"What do you mean you've hidden people?" she asked. "Hidden them from the tsar?"

"The Circle, Vera. I hid members of the Circle."

"The people who betrayed you?" They'd always spoken of that part of their lives in whispers. She did so now.

"I was not falsely accused by them; I was one of them."

Shock silenced her.

"I gave a number of them forged identification papers, which allowed them to escape, to hide, to never be discovered. They, and the exiles I have hidden since, have never been uncovered by their enemies."

"But why—you said—" She shook her head, unable to make sense of it. This wasn't what she'd always been told of their past.

"That I was connected with them was known, and that connection was strongest in the area of their writings, which I printed." Papa ran a hand down his beard. "Shaking off all suspicion depended upon a reputation for distrusting, disliking, and even being disgusted by writers in particular."

"It was a lie?"

"An absolutely necessary one," he said. "I was hiding *us* as well."

"You were one of them?" She could not reconcile it.

"The Circle was a varied group. Writers. Revolutionaries. Intellectuals. Even printers."

For years, he had left off this part of his explanations. "But your name does not appear on the lists of the members."

"It does," he said firmly. "After a manner."

"Oh, saints." The words whooshed from Brogan. "Sorokin isn't your true surname."

Papa adjusted his spectacles. "The less said on that the better."

Criminy. Vera was almost too overwhelmed to think, to understand what was being said.

"The Circle aren't the only ones I've hidden away. Didn't you ever wonder how it was I had so many printing consultations, but the shop was still struggling?"

"They weren't customers." She realized the truth even as she spoke it.

The children emerged from the back room, their coats on, and the scarves Brogan had gifted them wrapped around their necks.

"I'll keep the little ones safe," Papa promised once more. "Save our neighbors." He looked to Brogan. "And, whatever you do, get the letter and the list out of Chelmsford's house. That scheme *must* be stopped."

On that shocking last request, Papa took a child's hand in each of his and left without another word or glance.

"Merciful heavens." Vera pressed her hands to either side of her face. "What next?"

Brogan took a step closer and leaned in, his nearness warming her. "If you're willing to help, I believe we can manage your da's request."

She looked to him. "How in heaven's name do we sneak forged documents out of the private residence of a former Lord High Chancellor?"

He tossed out one of his half-formed, eye-twinkling smiles. "Very carefully."

CHAPTER 23

For two days Brogan had been coming to the shop to help Vera look after it, do her work, and to keep her company. Papa and the children were gone, and Vera hadn't heard a word from them. At times she would sit and stare off into nothing, attempting to wrap her mind around all she had learned in so short a time.

The much-despised Petrashevsky Circle was not, as she'd always believed, her family's enemy, but her family's past. Papa hadn't been betrayed by them; he was one of them. And his distance from the Russian community in London, his insistence that she not interact with writers and authors, and likely even those moments throughout her life when he'd slipped away during the day on business and returned without new printing jobs or clients had all been part of his efforts to hide and protect people.

The neighborhood was on edge, worried, even though they were more hopeful than they had been. They'd contacted friends, family, colleagues, and acquaintances in various corners of London. Reports were trickling back in that the extortion scheme had popped up in many of those areas at about the same time it had in Soho. The pattern was the same; the results were the same. Vera was more than a little worried that she'd taken on a fight she was not at all sure she could win.

When her confidence would flag, Brogan would give her a nod or a smile, sometimes he would simply tell her that she was strong enough for this battle. And through it all, though he didn't say it in specific words, he gave her every assurance that he would not leave her to fight alone.

On the third night after Papa had slipped away with Licorice and Olly, Vera was at Brogan and Móirín's flat, where she'd been spending her nights. She was dressed in her finest gown. Brogan, she knew, was also putting on his nicest clothes.

He had, though she did not know how, arranged for them to meet with Lord Chelmsford that evening in his house. Vera was nervous. She had never called on someone of such importance before. But her Papa's insistence that they had to get the forged papers out of the house solidified her determination to see this through.

She emerged from the bedchamber she'd been using and descended the stairs with as much confidence as she could muster. Brogan was waiting for her in the entryway. She'd never seen him dressed so keenly. He was never sloppy or slovenly by any means, but his appearance was always more humble than it was just then. That night he could've easily passed for a member of Society.

He smiled softly when he saw her. "You look beautiful, Vera."

Something about his simple, pleased expression warmed her. "I likely also look terrified. Our task tonight is a bit beyond my experience."

He neither dismissed her worries nor belittled her abilities. He simply nodded, quite as one would when understanding on a deep level the feelings of someone else.

"Fortunately, our task tonight is a straightforward one. Make this call. Engage in conversation. Learn what we can about the events mentioned in the counterfeit document without tipping our hand. Distract Lord Chelmsford long enough for the papers to be stolen."

She rolled her eyes theatrically. "Is that all?" she asked dryly.

He laughed lightly. "I won't argue that it's without risk or not the least complicated. But I do think we're equal to it."

"I hope you're right."

Brogan snatched an umbrella from the stand near the door and handed it to her. "It's been drizzling on and off this evening," he said. "I'd not want you to be rained on."

"Thank you."

He held the door for her. As she passed, his hand brushed lightly against her back. Her breath caught at the sizzle of his touch, the unexpected shot of energy emanating from that simple caress.

"The stoop's wet," he warned. "Tread carefully."

He was showing her consideration that any decent person would extend, and yet, it was the sort of thing he did all the time. He treated the customers with kindness that went beyond wishing to maintain connections with those who did business there. He was thoughtful and considerate of all the urchins who regularly spent time in the shop. He'd been patient and forgiving with Papa. Again and again her mind harkened back to what Licorice had said. He had lied about his name, but he'd never lied about who he was. That was proving quite true.

They walked along the dim evening streets in the direction of Lord Chelmsford's home. The year was coming to a close, and thus the days had grown quite short. She slipped her arm through his, telling herself that it simply made them look like a couple out for a stroll and would reduce the chances of anyone taking much notice of them. But she also took comfort in the touch, and the nearness of him as they walked.

"I hope this Phantom Fox you've engaged for the night is able to do his part," she whispered.

"No sneak thief in all of London is more reliable," he said.

"I still find it a bit odd that you're so trusting of a thief."

"And I'm more than a bit surprised—pleasantly so—that you're being so trusting of a writer."

She could appreciate that. "People are more than their labels, is what you're saying."

"They are, indeed."

He stopped them at the side of a cart and purchased a small bag of hot chestnuts. It was the first time since their falling out that he'd undertaken the once-familiar gesture.

"Thank you, Brogan."

He dipped his head. "I know 'tis a source of soreness between us, but I can't tell you how much I love hearing you say m'actual name. I wanted to tell you so many times, but by the time I realized the secret would be safe with you, I didn't know how to escape its tendrils."

Between chestnuts, she asked him the question that had been hanging awkwardly between them.

"Were you ever going to tell me? If I hadn't stumbled across the truth of it, would you have simply let me go on calling you Ganor?"

"I would have told you the truth, I swear to it. I hadn't formulated the how, but I'd already determined I needed to. 'Twasn't merely the awkwardness of explaining the lie. 'Twas also the difficulty of knowing full well your da's dislike of writers, and the knowledge that it came about because you both believed those in my profession aren't trustworthy. That I'd lied to you would only have added to that view."

"It seems rather fitting, don't it, that even *that* proved to be a lie. And that you weren't the only one using a false name. I had no idea I was too." In the days since that shocking revelation, she'd found herself wondering what her actual surname was. What it had been before they'd left St. Petersburg. If Papa would ever tell her the truth of that, or if she would go through life never knowing what her actual name was.

"How heavy that deception must've weighed on your da's mind. To be misleading his child all these years, all the while worried that if the secrets were known you'd be in danger."

She hadn't thought of it that way. It must've been a struggle for him. "And he kept a distance from the Russian community here in London, afraid he'd tip those who meant harm to the people he was protecting. He commented now and then about how little of Russia I seem to carry with me. I always assumed that was him being disappointed in me. But seems now it was more a matter of his sorrow at not being able to give me a connection to our homeland."

Brogan set his arm about her waist, allowing her to walk tucked up against him, protected from the biting cold air, while still giving her the freedom to eat the chestnuts he had given her. The gesture was small. He was not the flashy sort, whose good deeds were known by all. His kindnesses were found in small and simple acts.

"I suspect, Vera, things will be different between you and your da when you're together again. He'll be more open, more trusting. Perhaps he'll finally share more of his history with you."

"I hope so," she said. "I've never felt a connection to where I come from. That's sat as a void in my heart."

"No matter how far one wanders from home, the heart still longs to know it." It was a beautiful sentiment. He often said things she thought very poetic. How was it she hadn't twigged that he was a writer when he had such a way with words?

The idea bubbled as a bit of silent laughter. The answer had been in front of her all along.

"'Tis good to see you smile, Vera. You haven't done much of it this past while."

"It's likely because you haven't been around. I don't know what it is about you, but even in heavy and difficult moments, you've a lightening effect on a person's heart."

"That may very well be the kindest thing anyone has said to me."

Though she couldn't see him well on account of it being dusk and them being at a distance from the nearest streetlamp, the tone of his voice told her he was likely blushing at the compliment.

"I'm not good for many things, but I do hope I offer people a spot of happiness."

"On the contrary, you're good for a great many things." She held up her now-empty bag of chestnuts. "Delicious indulgences, for example."

He laughed. "I've never known anyone with your love for hot chestnuts."

"And I've never had anyone twig my weakness as quickly as you did."

They walked on, talking of little nothings. It was the easy and comfortable companionship they'd known before his secret had been whispered in her ear. She was finding herself more and more able to accept the fact that he'd hidden his identity. She understood why he had; she wouldn't've hired him if she'd known who he was. He'd been in a difficult bind.

He was good and kindhearted. Which made reconciling the fact that he was also a murderer that much more difficult. She believed what he'd told her of the horrid man in Dublin who had been hurting his sister. She could understand his desire to protect Móirín. But there were so many gaps in the story. Had it been a crime undertaken in a moment of anger? Or an accident? Had it been a brawl in which both men fought, and he happened to be the one who emerged alive? Had it been coldhearted and planned?

There was so much she didn't know, but when he'd briefly explained it to her, there'd been no denying he did not wish to discuss details.

It was an admitted strain on her trust. But for the moment, she would take comfort in knowing she had in him an ally, and that he'd proven himself worthy of trust in other areas. Leaning on that, she could move forward.

She could face the task ahead of them.

CHAPTER 24

The entryway of Lord Chelmsford's house was, by far, the grandest place Vera had ever been in. And this was simply the landing place for visitors who weren't yet certain of their welcome.

"I feel like an imposter," she whispered.

"If there's one thing an Irishman living in England learns quickly, it's that he does best to pretend he's wanted and welcome. Otherwise, everyone around him will insist he's not."

"I can imagine the members of every immigrant community would heartily agree with that strategy."

Brogan gave a minute nod.

In the next moment, a butler invited them to follow him to a very elegant drawing room, where Lord Chelmsford was waiting. The space was overly large for three people to meet for a short conversation, but she'd often heard the drawing rooms of the upper class were meant to impress. This one most certainly did, as did its occupant. He was dressed quite fine with a very regal bearing. He greeted them with a dip of his head and genteel words of welcome.

Brogan saw her seated, then sat directly beside her. His suggestion repeated in her mind. *Act as if you belong, and Lord Chelmsford will believe it.*

"I was most intrigued by your note requesting this interview," Lord Chelmsford said.

"We do not mean to take too much of your time, my lord," Brogan said. "We wish simply to express our very deep gratitude at your public support for the creation of the London Fire Engine Establishment. Captain Shaw is a friend of mine, and I'm pleased that he was chosen to head it. I have no doubt your influence was crucial in this."

Vera was beginning to understand how Brogan had managed this call. He'd tossed out Captain Shaw's name, who was a man of some importance. He'd also discovered that Lord Chelmsford had spoken in favor of the recently passed law, something that likely had taken some effort to learn, as Lord Chelmsford wasn't currently in parliament or the cabinet. Writing a note expressing his wish to talk about the goodness of this gentleman in supporting the cause would've softened Lord Chelmsford to the request.

Brogan continued his explanation. "There was, unfortunately, a very devastating fire on our street a short while ago. The tragedy of it was only made worse by the fact that the private brigades ignored the flames on account of the building not boasting a fire mark."

Lord Chelmsford shook his head, his expression one of sincere regret. "Even those who argue that such services should only be afforded to those who can pay for them must be willing to admit that any fire left to burn out of control threatens every building and every life nearby. Fighting fires is a public service and should be treated and funded as such."

"I could not agree more." Brogan's Irish accent was still obvious, but his word choice was a bit more formal than usual. He was adapting to the situation. She would do well to determine her wisest role and adapt as well.

"Have you had an opportunity to speak with Captain Shaw about the changes that will take effect in a few weeks?" Lord Chelmsford asked Brogan.

The discussion turned to fire brigades, safety techniques, and the character of Captain Shaw and the London Fire Engine Establishment. Through it all, Vera offered only a few quick interjections, not wishing to disrupt the flow, not knowing if Lord Chelmsford was one of those gentlemen who felt it best for women to keep quiet. She followed Brogan's lead in this, just as he followed hers in the matter of her neighbors' safety.

She peered now and then at the clock on the mantelpiece, watching the minutes tick by. How long would they need to keep this up? How could they possibly know when this Phantom Fox had managed his task?

"Though I didn't grow up in London," Brogan said, "I am still quite familiar with the Radlett murder. Your work on that case is quite well spoken of, even in Ireland."

It was an important change of topic. They were meant to learn what they could about the case mentioned in the forged document.

"I am ashamed to admit," Vera said, "I'm not acquainted with it. A few details here and there, yes, but overall, that case is a mystery to me."

Brogan took her hand and squeezed it, decidedly giving the impression of a tender connection between them. It would likely help Lord Chelmsford feel comfortable conversing with the two of them.

"I could tell her of it," Brogan said, "but I would not wish to deprive her of the opportunity to hear about it from your lips, Lord Chelmsford. What an opportunity that is."

While Lord Chelmsford did hesitate, he did not seem truly opposed to sharing details. What followed was a very intricate recounting of what she knew had been a notorious event. A man convinced a local solicitor, to whom he owed a great gambling debt, to join him and two friends for a weekend of cards. Near to their destination, the man shot the solicitor, but failed to kill him. He finished his sinister deed by beating the man to death. He and his two friends hid the body in a nearby pond before continuing on to their destination and enjoying a hot dinner and a night of lighthearted revelry, despite the atrocities still fresh in their minds.

The three of them were soon connected with the murder, and one of the men—Joseph Hunt, who owned a local inn—led authorities to the body of the victim, whom the villains had also robbed. Lord Chelmsford, a young barrister at the time, had been tasked with representing Joseph Hunt. Though Mr. Hunt had been the most cooperative and helpful of the three men, it was the other accomplice who was offered freedom in exchange for turning King's evidence. The murderer was hanged. The other accomplice went free.

"What was Mr. Hunt's punishment in the end?" Vera asked.

"Transportation for life. He was sent to Botany Bay, as many other criminals are."

"Did he have any family here?" Vera asked.

"None of note," Lord Chelmsford said. "He was well liked, though, by the staff and regulars at his tavern. Many of them seemed to regret his role in the crime and his sentence. One of the young women who worked at the tavern even cried when his sentence was handed down."

Vera nodded slowly. "Life is often cruel, isn't it? One cannot help but be aware that crimes impact so many innocent people. The family of the victim will mourn the loss of their loved one. The family of the guilty mourn as well. The people living nearby struggle afterward to feel safe. So many innocent people's lives change forever."

Lord Chelmsford looked at her with a kind expression one might receive from an uncle or grandfather. He was of an age to have been either one, though there was nothing feeble about him. "You have a kind heart, miss. Not everyone recognizes how many unseen victims there are."

"The nation is fortunate to have barristers such as yourself," Brogan said, "who are not merely gifted at what they do, but execute their duties with needed compassion. That is an important combination."

"Not everyone is pleased with the work I have done." Lord Chelmsford seemed to inwardly sigh.

Heavens, this was a fortunate direction for the conversation to take. Vera didn't mean to let it slip away. "Truly? Who could be displeased?"

"Any number of people. Those who were upset that I failed to gain a conviction. Those who feel a punishment was too harsh or too lenient. Those who were guilty as sin, but fully expected me to free them of the natural consequences of their actions."

"I'm certain you did your very best work," Vera said.

"If everyone had your generous heart, I believe we would make strides toward a more just system than we have now."

Brogan squeezed her hand but addressed Lord Chelmsford. "We are taking up your time, Lord Chelmsford. Thank you for seeing us."

"My pleasure."

Lord Chelmsford stood along with them and saw them to the drawing room door. He offered a friendly farewell, which they returned in kind.

Once on the pavement, they strolled leisurely down the street and around the nearby corner. Brogan then stopped and tucked them both up against a tall hedge, casting them fully in shadow.

"Do you think the Phantom Fox had enough time?" Vera asked in a nearly silent whisper.

"I was told to distract Chelmsford for at least fifteen minutes. We managed twenty-five."

"How will you know if the thief was successful?"

"I won't for a time," he said.

Across the street, two men emerged from the shadows and moved quickly and silently to where they stood. Vera recognized them in the brief moments their faces were illuminated. It was Fletcher Walker and Stone, the other two authors who were present when she'd been told about Papa's forgeries.

"What did you learn?" Fletcher asked, his voice low but not a whisper.

"We managed a quick discussion of the Radlett murder, particularly about Joseph Hunt."

"Hunt's name is on that forged list," Stone said. His American accent always caught Vera off guard. It wasn't one she heard around London, but she liked the sound of it.

"Chelmsford talked about people not always being pleased with the results of cases he's worked," Brogan said. "People were upset that Joseph Hunt was transported."

"But that was decades ago," Vera said. "I'd be full surprised if someone were seeking vengeance for it now. Mr. Hunt's likely not even alive any longer. The people upset about him might not be either."

"I know it," Brogan said. "I wonder if it's a more recent case someone's fuming over instead. The blackmailer may want to discredit Chelmsford, make him seem an object of ridicule and pity."

"The Radlett case was one of his most famous," Fletcher said. "Casting doubt on it'd do damage, for sure and certain."

"The two men who're connected to our troubles are criminals, yeah?" Vera pressed. "It makes sense blokes like them'd have beef with a barrister. Maybe avenging a wrong they feel was done to them or another of their criminal confederates."

"Any word from our phantom friend?" Fletcher asked.

"Not as yet," Brogan said.

Seemed all three of them knew the legendary sneak thief. Papa had insisted authors couldn't be trusted because they were dishonest. It seemed to her they were secret keepers more than they were liars.

The group walked casually toward the mews. The night was quiet, but not silent. Vera kept an eye on their surroundings. She suspected the other three were doing the same.

Without warning, a man sprinted around the corner and collided with Stone. Their American friend was a large man, built solid as a mountain. The collision sent him a single step backward, but left the other man sprawled on the pavement.

Quick as a flash, Fletcher grabbed him and yanked him to his feet.

"No reason to rough me," the man said, frantic. "Let me go, bloke."

"Not a chance of it, mate." Fletcher shook him a little bit. "Hold up your hands."

"Why?" he demanded

"Because you're outnumbered," Brogan said. "Do as he says, or you'll discover all of us are armed."

Vera didn't know if that was true, but it was a useful bluff.

Head darting about, the man held up his hands slowly. Five fingers on the left. *Four* on the right.

Brogan muttered something Vera suspected was an Irish curse. This was the notorious Four-Finger Mike.

"Stone," Fletcher said. "Catch up to our friend. Make certain all's well."

Stone left without hesitation. Vera didn't need an explanation. It was possible this criminal was not the only one nearby, which meant the Phantom Fox might've been followed.

In Fletcher's tiny moment of distraction in sending Stone off, Four-Finger Mike managed to produce a small knife, and before even a single word of warning could be issued, he'd swung backward and wounded Fletcher's arm.

Fletcher loosened his grip, and in an instant, the miscreant was free.

He made to run, but Brogan grabbed hold of his coat. Four-Finger Mike struggled, and the fabric ripped. He spun about, slipping his arms from the garment. He would be gone in an instant if something wasn't done.

Vera held her umbrella like a club and swung with all her might at the man's knees. She then jammed the handle into his middle. He bent forward, grabbing his gut. She raised the umbrella over her head and slammed it against his upper back. It was not the most efficient weapon, but it slowed him enough for Fletcher and Brogan to rejoin the brawl.

In an effort too well-coordinated for this to be the first time the two men had fought side-by-side, they quickly had Four-Finger Mike on the ground, his arms tied behind him with his own coat, his nose bleeding, and every ounce of fight drained from him.

"You've made a dangerous enemy, my friend," Fletcher said. "And this time, you won't escape."

"You know nothing of enemies." Even in his current state, Four-Finger Mike was defiant. "Toss me over to the blue-bottles if you want, won't make no difference."

"Locking up a man with as many marks on his record as you, with as much influence in the criminal world, not make a difference?" Brogan kept his tone calm. "You give yourself too little credit."

"You have no idea the tempest that's coming for you."

Stone returned, a bit winded, but still clearly agile and determined.

"All's well?" Fletcher asked.

"All," Stone said.

"There's a police station not far from here," Fletcher said. "Let's the two of us deliver this ribbon-tied present to them, shall we?"

"It'd be a pleasure," Stone said.

With that, the two men dragged their catch down the dark streets.

Brogan's attention turned immediately to Vera. "Are you injured?"

"Not a bit," she said.

Brogan let out a quick breath filled with relief. "I'd no idea Four-Finger'd be hanging about. I'd not meant to put you at risk."

She shook her head. "I had an umbrella, so I was well armed."

He chuckled. "I hadn't realized you were so handy with that thing."

"Neither had I." She hooked her arm through his, and he began walking again, the same casual, connected arrangement they'd assumed before, though both of them were a bit worse for wear.

"Do you remember what Clare said when she delivered that last note?" Vera asked.

"She said we couldn't stop the Mastiff. She said that a storm that was coming was—Oh, saints."

"Precisely." Vera could see he'd made the connection she had. "Four-Finger Mike said much the same thing, that we have no idea the tempest that's coming for us. The battle I've taken on is starting to feel too big and too dangerous."

He set his free hand atop hers, a nearby street lamp highlighting his scars. "You're not fighting alone."

Thank the heavens for that.

"There's strength in numbers," he added.

Strength, yes. But also chaos. Sooner or later the gale force winds would whip into the tempest they'd been warned of. What if they weren't ready for it?

THE MERCHANT AND THE ROGUE

by Mr. King

Installment VI
in which Time runs short and our Heroine
is faced with unfathomable Danger!

The damage to the confectionery shop was significant
enough that Tallulah had not the time to resume her candy
making or baking despite the passage of three days. The villagers had been remarkably kind and generous. They had
begun cleaning while she'd been in the pub learning the horrible truth of their situation. They'd continued their efforts
for hours afterward and into the next day. Given time, she'd
have the means to replace the glass in the front window. For
now, the town had kindly supplied her with enough greased
paper to fill the gaping hole left by the squire.

A *fear dearg* of all things. And in England rather than
Ireland. The Fae could, of course, travel, but didn't usually
go so far afield. Had she encountered in her homeland what
she had in Chippingwich, she would have recognized the
signs, would have known much sooner what they were facing. Then again, were she in Ireland, *everyone* would have

realized what they were facing, and she wouldn't be struggling with the enormity of defeating the monster on her own.

"There are many reasons the Fae avoid the mortal realm, iron being chief among them." She could hear her gran's words in her mind. "Iron bends the Fae. It twists them about, interferes with their magic. The most dangerous among them can only be felled by weapons of iron."

Heaven help them all if Kirby and Royston were unable to obtain an iron axe or sword. *Fear dearg* grew bolder with every bit of mischief and torment. They came to enjoy the misery they caused, yet quickly found it insufficient. They grew worse and worse with time, and this *fear dearg* had been at his current mischief for nearly a century. That the village suspected their monster-turned-squire had killed the last shop owner to push back against him didn't surprise her, but it did worry her. The squire would soon grow quite bold in that respect as well. Chippingwich would move from being tormented to being decimated.

The door, splintered but still functioning, opened. Her heart hammered on the instant but settled when Royston stepped inside.

He sauntered toward her, the same dandified gait he'd employed when first they'd met. It was a disguise; she could see that so clearly now.

"What news have you?" she asked once he'd reached her.

"My shipment of fabrics arrived today," he said. "*Only* the fabrics."

She rubbed at the back of her neck. "Without the

remainder of that shipment, we are in dire straits." They simply had to have an iron weapon.

"I do believe Kirby secured what we were looking for. It simply has not reached us yet."

She sighed. "Let us hope we receive that shipment in time."

"And with no indication of what's inside," he added.

Saints, that'd be a disaster. "We cannot risk raising a certain . . . person's suspicions."

He tugged at his lace-edged cuffs. "Tosh. I meant only that it's far more enjoyable to open a packet when one has no idea what might be inside."

How was it she hadn't seen through these antics sooner? He had managed to fool the *fear dearg* but had also pulled the wool over her eyes. "If you have no idea what is inside the packet we are anticipating, then I have concerns about your intelligence."

He chuckled. "Let us hope the squire harbors those same doubts."

"About both of us," she said.

Royston took her hand and raised it to his lips, pressing a warm kiss to the backs of her fingers. "I do not believe I have ever met your equal, Tallulah O'Doyle. You are brave and kind and, yes, intelligent."

"And you, Royston Prescott, are showing yourself to have excellent taste."

Again, he lightly laughed. With obvious reluctance, he slipped his hand from hers and stepped toward the door. "I will watch for our delivery. In the meantime, take care."

"I will say the same to you."

He dipped his head in a flourishing bow. A moment later, he was gone, and she was, once more, alone. Before the squire's destructive visit, her shop had seldom been empty. The villagers, bless them, had continued to come by, to look in on her, to offer what help they could. She loved the people of Chippingwich, and she was determined to free them from the grip of the dangerous monster in their midst, one they could not fully see for what it was.

"What a shame all your customers have fled." A whoosh of red and a waft of putridity accompanied the sardonic observation.

"Mr. Carman," she said, keeping her tone as calm and disinterested as ever. It wouldn't do to tip her hand before they were ready to truly do battle with the monster. "I have not yet begun replacing the candies and sweets and baked goods that were lost when the window broke. I do not know how soon I will do so."

"I only came to offer a friendly greeting." He turned his head toward her as he spoke, a shaft of light spilling across his face. It appeared as a double, both the human visage the villagers saw and the rat-like face of the *fear dearg* beneath. Each face faded in and out, repeatedly replaced by the other. His disguise was breaking down.

"You've offered your greeting," she said. "Now, I need to get back to the matter of repairing m' shop."

Squire Carman made a slow, dramatic turn, eyeing the room with a mock expression of concern. "A shame what happened."

As he turned, his cape rustled, and a rat's tail became momentarily visible. Why was it she was seeing so much more of the monster beneath the disguise? What had changed?

Perhaps knowing what he was made it more difficult to be fooled.

Or, perhaps, just as his mask had first cracked in her presence when he'd grown angry with her, the disguise fell to bits the more upset the *fear dearg* was. And if she was seeing him so clearly, then he was not as calm as he appeared.

"It would be a true shame if more damage occurred here," Mr. Carman said.

"Yes, it would." She held her ground, watching him warily and closely. Heavens, that tail of his wasn't hidden in the least. How odd that only she and Royston could see it.

"And yet, it seems unavoidable." The squire turned back slowly. His eyes glowed as they had before. His human face had grown nearly transparent. His disguise was all but gone.

"What makes it unavoidable?" she asked.

"The way you look at me." The *fear dearg* inched closer, his demonic gaze unblinking and hurling actual physical heat at her. "You hide it well, *bean*." That he called her by the Irish word for *woman* worried her. He understood that his origins in her homeland had offered her insights none of the others had. "You know what I am."

"Irish children are taught young the dangers of the Fae."

"And, yet, you've stumbled right into that danger."

Newly repaired shelves began to rattle. The paper in the window ripped. All the while, the *fear dearg* didn't look away from her, didn't take another step.

"I've a good arrangement here," the monster said. "I'll not let you destroy it."

"I've good friends and neighbors here," she said in return. "I'll not let you destroy them."

"I've not eaten any of them." His mouth turned up in a sinister smile, revealing sharp, jagged teeth. "Yet. But I'm running out of 'distinguished visitors.'"

Once a *fear dearg* discovered a liking for some bit of cruelty, he never lost his taste for it.

If only the iron weapon had arrived! What was she to do?

"Now"—the Crimson Man took a single step closer—"how to rid myself of both you and that ridiculous haberdasher at once."

"What has that rogue to do with anything?"

"He knows what I am, just as I know what he is." The *fear dearg* flipped back one side of his cape. "I suspect I'll have to invite him to cook dinner."

Invite him to cook dinner. She knew what that meant. Every Irish child knew what that meant. Any human invited to cook dinner for a Crimson Man found themselves roasting a fellow human over a spit. And if Royston were invited to cook, she'd no doubt *she* would be the unfortunate main course.

The new position of the squire's cape revealed something Tallulah had not seen him carrying before: a burlap bag. She ought to have known he had one. All *fear dearg* carried them. Always. And always for the same purpose: kidnapping and hauling off their human victims. If she was seeing it now, then she was moments away from being stuffed inside.

"I've delayed this bit of mischief for a long time."

Mischief. Not a strong enough word for what she knew would come next when that burlap sack appeared.

There was a means of preventing it, though. She had been told there was. But what was the method? It didn't stop *fear dearg* entirely, but it prevented being kidnapped. Heavens, what was it?

"You played me a dirty trick sending off the little ones." His hand inched back toward his bag. "I *do* know that children are delicious."

It was something she was meant to say. Her gran had told her. 'Twas a particular phrase.

He came closer, reaching for the bag.

What was it? *What was it?*

His free hand reached for her. Once he caught hold, there would be no escape.

Across the years, the voice of her gran whispered to her. Tallulah spoke her words as they entered her thoughts. *"Na dean fochmoid fàin."*

He froze, his expression turning putrid with anger. "That will save you from the confines of my burlap bag, but you may very well wish you were there."

The chairs at the table flew at her. She dove out of the way, only to have something else deal her a blow. She could hear the heavy, scurrying footsteps of the Crimson Man. He couldn't abduct her, but that didn't mean he couldn't kill her.

She groped around until she found something heavy that could fit in her hand—a shattered chair leg. Tallulah rolled enough to lean on her opposite hip and swing the leg with all her might at the *fear dearg*. He nearly toppled but managed to remain on his rat-like feet.

The stumble was enough to grant her time to scramble to her feet, the chair leg—now cracked—still in her hand.

He spun about with a jerk, eyes glowing so brightly the entire shop was lit in red. "I am tiring of these games."

"Perhaps we ought to stop playing."

He shook his head, no longer bearing even a shadow of human shape. "My games end only one way."

"With me on a spit?"

A grotesque grin grew on his rat face. "I *will* enjoy that. I'll have to continue playing after you are gone."

Once *fear dearg* had a taste for something . . .

Royston stepped into the shop. "I propose, rather, *we* continue playing after *you* are gone."

"You will be easier to defeat," the Crimson Man declared. "You haven't the fire of this one."

"Perhaps not, but I do have this." He raised a mighty axe.

The monster was unconcerned. "'Though blade of stone or axe of steel, the Crimson Man you'll never kill.'"

Royston's face filled with pity. "How very misinformed you are."

With a chuckle that sent ripples of dread through every inch of Tallulah, the *fear dearg* threw his rodent head backward in amusement.

"I need him within swinging distance," Royston mouthed.

She circled back, holding her pitiful chair leg with as much confidence as she could muster. The monster eyed her doubtfully, amusedly. She swung the leg with no intention of actually hitting him.

"How very pathetic," their enemy said. "And how very futile."

"I am protected from your bag," she said. "I must protect him."

Realization filled those glowing red eyes. Tallulah swung more frantically, more wildly. With annoyance, he stepped farther from her, but not near enough to Royston.

The supposed rogue held the axe firmly in both hands, eyeing his target with a firmness of purpose that belied his assumed character.

"He is not safe from my bag." The *fear dearg* cackled and turned. "Abandon your pathetic axe. It will avail you nothing."

"I like it," Royston said, securing his grip. "It is unlike any weapon I've yet yielded."

Claws on his burlap bag, the Crimson Man began to close the gap between him and Royston. "And you and your unique weapon can both turn over a fire."

"I wouldn't recommend it," Royston said. "Iron can be difficult to digest."

The *fear dearg* stopped, frozen to the spot.

Tallulah took a giant step forward and swung the splintered leg hard against his back, sending him reeling forward. Royston did not miss his opportunity.

A swing of the axe.

An otherworldly cry.

The shaking of the very ground.

Then all was still, and dark, and quiet.

CHAPTER 25

Rain began falling during their walk home. Vera's umbrella was in no state to offer the least protection, so they arrived at the flat more than a little wet. Brogan emerged from his bedchamber, changed and dry; Vera was still in hers. Any doubt that he still looked a sight was put to rest when Móirín spotted him and immediately laughed.

"You should've seen me before I changed," he said. "M'best suit ruined, and I don't know if it'll ever recover."

"You're fretting over your clothes, but you'd do best to clean up your face."

Brogan eyed his vague reflection in the window. A bit of dirt and likely blood was smeared across his forehead. That had probably happened during the fight with Four-Finger Mike. His hat hadn't offered him much protection from the rain, but it had managed to prevent that smudge from washing away.

Móirín tossed him a dish rag. He scrubbed his face with it.

"Have you convinced Vera to trust you again?"

Brogan tossed the rag back at her before dropping onto an obliging chair. "To a degree. She has a history of reasons not to trust, and I've pricked at that. I think I'm making progress, though."

"I suspect you're making more progress than you realize."

Oh, how he wanted to believe she was right. But he didn't dare allow his hopes to soar. "Have you spoken with her about it, then?"

"I have eyes, don't I?"

"And what have your eyes done to solve this mystery? Read letters she's written explaining her feelings in great detail?" he asked dryly.

"I've watched her when she's with you. And I've watched you when you're with her." Móirín sat as well. "You're both a bit wary, but you're also both happier. 'Tis difficult to explain, but the two of you are somehow more yourselves when you're with each other. Too often people speak of love and romance as losing oneself in another person, of needing them to the point where who they are disappears. But that's not at all what I see in you. You both grow stronger, fiercer. You grow independent . . . together."

He thought he understood what she was saying, but his mind still spun. "She has faith in me. That helps me have faith in myself."

Móirín leaned forward, looking him directly in the eye. "I hope you know, Brogan, *I* have faith in you. Always have. You may be my younger brother, but you always looked out for me. You've done our parents proud."

Even as they'd died of starvation, their parents had made Móirín and Brogan promise never to abandon each other, to forge an unbreakable link. Brogan had never yet broken that promise. Móirín hadn't either.

"But now," Móirín said, "'tis time and past that we allow that vow to include building our own lives. There is a woman in this flat right now who you could have a wonderful future with. You'd be a better person with Vera, and I've no doubt you'd have the same impact on her. If I didn't encourage you to try, if I did anything to stand in the way, I'd be breaking my vow to our da and ma in horrible ways."

They'd talked lately about setting up their own homes, and though they hadn't said it out loud, the reason was clear in his mind. A bit of distance would give them a far better chance of finding love and building families of their own.

"I wish you all the luck in the world, Brog. You deserve it."

Brogan rose and added coal to the fire. He was cold from the soaking he'd received and hadn't the least doubt Vera would be as well.

Móirín joined him and offered a quick, affectionate hug. "I'll be praying for your success in proving yourself worthy of her affections."

"Prayers may be required," he said with a grin. "I'm hardly a catch, you know."

"I beg to differ." After one more quick squeeze of his shoulders, Móirín slipped from the room.

He wanted to believe his sister was bang on the mark, that Vera felt for him what he felt for her. He knew she wasn't indifferent; he wasn't so thickheaded as all that. But how deeply did her affection run?

There remained uncertainty between them. And his

membership in the Dread Penny Society meant he'd have to tell her half-truths again. He didn't like that at all. And yet the DPS saved people. That work was important to him. The Dreadfuls had organized a watch on Old Compton Street, which they hoped would prevent a repeat of the violence that had occurred there mere days earlier. Protecting Vera, and so many others, required that he keep things from her. But he didn't like it.

"Thank heavens you've built a fire," Vera said from behind him.

He spun around. Despite the heaviness of his thoughts, the simple sight of her settled his mind and warmed his heart. Móirín had said he was more himself with Vera than when he was alone. He was coming to understand that better. Having her near didn't eliminate his worries, didn't solve his problems, but it helped him face them.

"That was quite a soaking we took." She sat on the sofa near the fireplace. "What an evening it's been."

He crossed and sat beside her. "If you take ill from this, I'll never forgive myself."

She shook her head. "You needn't worry about that. The rain was hardly the biggest risk we took tonight, and both of us took those risks willingly. I only hope it's enough to lead to our success."

"Four-Finger Mike's words keep returning to my thoughts. 'The tempest that is coming.' He must've realized we'd likely stopped their blackmail plot, but he didn't seem the least convinced that it would change much. I'm not sure what comes next."

"If we're truly fortunate, the purchase of a new umbrella." Her eyes danced with a held-back laugh.

He liked when she was in a teasing mood. He took her hand in his and held it, taking comfort in the simple touch. "Have I told you how impressed I was with your expertise as an umbrella fighter?"

"You have. And I'll return the compliment and say that you're impressive at throwing fives."

"A Dublin lad either learned quickly how to fight, or he didn't survive."

She leaned her head wearily against his shoulder, grateful for the solid strength of this man. "Life is difficult at times, ain't it?"

"A right struggle," he agreed. "But it has lovely moments as well."

"Like meeting someone who'll buy hot chestnuts quite regularly."

He smiled; how could he help it? "Or meeting someone who's willing to forgive a bloke for being bacon-brained."

She didn't move from her cozy position tucked up against him. "You're not so soft-skulled as all that. And you're very warm just now, which I deeply appreciate."

"Any time you need me to warm you, my Vera, you simply say the word." He released her hand and wrapped his arm around her.

"My Vera," she repeated on a whisper. She turned, though not enough to dislodge his arm, and looked at him. "Do you truly think of me that way?"

"I do," he said. "You mean the world to me, and I count myself fortunate that you allow me any part of your world."

"I'm beginning to think you like me." Her attempt at a jest emerged shaky, the sort of quiver that came from anticipation and hope more than worry.

With his free hand, he cupped her jaw just below her ear and ran his thumb slowly, softly along her cheek. "I've not merely *liked* you for ages now."

He leaned toward her and pressed a lingering kiss to her temple, then her cheek.

"My Vera," he whispered.

He strung kisses along her jaw. She breathed out his name. Brogan kissed her lips, warm and fervent. He wrapped both arms around her, amazed at how perfectly she fit, at how wonderful she felt, how sweet her lips tasted.

She kissed him in return, earnest and heart-full.

He had no idea what lay ahead of them. But in that moment, he chose to hope for the best.

CHAPTER 26

The next day at the shop was filled with stolen glances and hardly hidden smiles. Now and then, when Brogan slipped past Vera, he would take her hand and lightly kiss her fingers. She loved it, but she also deeply hoped to be kissed again like she had been the night before. Her wary heart had melted in that moment, choosing to believe in this man who rescued children, fed the poor, and saved working people from certain misery.

As closing time approached, she thought perhaps she would get her wish. But Móirín arrived just before Vera meant to lock the door.

"Don't hold supper for me," Brogan said to his sister. "I've a few bits of business to see to, and I'm likely to be back late." He turned to Vera. "I'll be quick as I can be, so I can see you before you settle in for the night."

She raised a shoulder in a half-shrug. "You're assuming *I* want to see *you*."

Brogan slipped close enough to pull her to him, though only his arm and her waist touched. "Don't you?"

Vera held his gaze. She didn't answer beyond a slow-spreading smile.

"What if I vow to bring you a bag of hot chestnuts?"

She let her smile grow to a grin, even laughed a little. She'd done that more often since she'd met him.

With his free hand, he took hers and raised it to his lips. He kissed the back of her hand, her knuckles, the tips of her fingers. A breath quivered from her. He turned her hand over and brushed the lightest of kisses on the inside of her wrist.

"Blessed fields, you two," Móirín's voice interrupted. "You're fit to make me vomit, you are."

Brogan kept Vera's hand in his but ceased his attentions. "Sisters are the worst," he muttered with a laugh.

"This sister's doing you a favor, lad, so you'd best not get on m'bad side."

He met Vera's eyes. "Don't let her boss you about."

"I won't."

He gave her hand one more quick kiss. "I'll try not to be back too late."

On that, he slipped from the shop. The moment he was gone, Móirín sat at the table and motioned for Vera to do the same.

"I need to close up," Vera said.

"We need to talk first."

No one could ever accuse Móirín of being weak-willed. Little wonder she'd so bravely assisted her brother in hiding from the Peelers.

Móirín didn't keep her waiting. "My brother's in love with you." The bold declaration came without any hint of blush or hesitation. "And, having watched you watch him, I know 'tis a mutual feeling. I also know you've a few concerns due to m'brother's often maddening sense of loyalty and infuriating selflessness."

Vera didn't know whether to laugh or be shocked.

"Let me see if I can't sum up a conversation you've likely had with him recently." She folded her hands on the tabletop. "He told you we grew up in a rough area of Dublin, that I was employed at Guinness. He explained that a man began causing problems and that same man was killed. A murder charge was levied along with a helping-a-murderer charge, and he and I fled to London."

"Not quite word for word," Vera said, "but that's the bits and baubles of it."

"And, while you've come to realize what a good heart he has and have found in your own heart a willingness to forgive him for having given you a false name, you're still struggling with his having killed someone."

She sighed. "It is a difficult thing to have rattling about in my chest. Came as a surprise."

"Then allow me to surprise you further." Móirín's expression remained stoic. "Brogan didn't kill anyone."

"But the man in Dublin who was causing you so much grief—"

Móirín held up a hand to cut off the objection. "*Brogan* is not the one who is wanted for murder," she said. "I am."

A million questions flew through her mind. "I am almost certain he told me *he* was—" But suddenly she wasn't certain. Perhaps he'd implied it. Or perhaps she'd inferred it.

"He lets people believe he killed my assailant. I think if he could manage it, he would try to convince the Peelers that he was the one who did it. Brogan protects people; it's what he does, even at great cost to himself."

"I know." She spoke the realization as she had it. Brogan helped people. She'd seen it time and again. "It's one of the things I—"

She stopped the words before they emerged.

Móirín finished for her. "One of the things you love about him."

Heat crept over Vera's face, putting truth to Móirín's assumptions.

"You'll find that helping people is a Donnelly trait." Móirín lifted the edge of her dress enough to reach into her boot and pull out a knife. She set it on the table next to her.

"Are you expecting trouble?" Vera eyed the weapon.

"Always." Móirín bent her arm and slipped her hand beneath the back collar of her dress. She pulled out a thick, black rod, roughly eight inches long. She held it out to Vera. "A fighting stick, you'll find, is a useful thing."

"I'd always imagined a shillelagh being longer."

Móirín smiled. "'Tisn't an ordinary shillelagh. I made this one m'self." She placed one hand on each end of the stick and gave a firm outward tug. The stick pulled long, like a telescope. She twisted each end until a click sounded. Móirín tossed it in the air and caught it.

"There you are. An extremely portable and fighting-ready shillelagh." She spun it about and handed it to her. "Safer than a gun for one who's not experienced with a firearm, and better suited to you than a knife."

Vera accepted the fighting stick, curious about Móirín's

invention. "Do you spend a lot of time twiggin' which weapon is best suited to a person?"

"More than you might think." In one fluid movement, Móirín snatched up her knife and stood. In that same instant, the door flew open and a large man with an inarguably angry expression stormed inside.

Surprise touched the ruffian's face when he spotted Móirín.

"Oh, dear." Móirín shook her head in a dramatic show of pity. "You were planning on attacking a woman entirely on her own, weren't you? It's right sorry I am to upend your odds."

The man gave the smallest of smug shrugs. "Odds still ain't bad."

Three men stepped inside. Three large, sinister-looking men. Three equally sinister weapons.

"I ain't personally pleased with those odds," Vera said out the side of her mouth.

Móirín was unshaken. "We can hold our own."

Vera grasped the shillelagh in as firm a grip as possible, eyeing the arrivals with growing uncertainty. She hadn't Móirín's confidence. Or apparent ability.

"Finesse, Vera," Móirín said. "The shillelagh isn't your enemy. Throttling it won't help. Throttling *them*, however"— she pointed her knife at the huffs—"would help tremendously."

Móirín's calm tenacity was boosting Vera's.

"I'll do my best." Vera adjusted her grip.

"Why is it women can't stop chattering, even long enough

to die with some dignity?" the leader of the group grumbled. "Cain't even follow simple instructions in a note."

Ah. "I suspect you're the one who calls himself 'the Protector,'" Vera said.

A satisfied smile slid over the man's hardened features.

Móirín tossed back, "Some protector, coming after a woman thought to be alone but needing to have your wee friends along to protect *you*?"

His eyes darted to the dark-whiskered ruffian at his left, who shook his head.

"We ain't here for jawing," the Protector said. "We're here to do what we came to do."

All eyes turned to Vera.

She borrowed a page from Móirín and made a show of being entirely unconcerned while her racing heart desperately clawed at her frozen lungs. She held the shillelagh firm but not white-knuckled. She'd fight back, however imperfectly.

"Our goal," Móirín whispered out the side of her mouth, "is escape." Three men stepped closer. "Hold 'em off. Turn 'em 'round." Three weapons flashed ominously. "Then, by all that's holy, get out the door."

"I can manage a bit of walloping until we've a clear path."

"On with us, then." Móirín brandished her knife and took a single step closer to their assailants.

Vera followed her lead.

One of the brigands sliced at Móirín. Vera beat back his arm with her shillelagh. The near miss lit a fire under the Irishwoman. The fierceness with which she fought spoke of a lifetime of struggle. Vera took strength from Móirín's determination.

Large-armed men were coming from all directions. Clubs and knives flew and landed and dealt glancing blows. The desperation of the moment, the pulse of survival numbed her to the pain she knew she'd feel later, but only if they escaped.

Get out the door. That was their goal.

She matched Móirín's maneuvering. Fighting off the on-slaught just enough in the right direction to switch spots with their would-be assassins. One blow, one step, one moment at a time, they danced this sinister dance. The door was now behind Vera and her partner in struggle, the roughers in front of them.

"Out we go, mate." Móirín tugged her through the door and into the street.

The night was dark. Though the lamplighters had been by, Vera's eyes would need time to adjust. That would make defending herself more difficult. She could only hope the brutes had the same difficulty.

She and Móirín had only just turned to face the shop front when four shadows passed through the door.

"What do we do now?" Vera asked. "I don't have experience with this sort of thing."

"On the surface, 'twould seem best to run."

"But we ain't meaning to?" Vera guessed.

"We aren't *needing* to."

From the street behind, two men stepped to their side. Vera recognized one of them as Stone. The other, Vera didn't know.

"Bang-up timing," Móirín said.

"What of *my* timing?" That question was tossed out by Brogan. He'd only just stepped up on Móirín's other side.

Next to him, Fletcher brandished a cudgel. He pointed the short, thick fighting stick at the Protector. "This is getting to be a habit with you lot."

The Protector snapped a wire cord, the sort used for efficient and gruesome strangling. "That habit ends here. As do you."

"Leadership at its most cowardly," Brogan said, eyeing the man.

"He ain't the leader," Vera said. "He looks to Whiskers for direction."

The true head of the gang slipped back, allowing his flunkies to tackle the task.

"We've more weapons than you," the Protector said. "It'd be wise to hand over the woman we want and be on your way."

"We won't be doing anything of the sort," Brogan said. "Even if we were as feckless as you, *they* wouldn't hear of it."

He motioned to a crowd Vera hadn't noticed gathering around them.

Peter stood at the head of the group. "It's time we end this." He motioned the crowd forward.

In a rush of angry people, the roughs were forced from the shop front and out into the street. Others, apparently on the side of the Protector and his partners, took up the cause.

A melee took over the street. Utter chaos.

Vera tried directing away any children wandering into the fray. She couldn't bear for Burnt Ricky or Bob's Your Knuckle to be hurt.

Then someone she didn't know, who sounded far finer

than anyone from this corner of London, said something that stopped her in her tracks.

"That's the Mastiff."

Brogan turned. "Who is?"

The man motioned toward the shop overhang. The one Vera had named "Whiskers" stood there.

The Mastiff. The criminal mastermind. The one behind all their troubles. A man even the police feared.

"He's the key," Vera said to Brogan. "Clare and Four-Finger Mike said it's bigger than the trouble we know of. If we nab him, that stops so much more suffering."

They moved toward him.

"I'd advise you stay put," the Mastiff said. "For your own safety."

"We know who you are," Brogan said.

"Of course you do." The Mastiff smiled like a lion spotting his prey. "The problem is, there ain't nothing you can do about it."

Vera took a single step closer. "We can make certain you don't get away."

"The Irishman's bleeding heart will make certain I do." He casually moved past Peter's replacement cart. He raised his left hand and, slowly, pointed at the print shop.

He snapped his fingers.

A blast of hot orange flames burst from the shop. The front windows blew out, sending shards of glass through the air.

Pain seared through Vera.

And the world went black.

THE EAD ZOO

by Brogan Donnelly

Day Five

Sebastian Hines considered himself quite a paragon of gentlemanly achievement. That the keeper of the mammals at the Museum of Natural History had, in an official capacity, asked for him to call was yet another feather in his cap. He stepped inside what the uncouth locals referred to as the Dead Zoo, feeling quite pleased with himself.

The museum was not open to visitors that day, which made his presence there all the more flattering. Yes, he was sharing space with two delivery men, but he did not permit that to dampen his spirits. The men carefully set down a pane of glass beside a display case in need of mending.

Nearby, a grizzled janitor bent over a mop, applying himself with pointed and focused effort to cleaning something off the stone floor. It was not exalted company, but *they* were there as tradespeople. *He* was there as a sought-after guest.

"Do not mind Jonty," William Sheehan said as the new arrival approached. "He is so very dedicated to his work."

"No bother." Sebastian pressed a lace-edged handkerchief to his nose, managing to hide his look of displeasure. "I am curious as to why you've sent for me."

"I have encountered a mystery here at the Museum of Natural History that I cannot solve."

Sebastian was taken for a tour, past a display of a missing rodent, past a disgruntled Jonty working hard to clean something from the floor, past a display case in need of new glass. Past a taxidermied polar bear looking unblinkingly at a seal.

It had all happened before.

It would happen again.

Dear Reader, should you visit Dublin, should you jaunt past Merrion Square, should you wander into the Museum of Natural History, take care.

Not everything at the Dead Zoo . . . is dead.

CHAPTER 27

rogan dropped to his knees. "Vera." She was face-
down, blood soaking the back of her dress. "Vera."

Hollis hunched beside him. "What can I do?"

"I have to get her to Doc." He looked up at Hollis. "Fetch
Captain Shaw—the London Fire Engine Establishment
agreed to protect this neighborhood."

Hollis nodded and took off at a run.

Brogan caught sight of Peter. "The neighbors' fire plan—
put it in motion."

Vera moaned as Brogan turned her over. The sound
worried and relieved him all at the same time. Careful but
quick, he slipped his arms beneath her and picked her up.
The moisture against his arms sent a shiver through him. She
was losing a lot of blood.

What if Doc couldn't save her? What if Doc's personal
frustration with Brogan meant he wouldn't help?

He had to at least try.

He carried her as far as Greek Street. The explosion had
ended the street brawl, but the fire had heightened the utter

chaos. He was far enough away to have some hope of hailing a hackney. The fates were smiling; he spotted one almost immediately.

Vera didn't talk as they rushed toward Finsbury. Brogan kept up a one-sided conversation, pleading with her to stay awake, to stay with him, promising all would be well but not knowing if it was true.

The moment the hackney stopped at Doc's door, Brogan climbed out with Vera clasped in his soaked arms. He kicked at the door, praying the doctor was home.

Mrs. Simms, a nurse who worked for Doc, answered.

"She's dying." Brogan's words rushed out.

"Doc's in the sitting room." Mrs. Simms motioned him in.

He carried Vera directly there, having been to Doc's home often enough to not need instructions. Doc was already on his feet and standing by the examination table in the corner of the room.

He was never shaken, Doc. Never upended no matter what was brought to him. "Lay her down and tell me what happened."

Brogan carefully set Vera on the table.

"You're covered in blood," Doc said.

"It's hers. From her back."

Doc helped him roll her onto her stomach so he could see her wounds.

"'Twas an explosion in a building she was standing near. Knocked her off her feet. Glass and splintered wood flew everywhere."

"Then we're likely looking at burns and puncture

wounds." Doc pulled a pair of scissors from a drawer just as Mrs. Simms stepped inside the room. "We'll have to cut off her clothes. I suspect the injuries are extensive."

Mrs. Simms took action on the instant, snatching up a pair of scissors for herself. She spoke to Brogan without looking away from her work cutting through the outer layer of Vera's dress. "Best wait elsewhere. Doc's library's available."

He'd no desire to leave Vera. But he couldn't invade her privacy without her permission, and she wasn't in any state to give it. And he wouldn't stand in the way of Doc's efforts.

"We're wasting time, Brogan," Doc said impatiently.

Brogan bent down enough to whisper in Vera's ear. "Stay with me, love."

A half hour passed. Nothing.

An hour. Nothing, still.

Brogan was ready to jump out of his skin. He was no surgeon, but he felt certain Doc and Mrs. Simms would've completed their ministrations if Vera's state weren't critical.

His pacing brought him to the library door just as Móirín and Hollis stepped inside.

"How'd you get in the house?" Brogan asked. "Is Doc done—?"

"Hollis picked the lock," Móirín said. "An odd talent for a well-born gentleman, I must say."

"Well-born gentlemen get bored," Hollis said with a shrug. "How is Vera?" he asked Brogan.

"Hanged if I know. Doc tossed me out so he and Mrs.

Simms could . . . sew her up and treat her burns and I don't know what else." He rubbed at his weary face.

Hollis clapped his hand to Brogan's shoulder. "I'll look in and return with a report."

"Thank you." He dropped onto a threadbare wingback chair.

Móirín sat in the spindle-back chair nearby. "In twenty years, Brogan, you've not once abandoned me in a battle. You've never once left me to fend for myself. Until tonight."

Saints, he *had* abandoned her. "I . . . forgot you were there. I don't know what— Vera was in danger. She was bleeding. I didn't—"

Móirín set her hand on his where it rested on the chair arm. "'Twasn't a complaint."

"Then what was it?"

She smiled. "I've been waiting a long time for you to be ready to build your own life. To reclaim your dreams without thinking yourself selfish for doing so. I'm seeing that in you lately. I see it more and more when you're with her."

He let out a breath. "I'm afraid for her, Móirín. She was too weak and wounded for even a single word all the way here."

"I've come to know her a little these past weeks," Móirín said. "She's a fighter. Probably one of the reasons you've fallen for her, seeing as you're a fighter as well."

"A family trait." He could smile, however briefly. "How far did the fire spread?"

"The print shop and the rooms above were destroyed. Some damage was done to the buildings on either side, but the neighbors saved the street."

A spot of good luck there. "Vera will be pleased to know her fire plan worked."

"And she'll be pleased to know your arrangements with Captain Shaw played a part as well."

"His men came through?"

She nodded. "And he was there, personally."

"Any sign of Vera's da?"

"No."

He slumped in the chair, the weight of the day growing nearly unbearable. "I hope he's keeping the children safe."

"I've every confidence he is."

Brogan closed his eyes and just breathed. It might have been a minute; it might have been ten. His mind slowly calmed, enough, at least, for continuing the discussion.

"Was the battle still raging when you left or did the fire distract the combatants?" he asked.

"After the Mastiff slipped away, Stone stepped up onto an empty cart and called out to the crowd. Told the roughs their leader had abandoned them, left them to be burned to death in a fire he'd set. Stone suggested they either slip off and leave the fray or put themselves to a useful purpose and help put out the fire."

Brogan shook his head in amazement. "Stone is a force. The man is one of the smartest I've ever known."

"A bit terrifying too," Móirín said with a smile in her tone.

"Only because there's no doubting he could accomplish whatever he put his mind to, and he's not afraid of what people think of him." Brogan opened his eyes and looked at his sister. "I've heard the same said of you."

Móirín grew subdued, more contemplative. "Do you suppose Stone's ever killed a man?" She almost never spoke of that chapter of her life.

"I don't rightly know," he said. "But I'm full aware that a person can have that mark on the ledger and still be an inarguably good person."

"'Tis sweet that you think I'm a good person."

He sighed. "And 'tis frustrating that you don't."

"I hope you mean to build a life with Vera," Móirín said. "You two love each other and work well together. The both of you are happier when you're together. I've waited years to see you happy again."

"I left Ireland willingly," he assured her. "And I've not for a moment regretted that decision."

"You'd not have met Vera if you'd not left Dublin," she said. "That's one argument in favor. Don't let her slip away, Brog."

"If Doc doesn't let her, I won't either."

The heavens, apparently, didn't mean to leave him in suspense long. Hollis returned and said, "Doc says to go talk with him."

Brogan let out a tight breath as he stood. 'Twasn't a very reassuring report.

"All will be well," Móirín said. "You'll see."

He left the library and made his way with heavy step to the sitting room. The door was open in anticipation of him.

His eyes fell first on the examination table. Vera was lying there, on her side, her head supported by a pillow, a blanket pulled up to her shoulders.

"She ain't dead," Mrs. Simms said abruptly. "Set your mind at ease on that score."

"Thank you." Brogan stepped up beside the bed and set his hand lightly and carefully on Vera's shoulder. He looked to Dr. Milligan, standing nearby. "What are we facing?"

"She will live; I have no doubt about that."

Brogan closed his eyes briefly, whispering, "Thank the heavens."

"Her burns were not so terrible as I feared they'd be, but she was riddled with glass and wood. We've removed every bit we could, but I suspect, based on one particularly egregious wound, that there is something imbedded very deeply in her back. There is a possibility she has sustained damage to her spine. At the very least, to the muscles and ligaments surrounding it."

"'Tisn't terribly encouraging," Brogan said.

"She'll be in significant pain, perhaps permanently," Doc said. "How much worse it might be, I can only speculate."

Brogan nodded, his hand still resting softly on Vera's shoulder.

"She'll need a great deal of support as she navigates whatever this means for her future," Doc warned.

"As I mean for her future and mine to be intertwined, she'll have the support she needs."

Doc nodded. "I never for a moment imagined otherwise."

"For a confirmed bachelor, you have a remarkably good grasp of what it means to love so entirely," Brogan said.

Doc gave a quick, awkward nod and made quickly for the door.

"Did I embarrass him?" Brogan wondered aloud.

"There's one thing Doc don't allow discussion on," Mrs. Simms said as she, too, made for the door, "and that's the matter of his bachelorhood."

"Is he unhappy about being unattached?" Brogan asked. "He's always seemed to take pride in it."

"Proud posturing covers a multitude of secrets." On that mysterious declaration, the nurse left Brogan to watch over the woman he loved.

"Did you mean what you said?"

Hearing Vera's voice, when he'd been absolutely certain she was sleeping, startled him enough to jump.

She laughed a little. "Didn't think I was listening, did you?"

"You are forever surprising me, love."

Vera slowly, and with a wince of pain, pulled an arm out from under the blanket and slipped her hand in his. Seems they weren't entirely without sensation.

He raised her hand to his lips and tenderly kissed each finger. "You've worried me, Vera. 'Twas a terrifying possibility you wouldn't wake up."

"And now that I have?"

"I mean to stay with you as long as you'll allow it. I mean to do all I can to show you how much I love you."

"My father is a fugitive from the law," she warned.

"So is my sister. So am I."

She paused for the length of a breath. "There are many things I might not be able to do anymore."

"I did not fall in love with you because you could walk painlessly—or walk at all—or because you could lift boxes or reach high shelves or any such thing. You are and always will be you. And I *love* you."

"And I love you," she said.

"That is very fortuitous." He leaned over and kissed her forehead. "Loving each other is the greatest foundation for a life together I can think of."

"A life together?" she repeated on a whisper.

"If you're in favor," he said.

She closed her eyes and smiled feebly. "I am decidedly in favor."

He kissed her, gently on account of her injuries, but with earnest and deep feeling. He'd nearly lost her. He would thank the heavens every day he had her with him.

And he would kiss her every opportunity he had.

THE MERCHANT
AND THE ROGUE

by Mr. King

Installment VII
in which Fear becomes Hope and Worry turns to Jubilation!

The creature had disappeared. Vanished. Royston had swung his iron axe, and he knew he had hit his mark. But the moment the cries of agony from the otherworldly monster pierced the air, the beast dissolved into millions of granules of glowing red light before dissipating entirely. Nothing remained. There was no blood, no body, no remnants of a creature that had, for nearly one hundred years, ruled viciously in this area.

In but a moment, he turned to Tallulah. Where was she? Had she emerged unscathed? With the boldness and bravery that would have inspired the poets of old, she had attacked the monster without the needed weaponry, making certain the squire did not fully realize what Royston was preparing to do. They had worked together, taking on a desperate task. But she, far more than he, had been willing to embrace true danger.

"Tallulah?" The shop was not entirely dark, but there

was a heaviness in the air that made everything confused and difficult to navigate. He suspected it was the aftereffects of the death of the monster. The feeling would, no doubt, dissipate soon enough. In the meantime, he needed to know she was well and hale.

"Royston?" She spoke from so nearby he was shocked that he couldn't actually see her. He reached out a hand. His fingers brushed what he was certain were her fingers. "There you are."

"Is he gone?" she asked, slipping her fingers through his.

"He's gone, evaporated into tiny particles of glowing red."

"Do you see his bag?" she asked.

"I cannot see a thing."

"Search about for it. The bag contains magic of its own and must be burned."

He dropped down, feeling about on the floor, searching in the darkness. The space was growing less befuddling, but he still felt upended.

"Wait, I found it," she said. "Let's go outside. The lingering magic will make this task impossible in here."

He fumbled, tripped a bit, but made his way outside. She stepped out of the building just as he did, her arms burdened with an enormous burlap bag easily big enough for a person to fit inside.

All around the market cross, villagers spilled from buildings, eyes wide with worry and questions. Kirby stepped from the pub, his bushy white brows pulled with concern.

Royston turned to face them all and, in a ringing voice, declared, "The monster has been defeated. We are free!"

Shouts of jubilation rang out around them, the perfect juxtaposition to the horrible shrieks of an evil monster who had met his demise moments earlier.

"There remains yet one more thing to be done," Tallulah said. "We must destroy this bag, burn it to ashes." She dropped the bag on the ground in front of her. It made an enormous lump of rough fabric. "It is the last lingering remnants of his magic. It must not be permitted to remain."

The villagers needed no encouragement. Torches were lit in the various fires of the establishments all about, from the pub to the mercantile, from the milliner to the butcher. Royston himself slipped into the haberdashery and to the small fire at the back of the shop, and lit a torch of his own.

One by one, those who had been tortured and held hostage by the creature who would have used this bag to steal away every one of them if given a chance, lit it on fire. Again and again, they touched torches to the fabric and added to the growing flame that was consuming it.

The fire spat out flames of purest, deepest red. No smoke emerged. No sparks flew. There was nothing about this fire that was natural. But it was undeniably cleansing.

Royston stood beside Tallulah as the villagers sang and cheered and danced. Their joy changed the glow of the flame from crimson red to a soft pink. Rather than being attacked by the dark magic of the one-time squire, they were being lit by the soft glow of his final demise.

"They are free," Tallulah said. "They are safe."

"Chippingwich has waited a long time for you, Tallulah O'Doyle. Only with your knowledge and bravery were we at last able to defeat him."

"Your role in this was not insignificant," Tallulah said. "I believe the key was not me, but *us*."

"Us." He liked the sound of that. "We did show ourselves to be a remarkably good team."

She slipped her arm through his and rested her head against him. "Yes, we did."

"It may take time for your shop to open again," he said. "If we were to combine efforts, you could resume your business while waiting on the repairs."

She met his eye, clearly curious. "What are you proposing?"

"That we open the first Haberdashery and Confectionery Shop. We will begin a new trend, I'm certain of it. And being the fine team that we are, we will make an inarguable success of it."

A hint of a smile played over her features. "Is that the only thing you are proposing?"

He leaned in and, adopting the roguish tone he had long ago perfected, he said, "That is not remotely the only thing."

"I should very much like to hear your schemes." She didn't seem to harbor any lingering doubts about his character. She'd seen past the rogue he'd pretended to be to the person lurking beneath. And she seemed to like who she saw.

"Well, let me tell you the first and the last item on my list." He raised her hand to his lips and kissed her fingers. "The first part of my proposal is that you join me at the pub for dinner, and I will hold your hand and look lovingly into your eyes the way a man does when courting a woman."

"I like the beginning of this list," she said.

"Then you're going to love where the list ends." He slipped his arm free of hers and wrapped it instead around her waist.

"And where does it end?" she asked.

He rested his forehead against hers. "It doesn't. There's no end. This, Tallulah O'Doyle, is meant to last forever."

CHAPTER 28

Brogan brought Vera back to his and Móirín's flat to convalesce. Her life was not in danger, but what that life would look like remained to be seen. They'd only been home a matter of hours when two notes arrived: one for Brogan and one for Vera.

Sleep sat heavy on her features. She'd likely not keep her eyes open long enough to read hers.

"Would you like me to read it to you?" he offered.

"Please."

He unfolded the smudged and scuffed paper. The handwriting was haphazard and hasty.

> *Kotik,*
>
> *I am so proud of you. Now it is time for you to rest and heal. The children remain with me. Whispers are abundant on the street, warning me that the storm has not yet passed. Donnelly will safeguard you just as I will safeguard these little ones. If the fates are willing, we will reunite soon and rebuild.*

*Until then, be safe. Be vigilant. I will see you as
soon as it is safe.*

Pápochka

"The tempest is bigger than we know." Vera whispered
the warning they'd heard from both Clare and Four-Finger
Mike, the same warning that was echoed in her father's note.

Brogan pressed a kiss to her forehead. "You've an army,
my dear. You will not face that storm alone."

Her smile was weak. Her eyelids were heavy. "Promise I'll
have you. That is better than any army."

"You always will, my love." He kissed her lips, softly and
tenderly. "And with you, I'll have every dream I've ever hoped
for."

She released a slow breath. Her eyelids fluttered closed. In
the next moment, her expression relaxed with sleep.

He sat beside her bed for a few minutes longer, grateful
she was resting. Even more grateful she was alive. It had been
a near thing.

All was quiet. He leaned back in his chair and pulled
from his pocket the note he'd received. The wax seal on the
back was disconcertingly familiar. This note was from the
Dread Master.

As he unfolded it, a penny fell out onto his lap. He picked
it up, turning it around with his fingers. It was marked with
the design specific to the Dreadfuls. He'd handed his own
penny over to Fletcher at the time of his feigned resignation.

Brogan turned his attention back to the note.

Today. 2 o'clock. Parliament.

He knew in an instant what the brief message meant. The Dread Master was summoning him to DPS headquarters. The demand couldn't be ignored, and yet he hadn't the first idea how he would be received by his one-time colleagues. They'd overlooked their frustrations with him enough to help solve the matter of the blackmail and the Mastiff's violent grip on Old Compton Street. But allowing him back into their brotherhood was another thing altogether.

He slipped the note into his pocket and sat on the edge of Vera's bed. He placed a light kiss on her forehead, careful not to wake her. She had a long road of recovery ahead of her, and sleep would do her a world of good. She mightn't be entirely whole, but he had every confidence she would be well in time.

Brogan paused long enough in the kitchen to tell Móirín he'd be back as soon as he could and to ask her to look after Vera.

"She's like a sister to me, Brog. You don't even need to ask."

His mind set fully at ease over Vera's care, Brogan pulled on his coat and hat and made his way toward an uncertain reception. Each street closer to headquarters meant his heart pounded harder and his mind spun faster.

Doc had helped Vera because that was the kind of person he was, but that didn't mean he had forgiven Brogan's defection. And he was likely not the only one. Just because the Dread Master had summoned Brogan didn't mean he was free to tell them all about his assignment.

He stepped through the familiar blue door. Nolan was

dozing in his usual spot. A pile of pennies sat on the table where they were always placed.

Nolan opened a single eye. Brogan showed him the penny, and the man reached over and pressed the center of a flower engraved in the molding. A door slid open.

Brogan swallowed against the lump in his throat. He couldn't put this off forever.

He stepped into the room where the Dread Penny Society held all of their official meetings. It was designed to be a small-scale version of the House of Commons. Fletcher sat, as always, at the head of the room in the midst of them all, on a chair that resembled a throne. The room was as full as Brogan had seen it in a long time.

All eyes turned to him. Surprise was written on every face, along with a fair bit of distrust.

"Ah," Fletcher said, "the Prodigal Dreadful."

Brogan approached the throne and handed over the Dread Master's letter.

Fletch read it quickly. To the gathering, he said, "Seems, mates, we've solved the mystery of why there's been a call to quorum."

A call to quorum. That explained why so many DPS members were present.

"The Dread Master summoned Mr. Donnelly here," Fletcher explained to them all. "Which is likely why the Dread Master also sent me this." He pulled another missive from his pocket, this one still sealed. He opened it and read.

Dreadfuls,
   Today Brogan Donnelly returns among you,

*after having undertaken a task at my insistence.
Doing so required a separation from the society, one
he could believably ask for due to his longstanding
concern about the deceit needed to maintain the secrecy required.*

Whispers sounded all around the room. Eyes darted from
Brogan to Fletcher and back.

*His efforts saw Four-Finger Mike imprisoned,
two influential men of importance and standing
saved from a blackmail scheme, and the solving of
a mysterious ring of extortion. But these matters all
tie back to this organization. He took on this mission
alone to protect all of you. It is time you returned the
favor.*

*He remains a member, never having truly re-
signed. And it is for you to settle the question he has
been asking for years.*

DM

Fletcher tore up both the note he'd just read and the
one Brogan had delivered and dropped the tiny pieces into
a bottle. He would, without a doubt, burn the papers at the
end of the meeting.

He motioned to Brogan from his position on his pseudo-
throne. "We've a quorum. Time to make your case."

Brogan didn't waste a moment. He rose and stood firm
and confident in front of them all. "M'sister's helped in far
too many of our missions to not have pieced together some of
the secrets of our society. Hollis Darby's fiancée, Ana, helped

us steal documents from Lord Chelmsford and, not too long ago, helped Hollis and Fletcher with a dangerous undertaking, which has left her with questions he'll not have answers to. Chandan Kumar"—Brogan motioned to him—"has kept his activities with this society a secret from his wife for far longer than it is reasonable to ask. Doc's nurses help his efforts on our behalf but can't be told the whys or hows. This'll grow more complicated as our families grow more numerous. My sister is no longer the only lass in m'life I'm having to hide my membership from. I can't abide lying even more to the woman I'll soon marry."

A chorus of congratulations filled the room. Brogan hadn't time for the well-wishes, though he was grateful for them.

"We've long spoken of forming a sister organization, one that can be involved to some extent in our activities, our philanthropies, and our missions. Doing so allows us to give our loved ones an explanation of our absences and efforts that's neither a complete falsehood nor an utter refusal to give an answer. It must be done. We can wait no longer."

"You have always been the most vocal about this need," Hollis said. "I confess I hadn't taken the matter as seriously as I ought before my Ana became entwined in the issue. It is stickier than I realized."

Kumar rose. "I have children now, and I don't care to spend the rest of their lives lying to them. Being able to tell them something—and something true, at that—would make a world of difference."

"It's risky," Martin tossed back.

"I'll not deny that," Brogan said. "There'd be little point

in pretending we've not argued this before. 'Tis also well known amongst us that something being risky doesn't make it not worth tackling."

"True enough," Martin said.

Brogan fully expected a drawn-out debate; that had always been the result of raising this subject in the past.

Doc Milligan rose. "I have learned that Miss Sorokina, apparently soon to be Mrs. Donnelly, fought alongside our membership. She formed a coalition that stopped in its tracks a sinister plot hatched by this society's greatest enemy. She offered us information and insights we desperately needed. She stood shoulder-to-shoulder with Móirín Donnelly, another who has offered us invaluable assistance, despite our lies to her. If we agree to the formation of this sister organization for her sake alone, we will still be more than justified in doing so, and we will yet remain indebted to her."

For a moment, Brogan couldn't respond. Doc had been beyond frustrated with him and had even denounced him for his defection. Was it possible Brogan had already been forgiven?

"Gentlemen, and lady"—Fletcher tossed a smile to Elizabeth—"this matter has to be settled."

Brogan stood on the spot, tense and nervous.

"The Dread Master wishes to speak to this matter as well." And Fletcher pulled out yet another sealed missive.

Their mysterious leader could vote on such a matter, his vote holding the weight of two of theirs. His opinion held great sway. The contents of that letter could make or break the proposal.

Fletcher read aloud.

Dreadfuls,

The proposal made regarding an additional branch of our society is incomplete.

Brogan held his breath.

Working with a sister organization whilst keeping the membership of that organization ignorant of our more dangerous secrets cannot happen without careful coordination. It is essential.

Should the matter carry, two Dreadfuls should be appointed to oversee this complicated coordination. By way of suggestion: Brogan Donnelly and Barnabus Milligan. Donnelly has the most passion for the enterprise, while Milligan has a ready reason to oversee philanthropic efforts and would not raise suspicions in the sister-organization membership.

The decision, as always, rests with you. My vote is in the possession of your figurehead. Consider wisely, but vote now.

DM

Fletcher lowered the letter. He looked at Brogan and Doc in turn. "Would the two of you agree to take this on should the proposal pass?"

Doc dipped his head. "I would."

"Readily," Brogan said.

"Well, then." Fletcher tore up the letter, dumping it in the bottle with the other fragments. "We have heard Brogan's reasons. We have once more admitted the risk involved. And we have the Dread Master's thoughts. It's time this matter was decided once and for all."

Brogan's heart seemed to seize. This was a long-awaited moment of truth.

"All in favor, let it be known."

Hands were raised around the room. Brogan scanned quickly, looking for any that were not in agreement. He didn't want the group to fracture; he would rather step away than stop them from doing the important work they did.

"All opposed, let it be known," Fletcher said.

Not a single hand was raised. Not one.

"The resolution passes," Fletcher said.

Brogan looked across at Doc. "'Twill be a fine thing working together."

"Assuming you don't take on another secret mission and disappear again." The man was clearly not entirely joking.

Damage had been done. Brogan would have to work to regain the trust of his fellow Dreadfuls. Some would likely be harder to convince than others.

"The matter of the sister organization—whose name is yet to be determined—was our primary purpose in gathering today," Fletcher said. "But before we dismiss or move on to any other matters, I have yet one more letter to read, again from the Dread Master."

Four letters in one meeting. That had never happened before. Never.

The whole room went still.

Dreadfuls,
The events of the recent past have revealed the

enormity of the web in which we have found ourselves entangled. The Mastiff and his minions have greater reach than we realized. To his crimes of fraud, child labor, forced prostitution, arson, we must now add blackmail, forgeries, extortion, and rigging explosives meant to kill. He holds prisoner, still, the unfortunate Serena we have been attempting to rescue, as well as, we must assume, her children. He is unafraid to target even the most powerful in England. He will not hesitate to crush each one of us.

As we have been warned, a tempest is brewing, one greater than we've ever known. Pursuing our fight against him is, possibly, a bigger threat than some would wish to take on.

We either knowingly and willingly take on the danger of going after London's most notorious criminal, or we choose not to invite the war our efforts might very well cause.

Decide. And act.

DM

Fletcher stood, holding the letter in his hand. "Our work has never been without risk, but this is a level we hadn't anticipated. The Mastiff is a ruthless criminal, willing to kill and destroy in pursuit of total control of London. He has conspirators among the police and in the government. His power is growing, and with it the danger he poses." His gaze slid over the entire gathering. The group listened without so much as breathing. "As the Dread Master says, the time has come for each of us to decide if this threat is one we want to confront. I won't ask you to make that choice now. And I won't make you declare your decision in the presence of your fellow Dreadfuls, but the decision *must* be made. Before long, there will be no turning back. Ponder. Contemplate. Decide."

"We are the Dread Penny Society," Brogan said. "We do not relent."

"And we do not turn tail and run," Stone added.

"So long as the Mastiff plies his trade unchallenged," Fletcher said, "the people of London will never be safe. Going after him might free them, or it might simply see us killed. Once we take this step, there'll be no turning back."

It was a promise as much as a warning. Danger lay ahead. Greater than they'd ever known.

There was, indeed, no turning back.

ACKNOWLEDGMENTS

My deepest gratitude to

- The curators of Dublin's Museum of Natural History for answering questions and sharing my enthusiasm for this most creepy of museums. I absolutely loved the time I spent in its walls. And a further thank you to the people of Dublin for using their talent for dark humor to give this museum the utterly perfect nickname of "The Dead Zoo."

- Dublin's Leprechaun Museum, for preserving the folklore and mythology of Ireland, for a wonderful, tale-filled tour, and for expanding my already enormous love of Irish folktales.

- Braeden Jensen, for invaluable help with the Russian language. He saved me from several embarrassing errors and offered perfect insights. Any errors that might have slipped through are mine. Everything that is correct is thanks to him!

- The Crandall Printing Museum. I could not be happier to have found this gem so close to home.

ACKNOWLEDGMENTS

- Lisa Mangum and Jolene Perry for unparalleled editorial feedback, advice, and insights. I could not have managed to tell this tale without it!
- Pam and Bob for being the best advocates an author could hope for.
- The ladies of the Friday Write Group for getting me through 2020 with all its ups and downs and for keeping me writing when I felt like giving up.

DISCUSSION QUESTIONS

1. Brogan considers himself a "foot soldier," someone better suited to following orders than formulating strategies. What experiences in his life lead him to believe this? What proof is there that he is underestimating himself?

2. Vera is understandably upset when she discovers Brogan has been using a false name. She later learns that *she* has been unknowingly using one as well. How do you think this discovery will impact her relationship with Brogan and with her father?

3. Street children in the 19th century often took on unpleasant and dangerous work in order to survive. Had you heard of "pure finding" before? What dangers would pure finders have faced on the streets of London?

4. Mr. King's penny dreadful featured a *fear dearg*—a creature from Irish folklore. Many Irish mythological creatures were frightening. What role do you think "scary" tales play in children's stories?

5. Why do you think the Dread Master chose Brogan to undertake the rogue mission rather than one of the other Dreadfuls?

DISCUSSION QUESTIONS

6. The Dead Zoo is an actual museum in Dublin—Ireland's Museum of Natural History. It has remained relatively unchanged since the Victorian Era. If given the opportunity, would you spend the night alone in the Dead Zoo as Amos Cavey did?

7. Mr. Sorokin's last letter to Vera, along with the Dread Master's note to the DPS, indicated that greater danger lurks on the horizon. What troubles do you think lie ahead?

ABOUT THE AUTHOR

Sarah M. Eden is a *USA Today* best-selling author of witty and charming historical romances, including 2019's Foreword Reviews INDIE Awards Gold Winner for Romance, *The Lady and the Highwayman*, and 2020 Holt Medallion finalist, *Healing Hearts*. She is a two-time "Best of State" Gold Medal winner for fiction and a three-time Whitney Award winner. Combining her obsession with history and her affinity for tender love stories, Sarah loves crafting deep characters and heartfelt romances set against rich historical backdrops. She holds a bachelor's degree in research and happily spends hours perusing the reference shelves of her local library.

Read more adventures from

THE DREAD PENNY SOCIETY

BY

SARAH M. EDEN

Available wherever books are sold

SHADOW
MOUNTAIN